Project 20/20:
The Experiment

Karen Adler Feeley

Printed in the United States of America

ISBN 978-1-84728-531-7

<u>DEDICATION:</u>

To
Alex, Jessica, Max, Kaitlyn, & Kevin:
May all your dreams come true…

And especially

to Gabi,
who, without even knowing it, inspired me to write this
story.

<u>ACKNOWLEDGEMENTS:</u>

The author wishes to thank the following people:

- Tina Cokenour, who provided the much needed teen perspective;
- Heather Longhurst, who offered fantastic suggestions to improve the writing;
- Pat Curren, who gave great advice and stuck with me all the way to the end;
- Ruth & Herman Adler, my parents, whose love, support, and advice have sustained me throughout my life;

And most importantly, my loving husband....

- T. Jens Feeley, who has been my greatest cheerleader, confidant, and editor. Without his ongoing encouragement, patience, and ideas, this story never would have been written.

TABLE OF CONTENTS

Chapter 1: The Rules 9
Chapter 2: The Boys From Texas 20
Chapter 3: Lost In The Jungle..............................26
Chapter 4: Desperation 37
Chapter 5: The Adventure Begins 48
Chapter 6: The Commission 53
Chapter 7: Cruising...68
Chapter 8: On Call..81
Chapter 9: The Artist's Life................................88
Chapter 10: The Night Shift 96
Chapter 11: The Emergency Room 104
Chapter 12: The Awakening 112
Chapter 13: At Home...123
Chapter 14: The Exam 130
Chapter 15: The Diner Series.............................138
Chapter 16: Return to Alpha..............................150
Chapter 17: The Package 161
Chapter 18: At the Office 167
Chapter 19: The Negotiation 178
Chapter 20: The Encounter.................................187
Chapter 21: The Offer..195
Chapter 22: The Boxing Match 202
Chapter 23: The Lunch.......................................207
Chapter 24: The Dinner 216
Chapter 25: Writer's Block................................228
Chapter 26 In a New York Minute 237
Chapter 27: The Phone Call...............................243
Chapter 28: The Skinny......................................249
Chapter 29: The Show..258
Chapter 30: The Stakeout 269
Chapter 31: The Ax 280
Chapter 32: Success...288
Chapter 33: Wrap-Up 292

Chapter 1:
The Rules

September 1: New York

Sweat dripped down Lyle Reardon's forehead as he stared out the bedroom window of his business partner's apartment. The 80-degree heat and 70-percent humidity of this typical end-of-summer New York day was not troubling Lyle. Like most Manhattan apartments, the air conditioning was running full-blast. Instead, the flames of nervous energy burning deep inside his gut were making the sweat run down him like a broken water main. He was about to give the biggest speech of his entire nineteen-year-old life, and it terrified him. He would not be speaking in front of television cameras or even in front of a large auditorium, but still this speech would be the beginning of the ultimate test of the "boy wonder of the Upper East Side," and lately of New York University. He wondered whether he would be up to the challenge.

Lyle turned away from the window and paced the length of the bedroom, rubbing his sweaty palms on his plaid pants and fumbling with his glasses. Why couldn't Cheyenne give this speech, he whined to himself. He really hated talking in front of groups; it made his stomach twist in all kinds of knots. Public speaking had this mysterious ability to change him from an intelligent nineteen year old man into a babbling five year old kid. She, on the other hand, relished the limelight. Besides, she was supposed to be in charge of marketing!

He returned to his spot in front of the window. Watching the world continue on its normal course helped him relax. His shoulders moved away from his ears as he allowed himself to take some pride in what he and his two business partners had already accomplished. Only eight months ago, he had shown his new invention to his friend and neighbor, Cheyenne Tilden. Cheyenne impressed Lyle: When she got excited about something, nothing could hold her back. Within a week, she had arranged to show his creation to Mr. Auerbach, a family friend and prominent businessman. Now, Project 20/20, their new company, was about to embark on a real scientific experiment with live human subjects. If only he could overcome his fear of public speaking!

While he contemplated ways to excuse himself gracefully, Cheyenne snuck into the room and laid a soft hand on his shoulder. Lyle turned around and smiled meekly at the tall, dark-haired, eighteen-year-old whom he was delighted to call his business partner. Normally, no girl that pretty would even consider hanging out with him; yet they had spent more time together over this past half-year than most couples he knew. Sure, they weren't dating, but this was close enough for him.

"Are you ready?" she asked calmly. "Everybody is out there."

He sighed loudly and threw himself onto the bed in sheer nervousness. "Are you sure you don't want to present LES to everybody?" he pleaded. "You always enjoy being the center of attention. I'd very gladly let you have the spotlight."

"No, this is your moment to bask in the sun," she encouraged. "Hey, I know you're nervous about speaking in front of everybody, but look at it this way: you're in a familiar setting and half the audience is your friends. It's really not a big group: just four more people. Besides, don't you want to show off the great work you've done? Don't you want to get proper credit?"

Lyle sighed deeply, "I guess you're right. If I can invent such a crazy machine, I should be able to talk about it, right?"

"Right!" Cheyenne agreed. "C'mon! Everyone's dying to meet the man behind Project 20/20."

Cheyenne led Lyle to the living room and grandly introduced him. The visitors gasped momentarily at the slight and boyish-looking inventor, then applauded. Lyle's face blushed. He surveyed the room, searching for the courage to begin speaking. He spotted his two partners standing at opposite corners in the back of the room. On the right, stout Mr. Auerbach, with his white hair, standard khaki pants and white button-down shirt, smiled and nodded supportively at him. On the left, Cheyenne, wearing the latest fashion in casual skirts, leaned comfortably against the back wall.

Lyle gulped some air and forced his eyes to focus on the other people in the room. Marco Centano, of average height and good build, sat next to his taller and skinnier buddy Taylor Washington. Both wore jeans and short-sleeved shirts. In front of them sat April Hayes. In her matching short set, she looked like his dream girl come to life. He quickly turned his eyes to her left before she could read his thoughts. Karla Ruiz, the last participant, sat a little apart from the others. She seemed plainer than April, but he guessed that, despite her loose-fitting tie-dye sundress, she probably had a good figure.

In the back of the room, Cheyenne cleared her throat, tapped her watch, thrust her head forward, and, without a word, urged him to begin.

He took a deep breath. Then, as if Cheyenne had magically sent him some of her stage presence, he launched into the speech he had prepared.

"Good morning. Thank you for coming today and for agreeing to participate in Project 20/20. As Cheyenne said, I'm Lyle Rearback and I would like to introduce you to an awesome machine." At that, Lyle pulled twice on a white bed sheet to reveal his invention. "This is LES, the Life Experience Simulator, and it is my pride and joy. Come take a closer look if you want," he invited.

Taylor, Marco, April, and Karla walked around LES to view it from all angles. The base seemed to be an old 17-inch television in a wooden frame. A small satellite dish protruded from the front screen. Its central antenna, which was surrounded by mirrors, pointed directly towards the audience. The group circled around back and noticed a small metal door running halfway down from the top. They peered through the opening at the bottom to see a wide assortment of motherboards, transistors, springs, tubes, wires, and other components joined together in a complex maze. Along the side of the machine, they discovered a keyboard resting on a small metal shelf below a dashboard comprised of three dials, four indicators, and one big, red switch. Two heavy-duty black power cords, which were plugged into sockets on opposing walls, snaked the floor, crawled up each side of the set, and plugged into a pair of old-fashioned TV antennas that sat in a metal tray of green liquid on top of the machine.

Taylor nodded his head and whistled with appreciation.

Lyle continued his speech. "By adjusting these dials and entering key data, I am able to beam anyone to any point in the future for a glance at what may be. Unlike conventional time travel devices like we've all seen in the movies, LES has the distinct advantage of not wreaking havoc on the real world. You can interact with people and things as much as you want, and it will not affect the past or the future. Why? Because, as its name implies, it *simulates* the future.

Through the magic of quantum physics and biology, you will be physically transported to an alternative dimension, which I call the 'simworld.' Everything will seem real. You can interact as much or as little as you like and the people in the simworld will react appropriately. This enables us to offer you the unique opportunity to try out the future in a completely safe environment. I want to make sure you understand, though, that this machine is not a fancy crystal ball. It does not predict what the future definitely will be; it only allows you to see what will likely occur if you follow a particular course of action.

"Today, you and LES will make Project 20/20 a reality. With this experiment, we all stand to gain: you will be able to try careers for five months at a time, and we will learn how we can improve LES. Of course, we might be less successful, too. You might find that your career choices don't fit you, or you might make some serious mistakes along the way that you will regret. On our part, we might discover some — uh — unanticipated features with LES, although so far, we haven't had any problems. I want to repeat what Mr. Auerbach told you in your interviews with him: we cannot guarantee the success of Project 20/20. We will do all we can to mitigate any potential harm, but you must understand that this is an experiment. With this knowledge, do any of you wish to back out of the experiment? If so, please tell us now. If you do not say anything now, you will not have the chance to leave for another five months. Is anybody interested in leaving?"

Lyle waited several minutes to see if anybody would have a change of heart. Everyone looked back and forth at one another, at the machine, and at each of the Project 20/20 partners; but nobody uttered a word. After what seemed like an eternity, but what was probably only three minutes, Mr. Auerbach gave Lyle the signal to continue.

"Great. It looks like we have four brave and eager candidates here. Let me now review with you how the program will work. You probably have heard this before, but I think it's worth repeating. Each of you will be sent to live in the city and career of your choice for five months at a time. Because people's interest and success changes depending on whether they are at the start, at the height, or towards the end of one's prime, we also will let you choose where in your career you want to be placed. You will be physically transported— body and all—into the simworld and will find yourself waking up on a Sunday morning in your own bed. This will give you the opportunity to take a day to adjust to your new environment before the workweek begins.

"Once you are there, you will have all the necessary skills to do your chosen career. To all who see you, you will appear as an adult rather than a teenager, so you don't need to worry about not being old enough. No one else will know that you are from a different dimension or that you are participating in an experiment. Only you will know the truth."

Taylor shot up his hand and interrupted, "So you mean that we can know everything without having to go through school?"

Lyle nodded with pride. Taylor scratched his

chin as he plotted the possibilities of what he could do with all this excess knowledge so easily acquired.

Mr. Auerbach sensed what Taylor was thinking and realized he needed to be reigned in quickly. "Don't get too excited, there, Taylor. The knowledge is only temporary. Once you leave that simulated world, you lose the technical knowledge."

Karla whined, "So if we forget everything we know, what's the point in all this? Seems like kind of a waste of time to me. Maybe I will change my mind."

"Wait a minute, Karla," Cheyenne begged, concerned that the whole thing might fall apart if someone actually got up the courage to back out. "What's the point in doing that? What other options do you have? Do you really want to go back to your previous situation?"

Karla glared at her for that comment. Cheyenne sensed this and took a different approach. Addressing the whole group she added, "Believe me, it's not a waste of time. Although you don't get to keep the technical skills, you gain something much more valuable: you get to keep the memories of the experiences. If you try two careers, then you have twice as much experience under your belt. Think what an advantage that gives you over everybody else your age. While they're still floundering in jobs they later realize they don't like, you'll be working in a job that you do enjoy. While they're still making all the mistakes that you already made in the safe environment of the simworld, you'll be surpassing them because you'll already know better."

Now Marco raised his hand timidly. "You said we get to try two careers. How soon can we switch? What if you decide after only a month that you don't like the career you've chosen?"

"You can change careers at the end of five months," Lyle responded, grateful to have the chance to get back to his prepared remarks. "At that half-way point, we'll bring you back to the real world, which I call the 'alpha world,' for a check. We'll ask you questions about what you have been doing and about the transport. Then, you can choose whether you want to continue with the same career, change to something completely different, or leave the program altogether."

Marco crossed his arms over his chest and lowered his head as he considered this. "So if I'm really unhappy, I'm just out of luck for the next five months?" He began shaking his head slowly, "I don't know about that."

Mr. Auerbach intervened to soften Lyle's response. "You can do whatever you want in the simworld, including look for a new job. However, I would suggest that you try sticking with the career you've chosen."

"Are the five months real?" Karla inquired. "I mean, when we come back to the alpha world, will it still be today or will it be five months from now?"

"Even though you are in a simulated world and may be in a different month or year, time still passes at the same speed as it does here. That is why we have said that this project will take ten months: two careers at five months apiece." Lyle confirmed.

"How are you able to change what we know and don't know?" Taylor asked. "Is there some sort of mind-meld thing going on here, like in those bad science-fiction movies?"

"Not exactly," Lyle chuckled. "As you may recall from your biology classes, knowledge and memories are based on minute electrical paths worn into the neurons of your brain. Basically, we're temporarily re-wiring your mind." Lyle glanced around and noticed people's eyes glazing. "I can go into more technical detail if you'd like, but I think it would just bore you."

The group quickly shook their head negatively. That was enough to ponder for now.

"Are there any other questions?" Lyle continued. He hoped not.

Marco raised his hand. "You said that the only ones in the simworld who'll know we're in this experiment are the four of us, right?"

Lyle nodded.

"Well, if that's the case, shouldn't we get to know each other so we can recognize each other? I mean, no offense but, so far you've only told us about the machine. If I can't get out before the break, then I want to know who I can turn to for help. Is that ok?"

The others nodded their heads and whispered in agreement. Mr. Auerbach stepped forward to rescue Lyle. "Yes, that is indeed a good suggestion. Thank you, Marco. Why don't we take a few minutes for you to introduce yourselves? Perhaps you could also share

with everyone your reasons for wanting to participate."
He noticed the participants retreating into themselves as
they tried to think of something to say. "It doesn't have
to be anything new. Just tell everyone what you told me
in the interviews." The group nodded, smiled, and
relaxed a little at the suggestion. "Any volunteers to go
first?"

Taylor shot up from his seat and waved his arm
in the air. "I'll go! I'll go!" he volunteered excitedly, as
he grabbed Marco's arm with the other hand. "I'll
introduce us both!"

With a flourish of his arm in the direction of the
make-shift stage, Mr. Auerbach chuckled, "All right,
Taylor. You can go first."

Chapter 2:
The Boys From Texas

"Hi Everybody! I'm Taylor Washington, and this here's my best buddy, Marco Centano. We're Juniors at Crockett High in Dallas, Texas." Taylor shook everybody's hands warmly. "We're pleased to meet all of you and darn happy to be here. Aren't we Marco?"

Marco smiled and nodded sheepishly as he marvelled at how much Taylor sounded like a politician.

Taylor continued, "Lyle, that's one heck of an invention you've got there. I don't fully get all of the technical aspects of what you were saying, but I did catch your point about the experimental nature of this. I want to assure you that I...actually we...have never shied away from anything dangerous in our lives. Why, just last month we tried sky-diving. It doesn't get much more dangerous than jumping out of planes, now does it? The way I see it, if we thought it thrilling to fall from the sky, then think how much more amazing this experiment would be. After all, this involves seeing the future and figuring out what we want to do with our lives. How great is that, right, Marco?"

Marco nodded, "Yeah, and we get to skip school for a whole year, too."

Taylor turned around and shot Marco a look that

seemed to say "Let me do the talking." Marco stepped back and shoved his hands in his pockets. The look was not lost on the audience.

Turning back to face everyone else, Taylor smiled broadly and continued his monologue. "As I was saying, this program presents a great opportunity to short-cut many years of agony and find out what really works. I mean, I look around and I see so many people who have settled for a job. They go through life each day just waiting for the eight hours of work to be done so they can enjoy the remainder of their day."

"Do you really think most adults are that unhappy in their lives?" Karla interrupted, somewhat surprised at this revelation.

"Well, I don't know about everybody, but I know there sure are people like that. Take my dad, for instance. He's got no energy anymore. He comes home from his middle management job and he's exhausted. He eats dinner, watches TV, and sleeps. That's it. No hobbies, no interests anymore. You know why?"

"Because he works long and hard to support your family?" April guessed.

"No," Taylor shot back, fully animated now. "Because he's not doing what he enjoys. He wasn't always such a bump-on-a-log. He used to be fun. That was back when he worked as an engineer, designing and creating things. He loved that…and he was so good at it, too."

"So what happened? Why did he stop?" April inquired.

"He was so good at his job that they promoted him

to various levels of management. Now he's head of the whole engineering department."

"No wonder he's tired. That's a lot of responsibility," she retorted.

"He had lots of responsibility before. Only now he never gets the chance to get his hands dirty. Dad's too busy handling managerial issues to actually build anything anymore. That's what saps him of all his energy. My father's not much of a people-person." Taylor sighed. "I hope I don't end up like that."

April couldn't help nodding in agreement.

"What about you, Marco?" Mr. Auerbach asked, hoping to give the other boy a chance to speak.

"Me? Nope. I don't want to end up like that, either."

"How would you like to end up, then?"

"I don't know. I guess I want to be successful. I just don't know what I'd be good at. That's why I want to try this thing. Maybe it'll give me some ideas."

April couldn't help smirking at Marco's response. He might not be as smooth as his friend, she thought, but at least he's honest.

"What do you think would make you successful?" Mr. Auerbach inquired.

Marco shot his friend a panicked look for help. Taylor jumped in to save the day. He offered a complicated explanation of how success had financial, spiritual, social, intellectual, and familial implications. Ten minutes later, he concluded by stating that one could not be considered a success unless one had a job that could simultaneously provide financial security, intellectual excitement, social relevance, and still leave time to be an active and involved family member.

The more Taylor spoke, the more April's competitive juices flowed. Clearly, here was a man to be reckoned with, she decided. He had ambition written all over him, from the words he spoke to the way he carried himself. He stood erect, with shoulders back and chest out, bursting with pride. When he spoke, though, he had this knack of leaning forward just enough to make you feel like he was talking directly to you. His brown eyes danced around the room, connecting with every member of his audience. She wondered where he had learned to speak so well.

April always believed that clothes told a lot about a person. She assumed that Taylor must feel the same way, for his outfit seemed to underline the image he was trying to project: professional, purposeful, yet fun. His yellow polo shirt had no wrinkles and, combined with his dark jeans and leather shoes, conveyed to her his readiness for any situation that would confront him. How different, she mused, from his best friend in the white t-shirt, who silently slouched with his hands in the back pockets of his faded jeans. She reminded herself that this experiment involved no contest between participants. Even still, she knew right then, she would need to watch out for Taylor.

Finally finding an opportune moment to interrupt Taylor's speech, Mr. Auerbach redirected the question at Marco, hoping to give him a chance to shine.

Karla instantly sat up in her chair, grateful to Mr.

Auerbach for ending Taylor's speech and curious to learn more about the guy who kept trying to fade into the background. She had already made up her mind about Taylor. She couldn't stand people who droned on and on. It reminded her too much of most of her teachers. She always wished she could stand up in class and shout, "OK, I got the point. Move on!" Within five minutes of listening to Taylor, she had decided that he would make the perfect addition to her school's staff.

Marco, on the other hand, remained a mystery to her. If the two guys were such good friends, why did he allow Taylor to treat him like that? One good fistfight would adjust Taylor's attitude and give him a new respect for his friend, she figured. After all, she knew many guys like Taylor: big on talk and short on action. Karla compared Marco's strapping physique to Taylor's trimmer body and decided that Marco, though somewhat shorter, could probably take him in two punches if he really wanted to. Yet, she concluded, he had probably never even tried to stand up to this bully.

What were these two doing hanging out with each other, she wondered? She could see what Marco could bring to the relationship: he probably got them all the girls they needed. After all, he seemed to have one of those amazing combinations that drive girls crazy: good looks, a soft and peaceful nature, and just a bit of "bad boy" in him. But Taylor, what could a blowhard like that bring to the relationship?

Marco stepped forward, hands still in his pockets as he thought for a minute. He cleared his throat into his fist nervously and said, "I guess if I'm doing something that makes me happy, then I'm successful."

Karla nodded her head and smiled. She could relate to that completely.

Lyle looked nervously at his watch and stepped forward from behind his machine. "Thank you, guys, for …uh…sharing. It's getting late, though," he continued, pointing to his watch, "so maybe we should let one of the ladies have a chance to speak now." With a wave of his hand , he politely brushed them off the stage area. "Who would like to go next?" He tried to look nonchalantly at both of them, but privately hoped that April would volunteer. He couldn't wait to hear if her intellect matched her looks.

Lucky for him, she obliged. "Very well, then," he introduced as calmly as he could, given his pounding heart, "Everybody, meet April Hayes, from Los Angeles."

Chapter 3:
Lost In The Jungle

April Hayes smoothed her flower-print shorts as she headed for the front of the room. She paused momentarily, then a grin crawled across her face as a light bulb went on in her head. Taking a cue from Taylor, she tilted her torso forward slightly to bring in her audience. "Picture it!" she began suddenly, as her upright hands, facing the audience, separated as if lifting the curtain on the play she was about to begin.

"There I was, standing in an empty, roofless room with a chalkboard behind me. Only half my hair remained in the bun I had made that morning," she began as she quickly swept her right hand through her long, straight, blond hair for effect. "The wind had whipped the rest out of place. The rain had glued it to my face. My bangs dripped water incessantly. When I looked up, bullet-sized raindrops shot into my eyes. Though blurry, I could just barely make out green palm leaves blowing dangerously back and forth above the roofline to the rhythms of the wind. Water had painted my white blouse against my body, and my stockings felt like oily snake skin on my legs."

Karla and Cheyenne grimaced, knowing full well

the awful sensation of wet pantyhose against cold skin. Taylor smirked salaciously, as he pictured her perky B-cup-sized breasts and lovely size 4 stomach covered in a fine mist of wet, white cotton. Marco looked at Taylor's face and jabbed him in the ribs with his elbow. Taylor really needed to find a girlfriend quick, Marco joked to himself.

"At my feet, an English language textbook lay open to a lesson on conjugating verbs," April continued. "The rain had turned whatever had been written on the chalkboard into a series of broken, splattered lines. My feet made this giant *shlooop* sound as I tried lifting them out of the 2 inches of mud into which they had sunk.

"Confused, I trudged across the muddy floor and left the building. I couldn't believe what I saw! In front of me stood...or rather ...lay a village in shambles: Half a grass shack here, the other half there. People cowered in groups of threes and fives behind anything that might provide some shelter. The place stunk of animal feathers, mud and manure.

"The typhoon finally ended and everyone started to crawl out of their hiding places. Starving, frightened, little Asian children made their way over to me and started wailing. 'Teacher. Teacher. What now?' they cried as they tugged at the hem of my skirt. I felt awful. I had no idea what to do." She shook her head, "I wasn't prepared for this."

April's petite body started to shake as she remembered this. A tear dripped from her eye. Lyle wanted to comfort her, but Mr. Auerbach restrained him gently. April sniffed, then went on.

"Not knowing what else to do, I reached into my backpack, found 2 chocolate bars, and divided them among several of the kids. A boy with muddy arms and teary eyes pulled at my skirt with one hand and pointed to his broken leg with the other. I tried to fashion a brace for his leg out of a nearby fallen tree limb. Unfortunately, I didn't have any string to tie it onto his leg. I looked around and saw nothing that could help me. Desperate, I ripped my shirt into makeshift bandages and tied them around the boy's leg."

Taylor tilted his head slightly in approval, impressed at her quick thinking and survival skills.

"Sure, I helped that one boy, but that was just a drop in the bucket. Half the village needed medical attention. I didn't know what to do. I wanted to help more, but I just didn't know...." April rubbed her head in her hands to collect herself. The room stayed deathly silent, as everyone waited breathlessly to hear what happened next.

"I don't know why I thought of this... but I thought....maybe I could call for help. Surely the Red Cross could do something, right? I dug through my bag for my cell phone, but I couldn't find it. Thinking back, I don't think it would have done me any good anyway. After all, what kind of reception would there be in the middle of the jungle?" she joked nervously.

"I walked all over the village...which only took a few minutes...and looked for a telephone, but I found only a few broken ones. I thought of e-mail, but given that they were living in grass huts, I didn't think I'd find either a computer or electricity. I couldn't understand it. Why wasn't anybody helping them? Where were the police or the authorities? How would I help all of them all by myself?

"I grew tired, scared, and frustrated at my inability to help. I began pounding my hand into my forehead while yelling at myself. If only I'd come more prepared! How I wished I'd studied medicine instead of rushing off to teach English in the jungles! What had I been thinking? If I really felt the need to help them, why didn't I at least come over to do something useful, like showing them how to build toilets with running water?

"Of course, chastising oneself doesn't really do much to help matters in these situations, and I soon realized that. In times like that, you need action." She pounded her fist into her hand for emphasis. "You know, positive action that works toward solving the problem."

Taylor crossed his arms and nodded approvingly. He liked the way this girl thought. She seemed almost as in control as he would have been, he decided. The rest of the group sat mesmerized on the edge of their seats.

"OK. I knew I had to pull myself together, but I gotta tell you: it was hard. I really had no clue what to do. Desperate and terrified, I began running through the jungle and shouting for help. The rain had picked up again and pelted my face. I didn't really know where I was going and I could hardly see straight. I called out to the world but nobody answered. Only the wind howled in response. After what felt like 40 miles, I cried for help again. Fatigue overcame me and I began to lose my voice. I summoned what little energy I had left and shouted with all my might.

It felt like a lion's roar had just echoed through the jungle.

"Faintly, in the distance, I thought I heard a reply. 'Help! Help,' I cried, as loudly as I could. I heard it again: a response! 'We're coming!' it said. I couldn't tell where the voice was coming from. I looked around and found myself in the midst of bushes that were taller than my head, with leaves bigger than my outstretched palm. I had no idea how I'd gotten through that jumble, nor could I figure how they would ever find me. Soon, though, I heard footsteps. Before I could turn around, I felt large arms grab me. I struggled to go free, but the arms grew tighter around my chest and neck. I couldn't see my captor." April paused for effect.

Karla, who was by now sitting with her fingers clenched on her seat in anticipation, couldn't stand it any longer. "What happened? What did you do then?"

Much more calmly now, April answered, "I finally managed to loosen the grip. Just as I was about to break free, I suddenly felt the world start to spin around me. I grew dizzier and dizzier until I finally fainted. When I opened my eyes, I felt disoriented. The first thing I noticed was a pale yellow carpet."

"Had they drugged you and brought you somewhere?" Marco asked, confused.

"Not at all," smiled April slyly. "Turned out, it was all a dream. I had fallen out of bed and woke up looking up at my bed from the floor."

"Ugh!" sighed everybody in loud relief, as their bodies relaxed.

"All that for a dream?" whined Karla. "Girl, you

made my heart pound a mile a minute!"

"Well, imagine how mine must have felt!" April retorted. "I was completely confused. I spent the next few minutes trying to figure out how the flowered pastel wallpaper, spelling bee trophies, and academic achievement awards that I saw around me had made it all the way to this Asian gangster's prison. I finally recognized my mother's face next to mine and that's when it hit me what had happened."

"Wow," laughed Marco, "you sure got us good. Even Taylor bought into the whole story."

Taylor blushed a little at his own gullibility, but quickly recovered. "All right. I'll admit it. You got me, too. You're a good story-teller, but what does this all have to do with Project 20/20?"

"Don't you get it? It was a sign from my sub-conscious. My mom says that you can learn a lot from your dreams, if you bother to understand them."

Taylor rolled his eyes at what he perceived as new-age mumbo-jumbo. He had expected better from her. "So, what's it telling you: be a doctor instead of a teacher?"

"Not exactly. It's more complicated than that," April explained patiently. "The thing that kept sticking in my head throughout most of this dream was this tremendous sense of dread at having chosen the wrong path for my life. I kept saying to myself, 'If only this, if only that.... ' As I told this to my mother, it hit me that this 'if only' business reminded me of an ad I'd read right before I fell asleep. Turns out, it was the ad to participate in this experiment."

She reached into her pocket and pulled out a folded piece of magazine paper. "Did everybody see this ad?"

Karla shook her head no.

"Here. I'll read it to you." She turned towards Cheyenne and added, "That way you'll know which ad was effective." She unfolded the paper and read:

"If I only knew then what I know now."

"They say hindsight is 20/20..."

"If only I'd have known..."

How depressing are these sentences? Yet how many times have you heard adults say them when referring to choices they've made?

Have you ever thought to yourself, "Boy, I hope I never say something like that?"

The fact is, dear readers, you will always end up saying them. But wouldn't it be nice if you didn't have to say them about big life choices like your career?

Now you have that chance! Project 20/20 is an experimental program that lets you try different careers for an extended time. You will live away from your friends and family for ten months while you work full-time in up to 2 careers of your choice in a simulated real-world environment. You can choose to be anything from an actor to a zoologist.

While we do not guarantee that you will be successful in each career, we do guarantee that you will have a better understanding of each career's lifestyle by the time the experiment is finished.

If you are interested in participating in this unique opportunity, send an essay describing 2 careers you would like to try and why. Essays must not be more than 2 typed pages and must be post-marked no later than July 1. Send your responses to the following address:

Project 20/20
PO Box 2020
New York, NY 10010

Participants will be notified by the end of July.

Project 20/20: Making foresight 20/20!

"That ad really hit home with me. I mean that's what had been eating at me for most of this year. You see, you gotta understand my situation. Even though I'm 16, I just graduated high school. Sure, everybody thinks that's great, because it means you're smart and all that. Don't get me wrong, I'm not complaining."

"It sounds to me like you are," muttered Taylor, a little jealous despite himself.

"Ok, well maybe I am, but it's not what you think. You see, the problem is that I don't know what I want to do next."

"Neither do the rest of us. That's why we're here, right?" Marco offered.

"True, but there's a difference. Even though we're all about the same age, you have an extra year to decide what you want to do. I lost that when I skipped a year. All my friends my age have that extra year, and all my friends in my class are a year older and have already had that time. I'm getting short-changed."

"What's to decide?" Taylor inquired. "It's obvious what you'll do next: go on to a good college and excel there, too."

"Right, but what am I going to study? That's the big problem."

"Well, why not just pick something you like and are good at and study that?" asked Marco

"Because I like so many things and they all come pretty easy to me, it's hard for me to pick."

"So why not try one and if you don't like it, change to another? Or just study something general like Liberal Arts?" Karla asked, not feeling too much sympathy for April's supposed problems.

"My parents don't have that much money. It would be a waste of my energy and their money if I went there without a purpose in mind...at least that's what my father keeps telling me."

"And what does your mother say?" Mr. Auerbach inquired, a little saddened that her father would put that kind of pressure on her.

"She agrees that it doesn't make much sense to study when you don't know what you want to study, but she at least was more willing to consider other options."

"Why didn't you just ask to work for a year, or take a year off to find yourself? Lots of folks do that," Marco wondered aloud.

"I tried, but he wouldn't go for it. 'What are you going to do without a college degree,' he kept hammering me. 'Do you really want to flip burgers for a year? You're too good for that.' Or he'd say something like, 'Find yourself? You're right here. If you take a year off, what are you going to do? We don't have the money to send you all over the world, so you'll just end up sitting around watching TV all day. No daughter of mine is going to do that.' It's not true, you know. I wouldn't just sit around all day. I'm not that kind of person."

"So, how did you ever convince him to let you do this?" Taylor asked. It just didn't seem to make sense that a guy who was so conventional would allow his daughter to do something as experimental as this.

April smiled with great satisfaction. "Well, it's like my World History teacher used to say to us: Know thine enemy. My father's a stubborn, old mule, but he does have a soft spot for my mother. She's a bit unconventional…I think she must've been a hippie when she was young. I think they're proof that opposites do attract. She's also pretty clever and Dad really respects her opinion. I knew that if I could convince her, she'd find some way to work on him until he relented."

"So, how did you do it?" Taylor repeated.

"I started with an emotional plea. I showed her the ad and told her how my dream must be a manifestation of all the worries and pressures that I'd been feeling lately. (Mom's always super-sensitive about not harming my emotional well-being. I think she's afraid of any emotional damage they might have caused by skipping me ahead a grade.) Given that I was still shaking from my dream, when we started this discussion, it really didn't take too much additional work on my part to convince her of this."

April shifted her weight to her other hip and continued, "Then I appealed to her logical side. I explained to her that I'd be living away from home, just like if I were at college. I'd still get that part of my personal development and she and Dad would still get their long-anticipated freedom. (I find a little humor always goes a long way at softening her up.) I pointed out to her that if I did this, I'd be able to try out two careers of my choice. I could try one science and one language-related job and see which I like better. That would help me decide what to study. Plus, since I'd be working, I'd be doing something productive with my time.

"That at least got me far enough to enable me to investigate this further. I think my folks thought that I'd lose interest in the meantime. Boy, were they mistaken on that! The more I talked with Cheyenne and Mr. Auerbach, the more this seemed like just what I needed. Mr. Auerbach even met with my parents to explain the program to them."

Turning directly to Mr. Auerbach, she added, "Thanks, again, for doing that. It really made a big difference. Even my dad was impressed at the amount of precautions and preparations you guys were doing for this."

She turned back to the group, "Between my continued research, Mr. Auerbach's discussion, and my mom's constantly working on my dad, he finally relented and allowed me to participate. So," she smiled and threw her arms up in a Y-shape to frame her head and shoulders, here I am!"

Chapter 4:
Desperation

"Thank you, April, for that wonderful performance…I mean, introduction," joked Cheyenne. "Well, Karla, you're the only one left. Why don't you come up and introduce yourself?"

Karla Ruiz grimaced slightly, then slowly rose to her feet. How could she follow those acts, she wondered. She had neither April's drama-queen tendencies nor Taylor's oratorical talents, and, unlike Marco, she hadn't found a way to get someone else to do her work for her. She meandered towards center-stage, eyes glued to the floor, as she psyched herself up for what she had to do. If she couldn't even handle this, she chided herself, then maybe she shouldn't even attempt the program. Inhaling a big breath, she pushed her mousy-brown hair out of her eyes and tucked the strands behind her ears.

"My story's a little bit different than the rest of yours," she began, "but, in the end, we have similar reasons for participating."

Marco's hand shot up. "Excuse me," he interrupted, "but could you speak up a little? I'm having trouble hearing you."

"And while you're at it," added Taylor, "could you

please tell us your name?"

Karla blushed a little, took a deep breath again, looked up, and started over. "I'm sorry. My name is Karla Ruiz. Can you hear me better now?"

The group smiled and nodded.

"As I said, I heard about this program in a little bit different way than the rest of you. You see, Cheyenne is one of my best friends, and she encouraged me to apply. I never actually saw the advertisements, but once you've listened to Cheyenne talk, you might as well have been watching an infomercial!"

The newcomers smiled, but Mr. Auerbach and Lyle burst out laughing. She had hit the nail right on the head. This gave Karla the confidence to continue.

"Don't get me wrong. It's not like Cheyenne was just telling everybody she knew about this to drum up business. Quite the opposite, in fact. She'd been working on this for months before she even let me in on the secret."

"So how'd you get it out of her?" Marco inquired.

"Well, I really wasn't trying to. It just kind of came up in conversation. You see, before Cheyenne got involved in all of this, she and I would always meet for brunch on Saturdays at the Café Au Lait. It's this little coffeehouse in Greenwich Village. Man, I love that place!" Karla's brown eyes lit up as she described the restaurant. "Talk about ambience…man, that place has it. It feels like it's from another time. Unlike most coffee shops in Manhattan, people don't go there to order take-out coffee. The caffeine-buzzed go to Starbucks. People come here to absorb the aromas of the various blends, to delight in the delicate pastries, and to savor the serenity of this break from the city's turmoil. The place has been around forever. I hear that Jack Kerouac and many of his beatnik friends used to come here in the 1950s to read poetry."

"At a coffee shop?" Taylor interrupted snidely. "That doesn't make sense. I heard they only hung out at smoky bars, getting drunk or stoned."

"Maybe they went there to sober up," snipped Karla, annoyed that this guy was shattering her illusions about her favorite place. "Even if they didn't, they could have. It's that kind of a place. The wait staff is great: service is efficient, but they never rush you. You can stay there all day if you want, just contemplating life or enjoying the company of friends. That's how Cheyenne and I used to spend our Saturday afternoons, just hanging out there and catching up.

"Then, about eight months ago, things started to change. Cheyenne became all involved in this project and couldn't meet me every week. We only saw each other about four or five times during that period. That really stunk for me because I really looked forward to those meetings. Cheyenne has a wonderful way of putting everything in proper perspective, and I really needed that at that time. You see, things at home and at school were going from bad to worse for me and I had no one to talk to about it."

"Couldn't you talk to your Mom or Dad about it?" April asked gently.

"No," replied Karla sharply, causing April to open her eyes wide with surprise at the ferocity of the reply. "I told you, I'm not like the rest of you. I can't talk to my mom because she's a big part of the problem...and I can't talk to my father because the jerk ran out on my mother and me when I was six."

"Sorry...I didn't know," April responded meekly.

"No, I guess you wouldn't," Karla relented.

Uncomfortable with the minute or two of silence that ensued, Taylor tried to get the ball rolling again. "So what happened that made things go from bad to worse?"

"Unless you don't want to talk about it," offered Marco, worried that Karla might snap at them again.

"No, it's ok now. The problem was that my sixteenth birthday was approaching. For some, that means looking forward to driving, but for me, it meant freedom. Not freedom of the road, but freedom of thought. You see, in New York, you can drop out of school at sixteen...and that's what I intended to do. You gotta understand, I can't stand school. Not because I'm too dumb to do well, but because it bores me. It's too rigid and structured for my taste. I need freedom to think, and those jerks at school just want me to memorize formulas. That's not learning, that's just parroting. Math, science, history, grammar...all just parroting. Creative Writing and Art are the only two courses I can really tolerate. In the past, I've tried to get my mother to send me to one of the creative art magnet schools, but she never agreed. She always thought they were too flaky, or something. She forced me to stay in my local public school, so I swore that I would do so only as long as I had to. She tried brushing me off with one of those off-handed, 'OK. Whatever you say' type of remarks.

"So when it got to within six months of my birthday, I brought up the subject seriously. At first she ignored me or dismissed me. Then, one day, when I'd bugged her about it for the umpteenth time, she finally had it out with me. She yelled at me and went on about how no daughter of hers was going to be a quitter. She couldn't imagine anybody surviving in New York City without a college degree, much less a high school diploma."

Everyone but Marco nodded imperceptibly. They all agreed with Karla's mom, but nobody dared to say anything.

"The part that still irks me most is her vision of what my life should be," Karla complained, now rattling on, full steam ahead. "She thinks she has all the answers, but she doesn't get me at all. You know what she wants me to do? Finish high school, go on to college, and become an English teacher! Can you imagine: me, a teacher? Yuck! I can't even stand to be in school now. Why would I want to stay there for the rest of my life? If she had any sense of who I am, she'd realize I would make a wonderful painter or poet, but a lousy teacher." She paused, calming herself down. "That's why I needed to talk to Cheyenne. I had to get it off my chest somehow."

Taylor made a mental note to try to avoid this hot-tempered chick.

"We finally managed to get together for lunch one Saturday," Karla continued, "and poor Cheyenne really got an earful that day. She listened to me and instead of just doing the usual 'I hear you' sympathy routine, she actually came up with a good suggestion. You see, that's why I like Cheyenne: she's creative, like me, but much more energetic and positive. I need that counterbalance." She smiled appreciatively at her friend.

"Anyway, Cheyenne told me all about her neighbor Lyle had invented this quasi-time-travel device as part of an assignment for his Quantum Physics class at New York University. Naturally, I was skeptical of the whole thing at first. I mean, it does sound far-fetched, doesn't it? But then she explained how she'd actually tried this thing out herself. She went forward two weeks to see how she would do on a mid-term exam. In that world she ended up with an 86. The weird thing was that when she really got her results back, she had that exact score! The machine was right! Well, that caught my attention."

Marco pursed his lips in thought. Maybe this would be cooler than he thought. It probably would, if people like Taylor and Cheyenne were so psyched about it. After all, they were a lot smarter than him.

"Cheyenne went on to explain how she had convinced Lyle to start this company, with him in charge of the technical aspects and she in charge of marketing the new company. She also told me that she had convinced Mr. Auerbach to get involved. Do you realize who Mr. Auerbach is?" she asked the group, as she pointed her open hand in his direction.

Marco shrugged his shoulders, and Taylor remained stone-faced, but April smiled knowingly.

Karla turned towards Marco and Taylor and explained, "You remember a few years ago those TV commercials for Purrrfection cat food and Hope's Soap-on-a-Rope?"

Marco perked up. "Yeah! I remember those ads!" Now he was in familiar territory. "The cat food ad was hilarious and for the longest time I couldn't stop singing that stupid soap jingle."

"Well, that was him. Those were his ideas," Karla announced, as she proudly pointed to Mr. Auerbach. Mr. Auerbach smiled appreciatively and raised his hand in thanks.

Karla continued, "According to Cheyenne, he's also the guy who invented the Elima-Dust filter and the Travel-Lipo machine."

"Oh, right. I've seen them advertised on TV," Marco interjected. "The filter's supposed to suck up all the dust particles so you never have to dust again, right?"

Karla nodded in confirmation.

"What's this Travel-Lipo thing?" Taylor asked.

"It's like a little vacuum cleaner that you can attach to fat parts of your body and it sucks away the fat. It's like your own portable liposuction kit," April chimed in. "My mom has one of those and loves it."

Taylor pursed his lips and lifted an eyebrow as he gained a new-found appreciation for the old man in the back of the room.

Karla immediately recognized the look on Taylor's face: an almost god-like reverence for the big money-makers. She had seen it on so many of those Wall Street types and all over TV, and it always disgusted her. It always struck her that these people admired the size of the bank account, rather than those who did anything positive with that money. The starving artists with the brilliant ideas was always ignored and the charitable actions of the rich always were mentioned only in passing. She hated this attitude and didn't want Mr. Auerbach to fall victim to it, so she felt obliged to protect him, "Not only did he do very well with his inventions, but, according to Cheyenne, he decided to retire from advertising and start his own social charity called Young Entrepreneurs for America."

Taylor turned around in his seat excitedly. "YEA? You did that? I read about that in *BusinessWeek* a few months ago. I didn't realize that was you!" He turned around and explained to the rest of the group, "It's a foundation that's open to college students, but you have to submit an application explaining your idea for a new business. If accepted, you get a grant of some seed-money to help you start your company. You're also paired with a business executive who serves as a mentor. The goal is to encourage the development of more small businesses and to promote innovative thinking among tomorrow's business leaders."

"That's right," added Mr. Auerbach proudly. "And I was so impressed with what Lyle and Cheyenne had already planned and accomplished that I decided to mentor them myself."

Cheyenne recognized her friend's ploy to divert attention away from herself but didn't want her to get away with it. "Karla, as usual," interrupted Cheyenne, "was pretty skeptical about the whole thing initially. Convincing her to apply took a lot of persuasion but I ultimately succeeded. One thing you gotta realize about her: when she does make up her mind to do something, she goes at it 200%. I mean, you should hear the poem she wrote for her application. Come on, Karla, why don't you read it to us?"

Karla looked down at the ground and wiggled her foot around. "Oh, I don't know," she responded meekly. "It's not really a poem. Besides, these people don't want to hear that old whiny thing. I think everyone would rather just get on with the experiment, right?"

Marco leaned forward, elbows on his knees and partially raised his right hand. "Actually, I'd like to hear it," he said timidly. A pretty girl reciting her own poetry sounded like the perfect way to delay the inevitable.

"Great," Taylor thought to himself, as he crossed his arms and slouched in his chair, "there he goes again wasting my time flirting with the dowdy art chicks. Why can't he ever go after the hot babes?"

Encouraged by the interest, Karla relented. "OK. I'll read it. But you gotta remember I was in a really bad place when I wrote this. I'm better now, thanks to the hope this program has offered me." She reached in her pocket, pulled out a crumpled piece of paper, opened it up and began reading:

I am a seed: full of potential beauty and yet capable of nothing. With the proper nourishment I could grow and bring life and meaning to others. Left unprotected, however, I will become nothing more than a speck of dirt: another collectible for the street sweeper.

What do I see coming towards me? A

storm...no a hurricane...no... a tornado! It approaches, growing faster and faster. I watch as it gains force, turns into a funnel, and comes my way. I am helpless. In its wake I see only destruction, gloom, and sorrow. I cannot help but wonder what will happen to me. Will I be carried in its funnel to some exotic locale, blocks or even miles from here? Will its headwinds simply push me out of the path of the storm? Will I end up under a building, in one piece but unable to ever grow, destined to be something that sooner or later is swept out with the trash? Will I be caught in the immense power that is the tornado itself? Will I be blown to smithereens, never to have done anything in my life but wait patiently for the future?

If I were not a seed what would I be? I would choose something that would allow me to share my inner beauty more easily with my surroundings. I would be a painter, so that I could draw for others the images that are in my head. Perhaps I would be a singer, so those who could not see could enjoy with their ears the beauty I have to give.

I am not sure; I only know that right now I wish someone would step on me so I would not have to bear the anticipation of the approaching storm.

The room filled with a heavy silence as all sat in awe of Karla's words. "Anyway," she concluded solemnly, "I think Project 20/20 is better than any of the other alternatives I was considering, and my mom finally came to that same conclusion." She shoved the paper back in her pocket and quickly took her seat, wanting to fade into the rug.

Chapter 5:
The Adventure Begins

September 1: New York

Lyle slowly made his way back to the front of the room. He pushed up his glasses with his pointer finger, looked at his watch, and cleared his throat. "Well...er...um...thank you for sharing, Karla." He cleared his throat again. "But the day is moving on, isn't it? I suppose we really should get back to business. We need to send you off so you can start your new lives. Any volunteers to go first?" he asked, peering back and forth at his audience.

A hush fell over the room one more time. Each participant looked around with eyes full of anticipation, excitement, and fear. Who wanted to be the first to brave the machine and enter the simworld? Taylor wanted to see what would happen before he tried it. April still had doubts whether this really was a good idea. Marco was still trying to determine which of his careers he would try first. Karla knew that no world could be worse than the one in which she currently felt trapped. She could not wait to be sprung from her cage.

"I'll go," Karla volunteered, as the rest of the participants breathed a sigh of relief.

"Wonderful. In that case, please lie down on the

couch."

Once Karla had made herself comfortable, Lyle sat at a stool behind Les and began adjusting the knobs. The machine buzzed as it warmed up. "Well, Miss Brave One, what career would you like to try for the next five months?"

"I would like to be a painter."

Lyle typed something on a keyboard. "OK. Now, we need to tell LES how advanced you are in your career. Do you want to enter your life just when you are beginning your career, at the point when you are starting to gain some recognition for your work, at the height of your success, or after you have peaked?"

Karla needed to think about that for a moment. Did she want to see how one gets started in a career in painting or did she want to experience life at its best? Did she want to be there at the moment when she comes into her own or did she want to see what it would be like to be headed towards retirement? She had never considered this before.

"Since I've never done this before, I guess seeing if I like retirement is a little like putting the cart before the horse," she thought aloud. "I really want to know what I would be getting myself into with this career. If I take the height then I won't have a good picture of what it will take to succeed. Therefore, I think I would like to try entering right before I hit it big."

Lyle nodded in agreement and played with one of the dials. He typed some more than peered around the corner to look at Karla on the couch. "Where would you like to live?"

"That's easy! All new artists live in SoHo, in

Manhattan. I want to be among the trendsetters, so I would like to live in SoHo, too."

"Very well." Lyle did some more typing. Finally, he flipped the big, red switch. He listened as LES buzzed and hummed faster and louder. Soon, the machine was vibrating noisily. The lights in the room flickered and grew dim as LES sucked up electricity. Gradually, a stream of light shot out from the satellite dish and began to surround Karla. The light unfolded into a curtain of fog. Thirty seconds later, the machine was quiet again, the fog had lifted, the lights had returned to full strength, and Karla had disappeared.

The crowd gasped. Karla was really no longer there. Everybody but Lyle raced to the couch to touch it. Nobody could believe it. With all the electricity that had flown around the couch, not a thread of material was seared. In fact, the couch felt cool to the touch. It did not even look as if someone had been sitting in it. Every sign of Karla's existence in that space was erased.

"Next?" Lyle bellowed like a man behind a deli counter.

Taylor bounded onto the couch. Now that he saw what would happen, he could not wait to see what would greet him on the other side.

"I'll go," he declared. "I want to be a policeman."

"A policeman it will be," Lyle confirmed as he again typed in data. "How far along in your career path do you wish to be?"

"Put me right before I reach the highpoint of my career. I want to enjoy the feeling of becoming the best cop in town."

"Where would you like to live?"

That required a little bit more thought. He wanted to go where the crime-fighting action was sure to be good. If he picked a rural area, there might not be anything more exciting than an occasional burglary for the entire time. He would end up spending five months just waiting. As he thought about this magical new experience, he decided he might as well live somewhere different than Texas, where he had grown up. He was impressed by what little he had seen of New York yesterday. If he chose to stay in Manhattan, he could also use his time to sightsee and experience a new part of the country. "I'd like to live in Manhattan," he decided.

"As you like," Lyle answered as he entered data, adjusted the dials, and flicked the switch. Within a few minutes, the machine again began to buzz and whir louder and louder. Just as before, the lights grew dim and the electric fog encircled him. Just as with Karla, when the lights returned, Taylor was gone.

"April, are you ready to try this?" Mr. Auerbach offered.

"I guess so. I'll save you the questions. I'd like to be a doctor working at a hospital here in New York City. I'd like to begin right before I hit it big. That way I can see two different phases in five months."

Lyle smiled as he prepared to send April into her simworld. He liked a woman who knew what she wanted. He waved good-bye as she became enveloped in the electrical curtain.

"I guess it's my turn," Marco ventured after April disappeared.

"You're the last," confirmed Cheyenne. "What would you like to be?"

Marco stared at the floor as he made his way over to the couch. The moment of truth had arrived. Should he pick a career that he believed was more suitable for him or should he keep his promise to his friend? Why did he let Taylor talk him into this anyway? Why did he agree that they would both try the same first career? Was this going to be a waste of five months? Was one career as good as another? Was it worth potentially damaging a friendship to do what one wanted? What else would he want to be? In the few remaining moments he had, Marco made up his mind that loyalty, friendship, and integrity to one's promises were most important.

"I'd like to be a cop in New York, too."

"And at what point in your career would you like to be?" Lyle asked without looking up from behind his machine.

"I might as well see how far I can go, so right before I am at my peak would be good. Thank you."

As Marco disappeared into the other realm, the three founding members of Project 20/20 looked at each other and smiled.

Chapter 6:
The Commission

SimTime: September 1, New York

Karla rolled over slowly in her bed, stretched, and glared at the clock, trying to read the blurry numbers. 11:30 AM, she thought it said. She rolled back and closed her eyes. Karla hated waking up. Usually, though, her mother would have woken her hours ago.

Karla's bolted upright. No wonder her mother had not bothered her this morning! She was not in her mother's home; she was in the simworld! Karla jumped out of bed filled with newfound energy. Where was she? What was she? How was her life? So much to learn! So little time! Why had she already wasted so many hours of the one free day she had before work began? Where was work, for that matter?

Karla started by wandering around her apartment. She seemed to be living in an artist's studio loft. She was standing in a large central room with hardwood floors, bare walls, and a high ceiling. Obviously, she thought, this was one of those "pre-war" buildings built in the 1920's. Toward the north lay the bed where she had been sleeping. To the east a small refrigerator, sink, counter and stove stood in a row. Directly across from the kitchen she spotted the bathroom, and next to it, a small closet. Scattered throughout the remaining space were canvasses of half-started paintings on easels, paint canisters, paint brushes, rags, and assorted other art supplies. Behind the artwork, underneath the only window in the apartment, stood a tattered couch and coffee table, the only other furniture in the entire place.

The cluttered yet empty appearance of the apartment startled Karla a little at first, but as she studied the paintings, and considered her choice, she quickly came to accept her surroundings. How else would a painter about to hit it big in New York City live? She was lucky to have such a nice apartment in … where exactly was she? She looked out her window to the street corner: Greene and Spring Streets. What a great location! Right in the heart of SoHo, near her favorite art galleries and restaurants.

Karla scrounged through the kitchen cabinets for something to nibble. Her stomach grumbled but curiosity consumed her mind too much to let her sit and eat a leisurely breakfast. She grabbed a granola bar and nibbled at it semi-consciously as she wandered back to the easels and stared at the miscellaneous collection of lines and colors that seemed splashed on the canvas in an almost random fashion. What the heck could she be trying to draw, she wondered. She walked up close to the half-completed canvasses, stared hard at each, cocked her head sideways, closed one eye, took three steps back, cocked her head in the other direction, closed her other eye, blinked three times, and finally shrugged her shoulders. She had no idea where she was going with these canvases. What kind of painter was she?

Karla remembered Lyle's explanation of how the machine would supposedly imbue her with the necessary knowledge to do the career she had selected. Her lack of understanding made her wonder whether this had actually happened. Only one way to find out, she concluded. She picked up her palette and some paint and gave it a try. She squeezed the paint out of the tubes, located the correct paintbrushes, and blended the paints easily enough. Maybe it had worked. Then again, she had taken a few painting classes in the past. Maybe the hours of preparing paint had stuck with her.

After a few minutes, Karla felt ready for the big test. She selected a thick brush, dabbed some paint on it, walked back and forth in front of the selection of half-finished works until one finally called out to her, stopped, took a deep breath, and lifted the brush. Here goes nothing, she muttered. Swoosh. Swoosh. Two lines stood stark naked on the otherwise empty half of the canvas. Hmmm…she thought it would happen more magically than that. They didn't look like any emerging image. They just looked out of place. Where was this miraculous talent? Could Lyle have lied to her? Maybe the machine hadn't work right?

Beginning to grow seriously concerned that she might have made a dreadful mistake participating in this experiment, Karla decided a walk would calm her down. She tossed on a loose white cotton shirt and some overalls

from her closet and descended the stairs to the outside
world. Karla's suspicions grew as she viewed the world
outside her doorstep. If she had travelled to the future, why
were almost all the shops and galleries the same?
Shouldn't they have changed with the times?

As she wandered through the streets among the
Sunday afternoon tourists, she couldn't help feeling a
strange sensation in her stomach. She didn't know why,
but she thought someone was following her. She quickly
glanced over her left shoulder to see who was behind her,
then walked as non-chalantly as she could for half a block
before taking a more careful look behind her. Other than
some punk with orange spiked hair and a guy with a
hideous tie, nobody struck her as particularly unusual.
Karla shrugged her shoulders. Probably just her usual
anxiety, she decided.

Seeing tourists window-shopping at the art galleries
and eclectic boutiques gave Karla an idea: perhaps some of
her works were on display in a gallery. Karla decided then
and there on her mission for the day: search the galleries
for her paintings and stop panicking over failed
experiments and mysterious imaginary people.

The Dyansen Gallery stood three doors in front of
her at just this moment. She marched over there and
bravely stepped inside. The standard Erté art deco
sculptures and paintings lined the walls of the first room.
Typical, she thought dismissively. She quickly glanced
around each of the other rooms in the gallery: some
Warhols, Chagalls, and other super-famous artists lined the
walls. Karla shook her head slightly and walked out

quickly. They wouldn't have her works. She doubted she was that big yet.

Karla walked south on Mercer for several blocks, bypassing several other galleries that she knew represented similar big-name artists. Again, she felt like someone was tailing her. She stopped at a newspaper stand and looked behind her while thumbing through a magazine. She gasped! About five doors down from her stood that same man from before: well-built, wearing dark sunglasses, jeans, a light blue button-down shirt, and the worst tie she had ever seen. It looked like a paint factory had exploded on it. Karla threw down the magazine, and walked quickly away. "Calm down," she scolded herself. "It's Sunday in SoHo. Of course you're going to see oddly dressed people. Besides, do you think you're the only one who has thought to walk up and down this street? Get a grip!"

Quickening her pace, she turned left onto Broome Street. The sight made her smile with eager anticipation and forget her worries. The colored awnings of smaller galleries featuring younger artists hung like flags lining a parade route off both sides of this street. Karla guessed that someone here would be more likely to represent her. She marched with renewed optimism into the first gallery. Unlike Dyansen's, this store contained only one showroom filled with lots of paintings of hunt scenes. Karla immediately turned around and walked out. Too British for her taste.

The next gallery held very few paintings, and seemed to focus on sculptures only. Since Karla had not seen any clay or other sculpting tools in her apartment, she was pretty sure this place wouldn't help her on her quest. Block after block she walked, ruling out one place after another on the grounds that she didn't like their artwork and therefore wouldn't paint anything like that .

By 3:30 on this Indian summer afternoon, Karla was growing weary: she couldn't find any sign of her art and she still had that sinking feeling that someone was following her. Every time she had left a gallery, she had paused on the step to look around her. Each time she spotted the man in the ugly tie not too far away, but still closing in on her. She decided to turn down an alleyway to get away from him. After all, maybe she was paranoid and he just was looking around. If she picked an unusual route, maybe she could ditch him.

Walking quickly through the alley, she kept glancing over her shoulder. Why would anybody want to chase her, she wondered. She only had a few dollars in her pockets. She froze in her tracks as a thought hit her: she had just placed herself in the perfect location to be mugged. Her stomach dropped to her feet and kicked her legs in gear. She began running towards the end of the alley in a panic. How could she have been so stupid to go down an isolated path? She'd grown up in the city and knew better than that. The alleyway seemed to stretch forever in front of her. Her mind raced twice as fast as her feet: When would she reach the end? Why was he after her? Maybe she really was in some alternate world and she had done something to upset somebody. Maybe her future self had gotten involved with some druglord and now they were out to get her. What should she do?

Finally reaching the end of the alley, she turned right onto a normal city street. She didn't quite know where she was but it didn't really matter. She saw people and shops and felt more secure. Ducking into the first open door, she found herself inside the Launch Pad Gallery. Judging by the crowds of people and the drinks table, she figured that it must be new.

After gulping down two glasses of water, Karla began to feel more like herself again. While catching her breath and wiping the sweat from her forehead with a napkin, she studied her new surroundings. The gallery had the most interesting layout she had ever seen. The front desk stood guard in a small vestibule that ended in a T-intersection. Several small showrooms branched off to the left of the vestibule. To the right lay the main showroom. Assuming she had more of a chance of being in one of the smaller galleries, Karla turned left. The first room contained some impressive woodwork that resembled landscapes. The next room contained almost obscene watercolors of nude men. The third room contained abstract paintings. This looked a little like what she had seen in her apartment. Carefully examining the cards next to each painting, Karla tried to find anything with her name on it. None were hers. Karla sighed with rising disappointment.

Eventually, Karla wandered into the big room, which was teaming with people, all abuzz over the pieces they were viewing. The paintings in that chamber were three-dimensional, multi-colored, and abstract. They seemed to focus on the use of lines and design while still coming across as somewhat representational. Karla wasn't sure what to make of them. She was impressed by the technical mastery involved in putting together such pieces. She leaned in to take a closer look and gasped. There, in the corner of the canvas, she recognized her own signature. Fearful of going crazy, Karla quickly glanced at the name tag:

City Sunrise/Sunset
Oil and tempera on cardboard and canvas
Artist: Karla Ruiz
$800

Karla stumbled backwards two steps with disbelief. She quickly scoped out the other paintings in this main gallery. All were her creations. She felt elated, all her earlier worries melting like ice cream on a hot day. The experiment had worked. She hadn't been swindled. She could now claim true status as a showed artist. She paused, mid-glory. Somehow, though, it didn't feel right. First of all, she reasoned, she hadn't really created them herself. They were just miraculously planted there by LES. Would she really have the talent to create more works like this? Judging by her attempt earlier in the day, she seriously doubted it. More importantly, though, she did not even understand these paintings. Where was the so-called sunrise? She returned to the canvas to study it some more.

The more she stared at the piece, the more it began to make sense. The top half of the canvas consisted of hundreds of small folded cardboard triangles which were glued, points facing outward, to the canvas. The left sides of the triangles were painted different shades of pinks, oranges, and reds. She guessed that, when viewed from the left, these represented the sunrise. The other sides of the folds were painted with shades of blues, mauves, and reds which probably represented the sunset. The bottom half of the canvas represented the city. A group of larger, painted triangles of various sizes gave the impression of skyscrapers while a series of wild lines painted on top gave a sort of frenetic energy to the buildings.

Karla noticed an older gentleman standing next to her. "What do you think of this one?" she asked, trying to sound casual.

"Too busy for my taste," groused the old man. "Give me the old masters any day." He turned away, grabbed his wife by the arm, and exited the gallery.

Not too promising a start, Karla worried. She turned to a middle-aged woman next to her. "Interesting, eh?" Karla offered.

"Well, it certainly has an energy all its own, doesn't it?" the woman responded.

"Would you say you liked it?" Karla asked.

"I'm not sure 'like' is the word I'd choose. It's definitely 'different' and innovative, but I'm not sure I'd want to pay the $800 for it. I can't imagine displaying it in my living room. It does hold my attention, though. I'm curious to see the rest of this show." With that the woman excused herself and walked to one of the other paintings.

Karla began to feel a familiar knot tightening in her stomach. The negative reviews from her two-person survey cut short her initial euphoria. How was she going to hit it big if nobody liked her work? Was she going to have to die to gain fame? Maybe Lyle had programmed the computer incorrectly.

"Amazing. Utterly amazing." A man's voice broke Karla's train of thought. A young man in a Gucci suit and Rolex watch stood next to her, admiring *City Sunrise/Sunset*. "This is the best thing I've seen in months. It's so innovative…so complex. It's like a cross between Jackson Pollock, Pablo Picasso, and Yaakov Agam but yet it's so different.

Karla reeled. What a compliment…to be put in the same company with such distinguished artists! Life was great! She knew now that she had done the right thing in joining this experiment. How could she have ever doubted herself? Completely thrilled with her newfound identity, Karla flitted across the room, admiring each of her works. She studied them carefully, albeit somewhat erratically, as she tried to absorb her style so that she could recreate it in the future. After all, she couldn't just rest on her laurels, she reminded herself.

After what seemed like the happiest half-hour of her life, Karla skipped gleefully out of the gallery. Turning the corner to head down the street, a voice interrupted her reverie. "Karla Ruiz? I thought I'd find you here. Can we talk for a moment?"

Karla's heart skipped a beat. She stood face to face with ugly-tie-man. This was it, she steeled herself. She knew her happiness could not last long; it never did. At least she had enjoyed her last hour of life, she consoled herself. She gulped. What could she do? This tall, thirty-something-year-old man was standing directly in front of her. If she ran, all he had to do was reach out and grab her. If she kicked him in the crotch, that might work, but it might just antagonize him. Should she shout and create a scene? Yes, she decided, that might work.

"Stay away! Stay away, do you hear?" she shouted as loud as she could. "Don't touch me! I don't have any money!"

A few passers-by glanced at her but kept walking. Some others just crossed the street and avoided looking at this woman they thought was crazy.

"Shh! Shhh!" hissed the man. "Please, be quiet," he begged as he waved his hands in a downward motion like a conductor telling an orchestra to play quietly.

"What do you want from me?" she shouted hysterically. "Whatever you want, I don't have it! Who are you? Why are you following me? How do you know my name?"

"That's what I want to talk to you about. If you'll be quiet and walk with me, I'll tell you," he explained as calmly as he could, given the scene. "I promise I won't hurt you."

Sensing that her scene wasn't working in this city where people are afraid to get involved, she slowly relented. "All right, but make it quick. And we're staying on this street, you hear?"

"Fine. Thank you," he responded gratefully.

"Karla," the man began, "My name is Steve Ang. Does that name mean anything to you?"

"Not really," she responded suspiciously.

"Perhaps you've heard of my mother, Dr. Ping

Ang?"

"No."

Steve whistled in disbelief. "Wow. You must be newer than we thought. Hmm...I hope that's not going to be a problem," he thought aloud.

"Problem? For what?" asked Karla.

"Let me explain. My mother is a very prominent art collector here in New York. Despite her eccentricities, she's probably one of the best in the world at spotting new talents. She's also on the Board at both the Guggenheim and the Museum of Modern Art.

"Each year she hosts a party in February where she displays the works of three or four up-and-coming artists. Usually, it's a pretty safe bet to say that at least one of these featured artists later ends up on display at one of those two museums. In the past, she used to go around herself and speak directly with the gallery owners and the artists, but then she started getting too many pestering calls from amateur artists wanting to be in her shows. Frankly, it's kind of turned her into something of a recluse. She'll still go to galleries herself to look at the new artists, but she always goes in disguise. She has given up on talking with artists directly before she's commissioned them. That's where I come in."

"I'm not sure I follow," Karla responded.

"I handle all her business dealings..."

"If you handle all her business, then why were you following me all day today? Why didn't you just introduce yourself to me earlier in the day and not scare the pants off me?" she interrupted.

"I'm sorry. I didn't mean to frighten you. I was just heading to your building when you went out to walk. I tried to catch up with you but you kept ducking into galleries. I don't want to have the same problem my mother did so I avoid making offers in galleries, especially where I know the owner knows me. Then you kept running away, which made it hard to get your attention."

"Oh, don't worry. You got my attention all right. You mentioned an offer; is that what you wanted to talk to me about?"

"Yes. My mother spotted your works at the Launch Pad and was quite impressed with them. She'd like to make you an offer."

"An offer?" Karla could not believe her ears. "What kind of offer?"

"Well, more like a commission, but also kind of like entry into a contest. You see, she would like you to create five related paintings that can be displayed in a long corridor or museum gallery. She'll pay you 50%, or $3,000 up front and the remainder when all five are completed and delivered to her."

"Fantastic," Karla exclaimed. "This is too good to be true. My paintings are going to be on display at a major museum. You're kidding me, right?"

"Wait a minute," he cautioned, as he grabbed her arm to calm her down. "First of all, there's no guarantee yours will be the one that makes it to the museum. Remember, she's also going to display three other artists who have the same aspirations as you. Secondly, the catch is that if you don't have the paintings ready by a few days before her party, then the deal is dead."

"Dead?" Karla's eyes opened wide. "You mean if I don't finish all five on time she won't buy any of them?"

"That's right," Steve confirmed, nodding his head in agreement.

"When is the deadline?"

"January 31."

Karla gasped. How was she ever going to complete five paintings in five months? She could barely understand her own works, much less come up with 5 new ones! Why couldn't LES have made her a normal artist? Why couldn't she have just drawn portraits?

"Well, whaddya say? You in?"

"Gosh," Karla stammered and blushed, "I don't know what to say. It's so much…in such a short time. I don't know if I can…I mean, I'm sure I can, but the timeframe is so tight…It's so much to absorb."

The man laughed appreciatively and removed his oversized sunglasses to reveal the most beautiful set of Asian eyes that Karla had ever seen. "Look, one of my mother's rules is that the artist must be confident enough to accept the commission on the spot, or the offer dies when I walk away. However, I really put you through the wringer today…much more than I intended to. I'll tell you what I'll do for you. I'll pretend that I didn't talk to you today. You go home and think about it. I'll meet you tomorrow for breakfast at the Moonlight Diner at 9:00 and you can give me your answer then. OK?"

Karla smiled appreciatively and nodded.

"Great. See you then."

As Steve put on his glasses and walked away, Karla wondered how she ever could have been so afraid of such a kind and good-looking man.

Chapter 7:
Cruising

SimTime: September 1, New York

Taylor and Marco were cruising around the streets of lower Manhattan looking at the people, the buildings, and the cars. Everywhere they drove, vehicles cleared out of their way and heads turned to look at them. Taylor was enjoying his first evening on the beat: wearing a uniform, riding in a car with sirens and flashing lights, driving around town while listening to music, and getting paid for it to boot! At one hour into his first shift, Taylor was convinced that this was an awesome job. Marco sat in the car next to Taylor, listening to the dispatch radio and anxiously watching for potential trouble.

Lyle had rigged it so the two rookies would be on the same 7:00 PM – 3:00 AM shift.   Marco appreciated having the time to figure out their new lives. He had enjoyed walking around and feeling the energy of the big city. Along the way, he had decided to set a new goal for himself of visiting each of the music clubs in lower Manhattan at least once in the next five months. He figured he could pick up some tips from other guitarists.

Marco loved music. When he played his guitar, he

felt transported to another, more peaceful world. The tones the strings produced when plucked or strummed fascinated him. He could sit around for hours, playing with chord progressions. The sounds provided the perfect backdrop for contemplating the future, friends, music, and life. If he could figure out how, he would gladly spend the rest of his life just playing with his guitar. In the meantime, going to the clubs would at least give him some refuge from this crazy world of policing. He still wasn't quite sure why he'd agreed to Taylor's plan. Oh well, he figured, for five months he could handle anything.

For now, though, Marco was just grateful that LES had been kind enough to make Taylor and him not only work partners, but also roommates. This saved them both the trouble of having to explain, or avoid explaining, their situations to new partners. Marco also felt much more at ease knowing his best buddy, who was so smart and brave, would be nearby to look after him.

At two hours into their shift, Taylor was becoming restless. Here he was in Gotham itself and he had received no calls. He had learned in the pre-shift briefing that he and Marco were to stay in a 20-block radius. Already they had driven up and down each street at least once. He wanted action! If the dispatcher wasn't going to give them any, then he'd have to find it himself, he decided.

Taylor turned on the lights and sirens and charged through a red light. "What are you doing?!" Marco cried in alarm.

"Did you see that guy in the Camaro?" Taylor asked indignantly. "He just drove through a red light."

"So did you!" exclaimed Marco.

"Ah, but that's different! We're allowed. In fact, it's our duty. We need to stop such scofflaws from wreaking havoc on the traffic patterns of this fine city." Taylor rationalized authoritatively.

Marco shook his head in amazement. Here they were on their first day on the job and already Taylor was looking for trouble. Why couldn't he just continue to hang low and avoid any problems? Sensing that there was nothing more he could do at this point, he resigned himself to calling in the automobile stop.

"Cover me while I talk with the driver," Taylor ordered.

"Aye, aye," Marco muttered.

Marco watched as Taylor lumbered over to the stopped car and asked the driver for the license, registration, and insurance. Taylor certainly managed to get into the spirit of things very quickly. Marco was amazed how his buddy slipped into a power-crazed attitude as quickly as he slipped on his uniform.

Taylor returned to the car with the driver's papers. He turned the car's mounted computer terminal toward him and entered the driver's license. Within a few short moments, the driver's record came back as clear.

"Since he's got a good record, why don't you just give him a warning and let him go?" Marco suggested.

"Are you crazy? I'm about to give this guy two tickets: one for driving through a red light and another for having expired insurance."

"When did it expire?"

"Yesterday."

"Geez, are you crazy? The guy probably hasn't had the chance yet to put the new card in his car. Why don't you cut him a break?"

"I am. Technically, I should tow him, but I'm just giving him a ticket." Taylor grabbed his ticket book and strode back to the driver.

Marco sat there dumbfounded. Of all people, he never thought Taylor would be such a stickler for the law. How ironic, he thought, considering all the times Taylor had driven way above the speed limit. Marco couldn't bear to watch his partner hand the man the ticket. As he turned his head to the side, he noticed a suspicious-looking man walk past him for the third time since Taylor had pulled the car over. He felt compelled to watch this stringy-looking guy in the cheap suit and expensive briefcase walk up and down the street.

So obsessed had Marco become with this guy that he didn't even notice when Taylor returned to the car.

"What are you staring at so intently? Some pretty girls over there or something?" Taylor's voice boomed through Marco's head like a stereo turned to 10. Marco dismissed the sarcastic remark with a wave of his hand as if swatting at an annoying gnat.

"You wanted action, right?" Marco asked slowly.

"You bet! Whaddya got?" Taylor responded with increasing interest.

"See that guy over there walking away from us?" Marco said as he inconspicuously pointed in the direction of the suspect .

"Which one? There's gotta be at least 20 on this block."

"See the gangly-looking dude with the greasy ponytail? He's wearing a suit that looks two sizes too big but is carrying a pretty nice looking suitcase."

"Yeah, I see him. He's wearing Nikes, too, right? What about him?"

Marco hesitated. "I'm not quite sure...but.... there's something fishy about him."

Taylor raised his right eyebrow dubiously. "Why? He's probably some schmo on his way to work. What's the big deal?"

"You're probably right," Marco shrugged, "but ... it just doesn't make sense. Why would a guy who can afford such an expensive briefcase wear such a crummy outfit? If he's going to work, why is he wearing sneakers?"

Taylor glanced sideways at his buddy and sneered, "When did you become the fashion police? He's probably just wearing sneakers so he doesn't wear out his good shoes. I hear a lot of people do that in this city."

Marco turned to look directly at Taylor. "There's more to it than that. While you were busy ticketing Mr. Camaro, this guy walked past me three times already. If he were on his way to work, why would he be pacing these two blocks? And there's something else. He keeps peeping his head into every doorway and looking over his shoulder...like he's looking for someone."

Taylor stopped smirking. Maybe his partner was onto something. "So...uh...what do you think we should do?"

"Let's just hang here a few minutes and…..hmmm…that's interesting."

"What? What's interesting?" Taylor asked as he craned his neck towards the passenger window.

"See that last doorway before the corner? There's a stoner hanging out in it."

"We're near Greenwich Village. What's so unusual about that?"

"He wasn't there before. He must have snuck in there while I was talking to you. And look, our 'friend' is slowly making his way over towards that doorway!" Marco paused abruptly to process all that was happening. "You know, I think we're about to witness a drug deal go down. As soon as they exchange the goods for the money, let's go after them. I'll take the dealer and you can take the buyer."

"You're kidding, right?" Taylor was taken aback. Where had his friend acquired this new-found crime-sniffing talent? He'd never seen Marco so focused on anything outside of his guitar before.

Marco stared intently. "Get ready. Start opening the door slowly, but don't let anyone see that it's opened." He spoke in almost dazed manner. "Wait for my signal…They're shaking hands and talking …That's it! Did you see them slip each other the packages? OK! NOW! Let's go!"

Both men burst from the car and started running towards them. "STOP!! POLICE!!!" shouted Taylor as he waved his badge. At that exact instant, time slowed to a crawl for Marco. His eyes cringed momentarily at Taylor's stupidity in ruining the surprise. He watched in exasperation as the criminals jerked their heads in the direction of the noise, then took off in opposite directions. Marco felt his feet shift into overdrive as he chased after them. He vaguely heard Taylor shout from behind, "I'll take the one coming towards us. You get the other one going the other way."

Marco had never felt his senses this sharp before. For half a second, he felt scared at the almost out-of-body feeling he was experiencing, but then his focus continued to sharpen. He could see the stoner a block and a half ahead of him. Marco's legs propelled him so fast that his brain could barely keep up with his surroundings. People seemed to disappear from view. He locked on his target. He almost magically zigged to the right to avoid a blurred group of pedestrians than zagged to the left to avoid some fast-moving object. The target was getting closer…they were on the same block now. More speed. More zigging and zagging. Marco felt like he was flying.

His prey approached the next street. Marco had to catch him. Trucks blocked the intersection. This is it, thought Marco, I'll get him now! Marco closed to within a quarter-block of him when the guy made a sharp right turn and headed across town. "Out of the way," Marco managed to shout as he cleared the corner. His target grew even larger in his sights. Was he focusing even more extremely or was the guy really slowing down? The stoner seemed confused, looking left and right for a way out of a crowd of people who were stopped for a moving van blocking the sidewalk. Marco leaped towards him but missed. The guy turned right into an alleyway. Marco regained his balanced and shifted directions after him again. Where the heck is my backup, he wondered as he ran.

Meanwhile, Taylor pursued the dealer, who had narrowly avoided capture by turning left at the intersection just in front of where Marco and Taylor had split. Now Taylor understood why this guy had on Nikes: he ran like the wind. Taylor hurried after him, jumping over up-ended garbage cans and pushing people out of his way. He had never run so hard in his whole life. His ears were flooded with the sounds of the chase: his pounding heartbeat, his heavy breathing, the hammer-like striking of his feet on the cement, the abnormally loud clanking of the rolling garbage cans, the angry shouts of shoved pedestrians. When was this guy going to stop, he wondered. Taylor doubted he could keep this up much longer.

The dealer turned left into an alleyway and stopped briefly at the sight of his customer and the other cop running directly towards them. Taylor seized the moment and threw his baton at the dealer. The guy tripped but did not fall. He turned around and hurled his briefcase, catching Taylor square in the gut. Taylor reeled backwards, momentarily stunned and winded from the leather punch to his stomach.

"Switch!" yelled Marco to Taylor. "I've got yours. He's coming right at me!"

Marco dove into the dealer and chest-butted him to the ground. The two men wrestled around the alley floor, trading punches, while Taylor stretched his arms out sideways and managed to grab the stoner by the waist as he was running past. He slammed the stoner against the wall, then flipped him around and pushed his face into the bricks to cuff him just as Marco finally managed to pin the dealer on his stomach and cuff him, too.

*****

Back at the station, Taylor and Marco strutted like proud sports fishermen as they brought in their first catch of the day and tossed them into the holding cell. Having dropped off their catch, they headed to the squad room to write their reports and examine the contents of the bags.

"Holy crow!" Taylor exclaimed as he opened the briefcase. "What a find. This guy's a walking pharmacy! There's gotta be at least 4 pounds of cocaine and ten types of pills in here! How does he carry all this garbage around with him?"

Just then Lieutenant Thompson, the shift's Officer-In-Charge, strolled over to the desk and gently placed his hand on Marco's shoulder. "I assume this catch was primarily your doing, Centano?" he praised gruffly as he glanced askance at Taylor. "Geez, who needs the K-9 division when we've got drug sniffers like you!" He paused for a moment as he watched Taylor head to the restroom. "Hey, let's you and me take a walk for a minute."

Marco shrugged his shoulders, stood up, and walked down the corridor with the OIC. Lieutenant Thompson, a big burly ex-Marine who still kept his crew cut, enjoyed ruling the roost. He commanded a lot of power both from his subordinates and from his connections higher up the police department food chain. Around the squad, he was known as the one OIC to avoid. He demanded perfection and ran his shift with the precision that came from twenty years of military service. For several minutes nobody said anything as they walked. The suspense was killing Marco. He hated when conversations began with anything approaching "Can we talk?" Usually, this meant bad news. Not being able to stand it any longer, he finally broke down and asked, "Ok, I give. What's up?"

Thompson smirked, content in the knowledge that he'd won again. "I don't know if you realize this, but the Sergeant's exam is going to be given at the end of January. Considering the good work you've been doing lately, I think you should apply. There are a number of openings in the Narcotics division, and I think having the Sergeant's stripes could really help you. What do you say? Should we sign you up?"

Marco didn't know what to say. He was both relieved that the private conversation was for something positive but hated the idea of taking a test. It wasn't that he didn't have the discipline. It was just that facts never seemed to stick in his mind. Then, whenever he took a test, he always panicked. Still, when a boss offers an opportunity like this, how much choice does one have except to take it? Besides, he had asked Lyle to be placed just before he hit it big. If he did nothing, would he be wasting this opportunity?

"Well?" Thompson interrupted, "what do you say?"

"I'm a bit surprised. Can I think about it a little more before giving you an answer?" Marco broached.

"Geez, boy, this isn't rocket science! It's just an

exam! Don't you want to get ahead? You amaze me! Everybody else would be jumping at the chance, especially if the OIC was recommending it to them. Yet you want to mull it over like you're purchasing a home. No! You can't wait! It's now or never," Thompson bellowed.

Shocked by the sudden change in attitude, Marco jumped to attention as he announced with all the enthusiasm he could muster, "You're right, boss. Count me in."

"Good. That's what I thought you'd say," the lieutenant commented snidely. "Now go back and finish up the paperwork on your latest find!"

Taylor looked up from his report to see Marco returning to his desk with a strange look on his face.

"What's up, buddy? You've got that smashed face look you usually get mid-way through the school year? Did the Lieutenant chew you out?" Taylor inquired.

"No. In fact, quite the opposite. He told me he wants to put me up for promotion." Marco answered, still somewhat amazed by the whole turn of events.

Promoted, already? Taylor was surprised. If anyone should be promoted, it should be him. "That's great! But why do you look so scared?"

"He told me that in order to qualify I need to take the Sergeant's Exam."

"So?"

"So, you know very well that I stink at exams! What makes it worse is that he practically ordered me to take it. I thought I'd be done with tests once I was out of school. Now it's back to the same thing. Besides, I'm perfectly content at my current level. I didn't ask to get promoted, so why should I force myself to go through all this?"

Taylor immediately wondered why he hadn't been invited to take the exam. There was no question in his mind that he could pass it. After all, he'd never met a test he couldn't ace! If this would be easy enough for Marco to pass, then that was even more proof that he, too, could pass it and be promoted. Maybe the Lieutenant just hadn't had the opportunity to ask him, Taylor decided.

"Obviously, he has lots of confidence in your abilities, Marco. I wouldn't be too concerned about it. Besides, if you want to get ahead, you have to do what it takes, right? In this case, that means taking this test." Taylor paused a few minutes then added, "Hey, I've got an idea! How about I help you study for the test?"

"You'd do that for me? Why?" he asked incredulously.

"Hey, I'm your friend. That's what friends do."

"Yeah, but why would you want to study for a test you're not even going to take?"

"I'll tell you what. How about as long as I'm going to be helping you study, I sign up to take the test, too? Then it wouldn't be such a waste of time. Besides, then it would give us both more incentive to study."

Marco thought for a moment before answering. He still couldn't figure out why anyone would volunteer to do such a thing. Then again, Taylor liked all challenges. Maybe this was just another way of amusing himself. In any case, he felt lucky to have a good friend like Taylor to help him through life's rough spots. "OK, if that's what you really want to do, that would be a big help for me. Thanks for offering."

"Great! Now I'll just talk to the Lieutenant about registering for it."

Taylor leapt from his seat and marched with a devilish grin towards the OIC's room to make sure his name would appear on both the exam and promotions list.

Chapter 8:
On Call

SimTime: September 1, New York

Beep-Beep! Beep-Beep! Beep-Beep! Beep-Beep!

April Hayes looked around at the other tables in the small, upper West Side café where she was eating dinner. All around her, couples were talking and enjoying the fine food, yet nobody was turning off that annoying, loud, high-pitched beeper. Why didn't someone answer that? April gave up looking for the beeper's owner and returned to cutting her meat.

The steak and fries dinner seemed the perfect way to finish what had been a most fascinating day. What a relief it had been to wake up feeling whole and normal. She had spent her first waking hour examining every piece of her body, both directly and in the mirror. She could barely believe that Lyle's machine had actually physically transported her. Everything seemed to be in place, although she had to admit to being startled to see a somewhat older version of herself in the mirror. Actually, she looked pretty good for a thirty-year-old, but she just wasn't quite prepared to see a different reflection. Still, she had no tingling sensations, and time and gravity seemed to operate exactly as it had in the real world. Only the lack of memory of Saturday night and her new surrounding indicated that she was definitely somewhere else.

She had enjoyed looking around her apartment and familiarizing herself with her new world.   What she discovered had pleased her: she worked as an emergency room physician at St. Vincent's Hospital and lived by herself in a fairly spacious one-bedroom apartment on the Upper West Side of Manhattan. She seemed to be making pretty good money, for her place was decorated with nice furniture and pieces of art.

Beep-Beep! Beep-Beep! Beep-Beep! Beep-Beep!

The renewed sound of the mysterious beeper startled April. As she reached to pick up the napkin she had just dropped, she had a surprising revelation: that beeping noise was coming from inside *her* pocketbook. That was her beeper! No wonder everybody else seemed to ignore it. How stupid did she feel!

April shut off the pager, ran to a pay phone near the restroom, and dialed the number. She had no idea whom she was calling, but she figured she'd better play along.

"Hello, St. Vincent's Hospital. Can I help you?" a harried woman's voice answered the phone.

"Yes. This is April Hayes calling. I think someone paged me."

"Oh—hi, Dr. Hayes," the voice softened a little, "Listen, Dr. Freeloff asked me to call you to see if you could work an extra shift this evening. Dr. Mikito called in sick. Can you cover for her?"

What?   Was she really going to go into work

now…at 7:30 pm? She was supposed to have a full day off before beginning work, according to Lyle. Still, she had enjoyed a pretty full day, and being a doctor meant having to work when needed, so she guessed she didn't have much choice. She'd just dive into her new career a little earlier than expected. "Sure. I'll be there within the hour."

April swallowed the rest of her dinner in less than five minutes, paid the check, ran home to change, and grabbed a taxi to take her to the hospital. Now *this* should be interesting, she thought, realizing that she had no idea where to go or what to do. She couldn't ask where to store her things, since everyone else believed that she'd been there all the time. She hoped Lyle was right that LES would provide her with the necessary skills and knowledge. Oh well, she decided, she'd just have to wing it.

As the taxi pulled up into the driveway, April nervously retied her ponytail. Her stomach momentarily jumped into her throat, but she swallowed hard and pushed it back down where it belonged. No sense worrying now, she decided. After all, what was going to happen would happen and worrying wasn't going to change anything. Better to focus her energies on what she was actually doing. That had always worked well for her before, so she saw no reason to change now.   She handed the driver his money and left the car. Here we go, she thought as she painted a smile on her face and stepped through the hospital doors and into her new life.

The admittance nurse saw her and immediately buzzed her in from the waiting area of the emergency room. April walked through the hallways, evaluating her work environment as she went. Scrubbed floors and white walls greeted her. Some rooms had patients who were being treated by doctors, but others remained unoccupied. People walked around busy with their daily tasks, but no one seemed particularly rushed at the moment. She felt relieved to learn she had arrived at a slow period.

"Good evening, April," greeted a voice that seemed to come out of nowhere. "Thanks for coming in on such short notice. It's such a relief to know that there's always someone on whom you can rely. Care for a cup of coffee? I've got something I need to discuss with you."

"Thanks, yes," she responded cheerfully to the doctor who had approached from behind. April was just glad that someone would now walk her to the Doctor's Lounge before she had to ask for directions. She decided that this friendly, bald gentleman, whose nametag read Freeloff, must be the head doctor. He had the air of someone both knowledgeable and important.

"Are you enjoying your work here in the ER?" he asked as she put away her belongings in a locker with her name on it.

The question seemed a little premature to her, as she had just arrived, but she knew she had to act as if she'd always been here. "Oh yes. I like helping people at the moment when they're most in need." She figured that would be the appropriate response.

"You know, the administration here needs more doctors with your spirit and high level of skills," he complimented as he handed her a cup of coffee.

"Thank you," she blushed.

"I've been working here for 30 years and I've always had the same attitude as you. Lately, however, I find I'm growing a little tired of it. It's not that I don't like the work. It's just that I'm about to turn 65 and I'm getting to the point where I don't feel like working late shifts or being interrupted in the middle of meals for other people's emergencies. I know this is a bad attitude, but I guess it just comes with age."

April didn't know what to make of this surprise confession. Clearly, this man trusted her, but why was he telling her all this? "That's understandable. This is a hard life to do for so long. Why didn't you just go into private practice instead?"

"Good question. I guess I never felt like it. I'm a lot like you, April. I've always been in this for two main reasons: One, I like to help others, and two, I've always felt challenged here. I treat many more types of injuries and illnesses here in a week than I would in a month in private practice. I can tell you this much: I've never felt bored."

The two sipped their coffee. April didn't say anything because she didn't know what to say. Dr. Freeloff, on the other hand, fell silent as he contemplated his words. "Well, I might as well spill the beans before someone else comes in the room," he blurted. "Listen, I've spent many a year and more energy than I can imagine improving the emergency room medical practice at this hospital. I'd now like to dedicate my time to other pursuits before my own health starts deteriorating. I'm thinking about retiring, but before I do, I want to make sure that I leave this place in capable hands.

"April, I've been watching you for quite some time now. Your work is impeccable, your devotion unwavering, and your diplomacy outstanding. I think you would make an excellent head of ER. Would you be interested in becoming my replacement?"

The young doctor almost spit out the coffee she was drinking! Me? Head of ER, she marvelled. How great is that? What a wonderful opportunity! How nice to know she had done so well already. "I don't know if I could ever replace you, but I don't think I could turn down the opportunity to head such a prestigious department."

Dr. Freeloff looked pleased. "Good, but don't get too excited yet. It's by no means definite. I haven't even made it official yet, although I intend to do it in the next few weeks. Once it's official, the hospital will need to open the position to the public. You know, of course, that John McBain has been angling for this position for years. As soon as word comes out, he's going to go full-throttle to get it. He's been playing the political game for a long time, so he's got lots of friends in high places. Despite your good work, the top brass hasn't heard much about you. Therefore, you'll need to start making yourself known. Rest assured, you'll have my full backing. I'll do what I can to make things work in your favor, but I can't guarantee you'll get the position. You'll have to do your part to make that happen. In the meantime, I can at least appoint you as acting head. I must warn you, though: McBain can be ruthless.   Watch yourself... and more importantly, watch him."

"I understand, and I'm honored that you even considered me. Thank you very much."

Just then a nurse barged through the doors, announced that an ambulance was about to arrive with two car accident victims, and hustled back down the hall to prepare for the new patients. As the two doctors rose to meet the ambulance, Freeloff turned to April and added, "By the way, until this is official, I'd appreciate you keeping all of this under your hat."

"I understand," April nodded as she left the lounge to greet her first patient of the night.

Chapter 9:
The Artist's Life

SimTime: October 30, New York

Karla dabbed some orange oil paint in the upper left corner of her canvas. Taking a step back, she assessed her work so far. It definitely needs some more silver on the bottom right to counter the effect, she decided. With a broad brush stroke, she swooshed a long swirl of silver across the bottom. She loved that feeling. Every time she did one off those long whooshes of color, she felt the stress of the day slip away from her. She had never realized how much tension one could accumulate simply by waitressing. For the past month, however, she had been learning that lesson first hand by serving rude, impatient, and grumpy customers at the Moonlight Diner.

The fact alone that she was working there annoyed her to no end. She had not counted on doing anything except her painting. Unfortunately, her first four weeks had not gone according to plan. It started out promising enough, she recalled as she continued to paint. She smiled as she remembered the day she accepted the commission.

She had arrived at the diner about twenty minutes before her meeting with Steve Ang. She figured it was better to arrive first and wait than to be late. More nervous than she'd ever felt in her whole life, Karla scouted her surroundings. The chrome and vinyl décor screamed 1950's, but the surprising lack of grease and the sweet aroma of fresh baked goods suggested a more current approach to cooking. Despite the clean environment and reasonable menu, only a few tables had customers. She paced around the lobby, waiting for Steve to arrive. On one lap, she fiddled with the red and white striped mints by the cash register, then walked away. On her next return she stacked and unstacked the pennies on the chrome-covered counter. The waiter had given her a nasty look so she had moved away again and leaned on the glass door. She started drumming her fingers against the window to release some of her nervous energy. Obviously annoyed again, the waiter came over to her.

"Can I help you, miss?" he asked condescendingly.

"No thanks, I'm just waiting to meet somebody," she replied.

"Why don't you take a seat at a table and he can join you there?" he offered.

Having gotten the hint, she sat at a table facing the door. She alternated between drumming her fingers, tapping her foot, and looking at her watch. Ten minutes late…then twenty minutes late. Her stomach began to tighten again. Why wasn't he here yet? Had she blown it? Did his mother find out about their little plan and forbid him from coming? Why hadn't she just said yes? Why did she hesitate? Why was she so stupid to always do things like this? She began breathing heavily.

"Excuse me," the waiter had interrupted. "Are you ok? You look a little flushed."

"I'm fine," she muttered.

"Are you sure?" he inquired, looking closely at her. She nodded sullenly.

"Are you Karla Ruiz?" he asked.

"Yes," she responded. "How did you know?"

"A Mr. Steve Ang called a few minutes ago and asked me to let you know that he's running late and is stuck in traffic. He says he'll be here in about ten minutes and that you shouldn't worry. Looks like he called just in time, eh?"

Karla chuckled. "Ain't that the truth!"

"So… is he your boyfriend?" the waiter had asked cautiously.

Karla blushed. "No. He's just a … business associate."

"Ohhh," the waiter responded as he quickly took a seat across the table from her. "Say, is he any relation to Ping Ang?"

And so began her friendship with Drew. They talked non-stop until Steve arrived. She and Steve ate a delicious breakfast and talked business. At the end of the meal, she formally agreed to create five related paintings by January 31. Her patron gave her a partial payment up front to help cover the cost of supplies. After he left, Drew and she talked and laughed for another hour about everything under the sun. She left the diner happier than she had ever been. What a day! The gorgeous and rich Steve Ang had dined with her and kickstarted her career. To make matters even better, she finally made a friend in the artist community.

Karla sighed as her mind returned to the present. She dipped her brush in the paint again and continued adding dabs of color to the canvas. Unfortunately, her good luck hadn't lasted much beyond that. She had spent the next month trying to come up with an idea that would work across five different canvasses; yet nothing came to her. She remembered how she had tried everything from sitting in front of her canvas, to doodling on paper in bed, to sitting on park benches all over New York City, to talking with other artists around the city in clubs and cafes. Although she had enjoyed many nice walks and fascinating conversations, nothing had helped. In fact, by the end of September, the only thing she had succeeded in doing was running out of money.

Finally realizing that nobody was going to give her any more money, she admitted she would need to work at a real job and then paint during her off-hours. Drew had been on her case about this for several weeks now. He had offered several times to get her a job at his diner but she had refused. After all, she had not come to this place to wait tables; she'd come to paint. Eventually, though, the reality of the situation forced her to take Drew up on his offer. She figured waiting tables would give her the necessary cash and still leave her with enough energy for painting. Boy, was she ever wrong! Most days, it felt like a struggle to keep her eyes open.

Karla surveyed her canvas again and realized it needed more texture. She searched around her apartment for something different to throw on it. She rummaged through piles of clothes, assorted art supplies, and various pieces of junk that had accumulated around the place until she stumbled upon a matchbox from the Moonlight Diner. She fondled the matchbox lovingly. It reminded her of how the idea for her "diner series" had hit her.

It happened less than a week after she started working. The dinner rush had finally passed and she plunked herself on a stool to recover from all the running and carrying she had just finished. She poured herself a cup of coffee and fell into a sullen mood which caused her to take a hard look at her surroundings. Like a strong wave at the beach, an idea struck her when she least expected it: here was this 1950's style diner, full of chrome and jukeboxes, in the middle of a modern city. The full moon on the matchbox cover seemed somewhat ironic to her, as she almost never could see a moon that clearly in this city. During busy times, people from various walks of life shared one common experience between them: the diner itself. As she looked around again, recollections of the customers who had been at each table bombarded her brain. She felt these splats of memories congealing in her head into a single, large image for a multi-paneled painting. Sure, other artists had painted diners before, but she would do it differently. Hers would capture the mood and the atmosphere more than the actual images. She rushed home immediately and began sketching the design for her first panel.

That occurred almost a month ago, and already she had started the third of five paintings. She had desperately needed this type of creative breakthrough, as she had already fallen a month behind on her plan. It would be tight, but she finally had hope that she would indeed make her deadline.

Karla took a sip of red wine as she considered how she could incorporate this matchbox into her artwork. Whenever she painted, she liked to have a glass of wine near her bed. At those moments where she needed to free her mind, she would walk over to the bed and take a sip. This was something that Drew had taught her.

Drew was a truly fascinating fellow. Physically, he looked completely non-descript: average height, average weight, straight light brown hair, average nose, and glasses. His personality, though, made him stand out in a crowd. He played the saxophone and considered himself an expert in Zen Buddhism. She could listen to him for hours, for he seemed to have all the answers. One evening early on, for example, he had explained to her that sometimes, when one thinks too hard about a subject, instead of finding the answer, one inadvertently prevents the answer from arriving. At first she had not understood this. He compared it to finding a boyfriend: if you are desperately looking for someone with whom to share your life, no one will find you interesting. As soon as you give up looking and decide you don't need anybody, then all the guys become interested. It's the same way with solving problems: you can only look so much and then you just have to wait for the idea to hit you. One way to do this is to take your mind off your thoughts. Exercising, showering, or listening to music were just a few different "mental ice breakers," he had suggested.

At first, Karla didn't know whether or not to believe him. He was about as "artsy" as they come, and sometimes his ideas were too weird even for her. Ever since the diner theme had struck her when she wasn't even thinking about her paintings, however, she had been more inclined to believe him. She had decided to use mental ice breakers whenever she painted.

At first, she went out drinking with Drew to free her mind. She stopped that practice pretty quickly, though. Her single hours of "ice breaking" were increasingly turning into two or three hours at a time. When she came home, she had felt way too tired to paint, and that was putting her even further behind schedule. More importantly, though, she was concerned about Drew. Clearly, he wanted more than friendship from her, but she didn't want that. She had other plans in mind: finish the paintings, impress the Angs, get her works in the museum, and live happily ever after with that hunk Steve. Still, she did find that the wine helped her creativity. She decided to limited herself to one sip of wine for each creative stall she had during a night. As a precaution against drinking too much, she limited herself to no more than two glasses of wine per night if she were by herself.

Karla now sat on her bed, sipping her wine, and

toying with the matchbox. She turned it over and over in her hands while glancing at the canvas. What if she used many matchboxes together to create a giant moon, she mused. She could use the repeating picture of the moon to form a big lunar image. Then she could layer the matches in some sort of upright position and create an interesting textured effect of moonlight glistening down on the rest of the painting.

With little ado, she reached under her bed for a can of yellow-tinted shellac. As she ripped the matchbook in half and began dipping it slowly into the varnish, her eyelids grew very heavy. This really wasn't too surprising, considering how, for the past several weeks, she had worked from noon to 8:00 PM at the diner and then from 9:00 PM until 3:00 AM on her art. She glanced at the clock: 1:45 AM. Maybe, she consoled herself, she would just lie on the bed while she waited to apply the next coat of shellac. This would make her more comfortable but would still keep her productive.

Karla stared at the matchbox cover as she waited for it to dry. She tried to visualize this image juxtaposed 100 times over. The more she imagined, the clearer the image appeared. Eventually, the moon set and a bright, burning ball of gas emblazoned itself in her mind as the matchbox slipped away from her resting body.

Chapter 10:
The Night Shift

SimTime: October 30, New York

As Marco slammed the door shut, Taylor stepped on the gas, and their patrol car slipped out of the parking lot in front of the precinct headquarters. Six times in as many hours they had been to the station to write up business they had found on the streets. Tonight was one of those nights that gave New York its action-packed reputation. So far, they had already found a runaway child, busted two different drug deals, been the first on scene at an automobile accident, and busted up a bar scene.

"Can you believe that fight?" Taylor asked excitedly as they returned to their normal patrol. "I thought those things only happened in movies."

"Apparently, they're quite real," Marco responded, nursing a small lump he'd sustained on his arm while trying to throw his body between two brawling men.

"Geez…Do they have a rule in that club that all guys must be six feet tall and more than 200 pounds?" Taylor remarked. "I've never seen such a collection of gorillas outside a zoo. I didn't think we'd make it out of their alive."

"Neither did I." Marco chuckled slightly. "And if

it hadn't been for the ten other cops who backed us up, I don't think we would've."

"I know. It took six of us just to get that group of four to stop whacking each other over the head with the bar stools and liquor bottles."

Marco started smiling more as he thought about what he'd just survived. "Yeah, while you were busy saving furniture, the rest of us were trying to dig through a pile of men to get to the guy on the bottom who was being pounded to death. Man, you should've seen that guy's face. It looked like a pepperoni pizza."

Taylor laughed, partly at the image and partly in relief that Marco was finally seeing the fun side of all this. "Man, that's harsh! Then again, none of us came out of there unharmed. I think I caught a couple of fists in my face, too." He turned his head slightly and pointed toward his right eye.

Marco looked at his buddy's face. "Yup. You're definitely going to have a good shiner there in the morning."

"That's ok," Taylor smiled proudly. "It'll be my badge of honor." He paused briefly. "You gotta admit: even though that was crazy, it was kind of fun, too, wasn't it?"

"I'll admit to the crazy part," Marco answered sarcastically, as he tossed the police radio speaker from hand to hand.

"Oh, come on. You enjoyed it, too. I saw you diving right into the fray. Admit it, this was the best part of the whole evening."

"Hey, I just did what I had to. Frankly, the best part of the evening for me was reuniting that runaway with his mother. Did you see how happy she looked when they saw one another? That's more my speed." He looked out the window as they turned down Broadway.

"Pfffhhh," Taylor expelled, "You enjoyed it and you know it. You just don't want to admit it because it goes against that laid-back, musician image you're trying to cultivate. Deep down, though, you get a thrill out of this danger stuff as much as I do...maybe even more. Look at the way you always manage to find all the trouble."

He turned his head towards Taylor. "It's not like I go looking for it, you know. It just kind of finds me. I mean, I just see stuff and point it out."

Taylor turned right at the next light. "Yeah, but that's just it. You always spot the important things. I mean, the only crimes that I see are the real petty stuff like traffic violations. You see robberies and drug deals."

"That's only because I'm more observant than you. You're so busy looking for action that you don't notice what's happening around you. I like looking around, especially at people. That's why I always let you drive... so I can just stare out the window at the world. I guess when you do it long enough, you start to notice things. It's really no great talent, though."

Taylor glanced at the digital clock on the dashboard: 2:15 am. They still had another half a shift to go. He stretched his right arm up and back until it latched onto the metal prisoner guard behind his seat. Maybe his friend was right. Maybe he'd been so busy watching out for pedestrians and other traffic hazards that he hadn't had time to look at what was happening on the sidewalks. Maybe that's why he only noticed moving violations. Maybe he should let his partner drive for a while. He stretched his neck to the right and shot a quiet disdainful look to his partner. How could Marco know better? That never happened in the real world. What had Lyle programmed into the machine?

"What's that look for?" Marco asked defensively, catching Taylor's squinty eyes.

"Huh? What look?" Taylor answered just as defensively.

"That look! You were looking at me sideways through slanty eyes. It's the same look you always give our quarterback, Frank Richardson, and that super-smart kid Justin Lewis."

Taylor's face started to blush: caught red-handed, or rather, red-faced. "All right. You caught me," Taylor relented. "Truth is, I'm a little jealous of you lately." Taylor looked left as they approached an intersection. He could think of no other reasonable way to hide his embarrassment. Imagine: being jealous of Marco, of all people.

Marco couldn't believe it. "Me? You're jealous of me? Why?"

"I don't know. You just seem so different lately. More in control, and all. I'm not used to it."

"I'm the same person I've always been," he shrugged.

"No, you're not. I mean, I'm the one who was so sure he'd make a great cop, and yet you're clearly enjoying this more than I am."

Marco shook his head. "What makes you say that?"

"Well, it's obvious that you're better at this than I am. Everyone knows it. The Lieutenant practically threw the promotion on you, yet he thinks of me as just some second-rate cop."

Taylor started to fume as he remembered what a hard time he'd had convincing Thompson to let him take the Sergeant's Exam. Thompson practically laughed him out of the room at first. Then he as much as said that the only place Taylor might be wanted was the traffic division. How demeaning was that! He finally got the guy to agree by letting it slip that he was planning on helping Marco study. Eventually, Thompson admitted who wrote better reports and agreed that Taylor might be able to help Marco overcome his weaknesses. The Lieutenant finally endorsed Taylor's idea, but told him directly not to expect his support when it came promotion time. Taylor felt a little bad about having to disclose his buddy's secret like that, but at least he got his name on the list on time.

Marco fumbled with his nightstick. He'd never seen Taylor this way before: so open and vulnerable and maybe even angry. It made him quite uncomfortable. "Just 'cause I'm good doesn't mean I enjoy it." He wasn't sure if that would help any. It didn't come out quite the way he'd intended.

"Oh, come on. Admit it: you like the thrill of it all. You like being a cop."

"It's alright...except for all that paperwork. Heck, if it weren't for your help, I'd be in the office all shift."

Taylor pressed on the brakes as a traffic light turned red. "Great. So I'm good at paperwork. Big deal. So is a secretary. Where's the glory in that?"

Marco felt as if the rules of the universe had suddenly been reversed. He'd never had to give Taylor a pep talk before. It seemed almost unnatural. "Well, if you don't fill out the stuff just right, then all the criminals eventually go free. It's like a team: I rack 'em and you book 'em." He paused momentarily. "Except, of course, you help rack 'em, too."

Taylor turned on the radio and surfed the channels looking for good music. Anything to stop this conversation. The two rode in silence for almost an hour. Taylor groused to himself. Some great choice he had made. He stunk at his job, Marco pitied him, and his boss did not respect him. He'd show them all. He'd ace the sergeants' exam. Then they'd have to promote him.

Meanwhile, Marco sat silently looking out the window. He didn't understand Taylor's anger. After all, Taylor was getting the danger and action he wanted. So what if he had found most of it for Taylor. That's what friends are for. It's not like he himself was getting any great joy out of it. He'd much rather be hanging out in any of the music clubs they were currently passing. He'd heard some pretty amazing sounds over the past few weeks, but not as much as he would've liked. These darn night shifts kept getting in the way. Even when he had gotten a chance to go to the clubs, he couldn't enjoy them fully. He kept worrying about his upcoming exam. What if he did as poorly on it as he usually did on tests? Would it make Taylor feel better? What would Lieutenant Thompson do to him? More and more, he wished he'd had the courage to stand up to Thompson and just say no.

After about an hour, Taylor finally broke the silence. "You want to study after we get off shift?" Studying always made him feel better.

"Are you crazy?" Marco shot back. "It'll be after 6:00 in the morning. The only thing I'm going to want to do is sleep. How can you even think of studying then?"

"You know," he responded in a parental tone, "you haven't done any prep work yet. The test is only a few months away and there's a lot of stuff to memorize. When are you planning on starting?"

"Who appointed you my father? I don't know when I'll start. Maybe tomorrow afternoon before shift. At least I'll be awake then."

The two guys looked at each other with amazement. Neither could fully understand the other. One couldn't figure why the other cared so much, and the other couldn't understand why the former would waste a good opportunity. Both shrugged it off with the knowledge that their friendship survived because of their differences, not in spite of them.

As Taylor turned the corner onto Spring Street, Marco suddenly sat upright. "Stop the car! Wait! Stop the car!" he cried.

"What? Another drug deal? Come on, I'm too tired to write another report," Taylor whined.

"No. Look up at that building on the right. Does that look like smoke to you?"

Taylor pulled the car to the side and craned his neck to get a better look. "Oh my god! You're right. That building's on fire!"

Just then a thunderous crash boomed through the deserted street. Glass showered down on the empty sidewalk right next to the car. A flame reached out the window like a fist finding the end of a sleeve.

"I'll call it in. You grab the extinguisher. I'll meet you inside in a minute," Taylor ordered to Marco. He could've saved his breath. Marco had already sprung from the car and was running towards the building before the words had left Taylor's lips.

Chapter 11:
The Emergency Room

SimTime: October 30, New York

Dr. April Hayes threw her bloodied rubber gloves in the receptacle and exited the operating room. She strode directly to the reception area of the emergency department and marked herself as available on the big white assignment board. As she surveyed the board and noticed that most of the other doctors on duty had also become available within the last half-hour, she chuckled at the thought that emergencies in this city seem to operate on the same schedule as stop lights: spurts of traffic followed by momentary pauses to clear the passages. She liked the red lights, for it gave her a chance to think.

"Just finishing with your patient, Hayes?" cracked a snide voice behind her. "That's the third time this week I've stabilized big accident victims quicker than you, isn't it? I guess it just goes to show who really is the top doc around here."

"Either that, or who manages to always pick the easier cases," she snapped as she walked away from Dr. McBain.

Over the past month, he had certainly become the

bane of her existence. Dr. Freeloff had warned her to watch out for him. Ever since the announcement appointing her as Acting Chief of Emergency Medicine, McBain had declared all-out war. Everyone knew it, for he made no secret of his disappointment at not getting the position, his contempt for her, and his determination to take over as head of the department. That beady-eyed, stick of a man seemed to be shadowing her, ready to note her every mild imperfection and twist it into some major catastrophe which he then reported to the Board of Directors and the administration.

Luckily, she had heeded Dr. Freeloff's advice and had used the weeks in between their discussion and the formal announcement to endear herself to some of the administration. Although relieved to know that she had some strong backing upstairs, she felt uncomfortable that the top dogs now seemed to be divided into the McBain camp and the Hayes camp. This rivalry had gotten pretty nasty and come to something of a head at a hospital fundraiser the other night. That skinny toad interrupted and edged her out of every conversation. He also managed to mention to each board member how he had taken a mere 30 minutes to stabilize a stab victim at the very same time it had taken her almost an hour. Nevermind the fact that her victim had a punctured lung and his only had arm wounds.

April stepped outside for a breather before the next wave of traffic hit the ER. Besides, she needed to calm down after hearing McBain again. She didn't want to let him get under her skin, but sometimes she couldn't help it. The more tricks he pulled out of his hat to squelch her sincere efforts at improving the place, the more he grated on her. Sure, he was a Class-A snake-in-the-grass, but she really disliked the effects his efforts were having on the working environment. Not only had he managed to divide the administration, but he also had split the nurses and the doctors. If he had just gone along with her new policies, everyone would have been happier and healthier.

Take, for instance, her new healthier lifestyles initiative. Last week she announced a new policy against leaving junk food in public spaces for all staff to eat. She had no problem with sharing food or snacking while on shift. She just thought that if people had fruits and vegetables or other healthy snacks they'd feel better than if they munched on cake and walked around on short-lived sugar highs. The very next day, McBain walked into the nurses' station carrying 2 big boxes of fresh doughnuts. He was all smiles and cheer that day, and the nurses ate it up. In the end, she had to to rescind the policy after so many of the nurses complained to the administration about her.

April hated losing on anything, but she consoled herself that although McBain had won that skirmish, and was now much more popular with the nursing staff, her new paperwork completion policies had scored her the bigger victory with the administration and the doctors. Initially, she lost some of the doctors' goodwill when she insisted that everyone be more accurate and timely in submitting their paperwork. They accused her of selling out and turning bureaucratic on them. McBain, of course, led the way at riling the staff and complaining. Still, she had been able to persuade them that it would be in their best interests to follow her requests.

To soften the deal for them, she rearranged the shift schedules so the first hour of the next shift overlapped with the last hour of the previous shift. This way, the doctors could spend their last hour finishing their paperwork properly without patient care being jeopardized. Naturally, McBain balked at that. Although it took a lot of cajoling and persuasion to get this to work, in the end she had succeeded. The improved paperwork was handed in on time, which made the administrators very happy. Since they weren't sending papers back for correcting, the medical staff's workload eventually lightened, too. Only McBain failed to comply, which eventually made him look like more of a jerk to everyone else.

The electric door slid open and McBain joined her in the driveway. April stiffened. Break's over, she thought.

"Hello, John," she said as sweetly as she could muster. "Catching a breath of fresh air, too?"

"Yeah. That, too," he responded coolly. "Actually, I wanted to talk with you some more about your new rotation policy. I think maybe we can reach some common middle ground. Whaddya say?"

Momentarily taken aback at his moderate approach, April quickly grew suspicious. This seemed so out of character for him. Why would he finally become reasonable about something which really angered him? Nothing had gotten his rankles up more than her latest proposal. Over the past few weeks, she had noticed that doctors were being assigned primarily on a first-come-first-served basis. She quickly realized that many of the doctors felt tired and frustrated because they never received a break. She wanted to assign staff on a rotating basis, so that everyone would have at least a few minutes to recharge before rushing to the next emergency.

Dr. Mikito had warned her to expect a big fight from McBain on this because he had come up with the current plan. Boy, had Mikito been right on that! McBain had been using every dirty, underhanded trick in his book to prevent this one. He'd started so many rumors that she'd lost count somewhere after the one about how this was going to give each doctor more work and the one about lay-offs. He'd complained yet again to the Board about her and had tried to bribe the doctors and nurses into revolting against her.

"What do you have in mind?" she asked sweetly.

"I'm concerned that our patients won't receive the best help possible with this new approach. After all, most of the better doctors are able to process through patients quicker. If you use the first-come-first-served approach, then more people have access to the good doctors," he explained.

"Hmmm. I see what you're saying, and you may have a point there," April responded as diplomatically as she could. "And yet, this might not always be the case."

"How do you figure?"

"First of all, you're assuming that some of our doctors aren't very skilled. I'd like to think otherwise. Secondly, faster doesn't always mean better. Sometimes it means sloppier. But for the sake of argument, let's say it does mean better. Now you've got your really good doctor who, over the course of an hour, has worked his butt off on five patients. At the same time, you've got your so-so doctor who's only dealt with two. At the end of the hour, who do you think is going to be more tired: the good doctor or the so-so doctor? And as you and I both know, when do more mistakes occur? When people are tired and stressed. See what I'm getting at?"

"Yes, but what if Dr. X is next on rotation and he still has 5 other patients? How's he going to handle yet another?" McBain countered.

"You're right. We'll need to work in some rule about a maximum number of patients." April figured she'd concede this point, as she had already planned to build in just that sort of rule.

McBain smiled cockily, thinking that he was finally starting to make her see the wisdom of his ways. "And what about the doctor who finishes early and is not at the top of the rotation list? What's he going to do? Hang out and get paid for doing nothing?"

"It's called a break," she replied. "The doctor can use the time to go to the bathroom, regroup, check on other patients, fill out paper work so he doesn't have to wait until the end of the shift. There's plenty to do. You know that."

Before McBain could retort, a car screeched into the parking lot and a frantic man jumped out and ran over to them. "Doctor! Doctor! Please! Come quick! My wife … in the car…she's starting to deliver our baby…and there's blood!"

"I'll get Dr. Tate. John, go check on the mother,"

April ordered. The doctors ran in opposite directions.

April burst through the doors and ordered the admittance nurse, "Page Dr. Tate…emergency delivery!" She turned around to see a different lady run up holding her crying son.

"Help! My son fell out of his bunk bed while sleeping. I think he might have broken his arm."

April walked the woman and child into an examination room. Along the way she brought a young resident with them. "Don't cry. Everything's going to be fine. Dr. Singh is going to take a look at you and fix you all up," she explained calmly to the seven-year-old before leaving the room.

As she updated the assignment board, she could not help but think how the light had just turned green again. As if to prove her correct, two stretchers burst through the doors from the ambulance bay as if in a drag-race. "Fire victims," shouted the paramedic as she wheeled in a stretcher. "Two males so far, more to come. Smoke inhalation and second degree burns on these two…." Another set of paramedics rolled through the doors behind the first crew and began shouting out their statistics.

Within seconds the medical staff was flowing back and forth around the patients, the room humming with the energy of well-flowing rush hour traffic. April stood at the center of it, the big police officer directing the flow. She coordinated room and doctor assignments while performing triage. One patient, however, caught her eye. Unlike most of the victims, who suffered minor burns, this young lady, who looked vaguely familiar, had massive burns on her arms and legs and looked like she was about to go into shock. April declared, "I'll handle this one myself."

"What happened?" she asked to the two officers who were standing nearby.

"Chemical fire. We think she was in the room where it started. She was found lying on the bed. We're not sure if she fell asleep before or after the fire started," the taller one answered matter-of-factly.

"I guess it really doesn't matter at this point," April responded. "Right now, we just need to make her comfortable and prevent her condition from worsening."

As April started to roll the gurney away, the other policeman grabbed her arm, looked her directly in the eye with deep concern, and said, "Doctor, you *are* going to be able to help her, right? She's someone…um…rather special, if you know what I mean."

"She couldn't be in better hands. I'm the head of this department and I'll make sure she gets my own special attention. I'll do everything I can for her…and by the way, every patient is special to somebody," she advised in the assured tones of the able doctor that she was.

"Taking the heroic one for yourself again, are you, Dr. Hayes?" McBain muttered as he squeezed past her.

April shot him a quick and nasty warning look. As she wheeled the patient away, she turned back to Marco, nodded and winked to signal she understood his meaning.

Chapter 12:
The Awakening

SimTime: October 31, New York

Karla opened her eyes and looked around in confusion. Where was she, she wondered. This was not her apartment.

"Good morning, Karla. I'm Dr. April Hayes and you are in St. Vincent's Hospital. Do you know why you are here?"

Karla shook her head in ignorance.

"There was a fire last night in your building. An ambulance brought you here and I treated you for second and third degree burns and smoke inhalation."

Karla lifted her arm to shake her doctor's hand and a slight shriek escape from her lips. It felt like someone had just slit the skin at her elbows with a razor. As her arm came into view, tears welled up in her eyes. Her arms looked covered in a flesh-and-blood covered bubble-wrap.

"You'll be in some pain for the next few days until the wounds start to heal. We'll keep you here to monitor your progress. Later on, we can do some skin graft operations to help restore your arm."

Karla tried with all her might to avoid crying, but

had a difficult time of it. She had no idea what had happened. She woke up alone in a hospital with her arms looking hideous and feeling even worse. An upsetting thought struck her: If she was that badly burned, what happened to her paintings? Were they all destroyed?

The doctor looked sympathetically at her patient. She hated having to welcome people from a sleep to the news that they were in a hospital. The terror in their eyes made her want to hug them and cry with them. It took all her strength to remain sympathetic yet calm and professional at those moments. "Karla, you have some visitors who have been waiting for you to wake up. Is it all right if they come in?"

Karla couldn't imagine who would be waiting so patiently for her, but she was grateful that somebody cared. She nodded.

In a moment the doctor returned with two policemen, the shorter of whom was carrying a bouquet of flowers. "These are for you," he offered sheepishly.

"Thank you," she mustered while trying to hide her growing confusion.

"These two gentlemen were the first at the scene and valiantly ran through much of the building, knocking on doors and carrying people until the firemen arrived," April explained.

"Do you remember anything?" the taller officer asked.

Karla thought hard. She didn't think she had amnesia, but she definitely was having trouble putting all the pieces together. "I remember that I had been working on my paintings," she started. "I was in the middle of the third one when I had this great idea for how to add more texture and dimension to the work. You see, I wanted to take matchbox covers and dip them in shellac so they would become stiff...but I don't suppose you're really that interested in that."

"No, please, go on," encouraged the one who held the flowers. "What is the last thing you remember?"

"It was late at night, or rather early in the morning. I remember being tired, but I felt that I had to continue. I was in the middle of a creative moment and I didn't want to lose my train of thought. Besides, I had a lot of work to do and was running behind schedule. Anyway, the last thing I remember is that I had dipped the matchbox in the shellac and was waiting for it to harden so I could add the next coat." She paused for a minute to collect her thoughts. "After that, I'm afraid it's all a blank until just a few minutes ago. Do you know what happened?"

"The fire chief thinks it was a chemical fire," the taller cop explained officially. "The firemen said they found you lying down with part of your body hanging off the bed. They also mentioned finding an empty paint can and a space heater in different parts of the room."

"I had the space heater near my bed. The landlord had not yet turned on the building's heat for the winter, and I was cold. I figured I'd put it near my bed so it would be away from my paintings and could keep me cozy while I slept." She closed her eyes to help her recall what happened. "I was tired so I figured I'd just sit on my bed while I waited for the next dipping. I must have fallen asleep." She paused as she put the pieces together. "Oh my God! My hand must have slipped off the bed and knocked over the varnish when I fell asleep... Oh my god! You mean I started the fire?" She started sobbing uncontrollably. "I'm such a loser. I can't believe I accidentally burned a building. I'm so in trouble. I'm ruined...and I didn't even have that much to start with!"

April couldn't help herself. She leaned over and hugged her patient. "There, there. Everything's going to be all right. Shhhh. Accidents happen. You'll be okay."

Karla cried for several minutes while April hugged and rocked her back and forth. The guys stood there uncomfortably, not quite sure what to do with a hysterical woman. Finally, Karla managed to pull herself together a little.

"I'm really very sorry for what I did. I feel just awful. Thank you, though, for helping me to understand...and thank you for rescuing me." Just as she said this, something odd struck her. She stared intently at the officers for quite some time. Finally, she ventured haltingly, "I know this is going to sound odd, but you look familiar. Do I know you from somewhere?"

The three visitors in the room glanced at each other and grinned. "We were wondering if you'd remember," April chuckled. "Does the term 'Project 20/20' mean anything   to   you?"

A pregnant pause filled the room as Karla searched through her memories some more. Gradually, a smile of recognition grew on her face. "I thought you looked familiar, and now I know why. You're the other three test subjects! How wild that the first time we run into each other would be when you all save me."

"Um…actually…we've all seen each other before," Taylor volunteered hesitantly. "You see, Marco and I are actually partners and roommates. We ride together everyday."

"Yeah, in fact, we're both studying for the Sergeant's Exam together. Taylor's always so great about helping me out with tests," Marco added. "And as for April, we've seen her around here a few times when we've brought in patients. When we came in with you, it struck us that nobody had any idea what you've been doing."

"I guess that makes sense. As a general rule, I try to avoid hospitals and police stations. Look what happens when I don't! I didn't realize that you had all picked to live in New York City, too, so I never even thought to look for you. Mainly, I've just been busy waitressing during the day to keep some money in my pockets and working on my artwork at night." Karla updated them on her life.

A faint knocking on the door caused everyone's heads to turn. A nervous, little head with glasses peered its way around the corner.

"Drew! You came, too? Thank God you're here! What would I do without you? Come in!" For the first time, a spark of happiness returned to Karla's eyes.

Drew presented her with a large bouquet of flowers that made Marco's seem paltry by comparison. "Here you go, honey. I thought these might cheer you up," he said as he gave her a big but gentle hug. He glanced around at the other visitors and stood upright. "Who are you?" he asked.

"We're friends of Karla's," Marco explained flatly. He didn't like the way this guy just barged in and lit up her world.

Drew looked suspiciously at them. "That's funny. Karla never mentioned she had friends who were cops."

"Well, she never mentioned you to us either," he responded with an edge to his voice.

Taylor turned towards his buddy with surprise. Where had that attitude come from? Almost nothing ever riled Marco. He was usually so pliable. Lately, though, he had seemed almost like a different person at times. Could it have been something in the way LES transported him? Not wanting to make a bad situation worse, Taylor tried to diffuse the two guys' tension. "Well, you know how it is. Different circles of friends, I guess," he chuckled nervously. "I'm Taylor. This here's Marco and April. We go way back with Karla….and you are…?"

"Drew. We…um…work together." He paused, then extended his hands to each of them. "Nice to meet you." He quickly turned his attention back to the patient and the two caught each other up on what had happened.

Marco grunted as he watched the scene and listened to the conversation. Great, he figured. Ever since they discovered her last night, he'd been waiting for the chance to talk to her. Now he finally had the chance to make a good first impression and this guy waltzes into the room, with his fancy flowers and big hugs. Not only that, but Karla really seemed to dig this guy. She kept holding his hand and talking. Marco sighed. Obviously, he'd lost out again. No point fighting matters. Like everything else, he'd just have to accept this and get on with life.

Karla's new, louder sobs refocused Marco on the current scene.

"My paintings…my paintings! What happened to them? How are they, Drew?"

"Tell you the truth, I don't really know." He titled his head towards the officers in the room. "They've sealed off your apartment, so nobody can take a look inside."

Karla reached out to the nearest policemen she could find and grabbed Marco's sleeve. "You're official. Tell me: did my paintings survive?"

"I don't really know either. We haven't been back since it happened." He glared back at Drew in response to his nasty look. "It's the firemen who have sealed it off. They're still investigating the scene." Jerk, thought Marco about Drew. He's trying to paint us as the bad guys.

"Yeah, it's pretty bad over there," Taylor added. "The door's only barely shut because the lock melted."

April shook her head slightly in amazement. Why had he just said that? That wouldn't make her feel any better.

As if on cue, Karla burst out in a new round of tears. "Melted the lock?! That's gotta mean that my paintings were destroyed completely! Aaarrgghh! What am I going to do?" She buried her head in Drew's stomach. "I'm ruined…ruined…. Everything's ruined."

"There, there, honey. I'm sure it's not as bad as all that," he consoled her, stroking her hair gently and immensely pleased that she felt comfortable enough to cry on him.

"But it is that bad," she retorted. "I was midway through my third painting. Now they're all completely destroyed. I'll have to re-create them plus make the other two all by January 31. That only leaves me three months to do five paintings. That's just barely enough time. What will Steve say? He'll be so disappointed in me. He'll never talk to me again. And then where will that leave me?"

Steve! Drew stiffened at the very mention of that name again. He'd never met this mystery man but he hated him already. Why was Karla completely infatuated with him? Sure, Steve Ang had good looks, power, prestige, and money, but he'd only talked to Karla once since he commissioned her works at the diner. Every time Drew made some headway in moving this relationship beyond mere friendship, that guy's name would come up in conversation.

"Oh, it'll be alright. I'm sure Steve will speak to you no less frequently than he currently does," Drew mildly attempted to comfort her on this point.

"But don't you get it? If he doesn't trust me, he won't like me. If he doesn't like me, his mother won't either. If his mother doesn't like me, my art will never get shown in a museum. It'll kill my career just as it was starting to take off." Besides, she added to herself, if he doesn't like me, he'll certainly never date me.

She tried to collect herself a little and control her sobbing. All this crying was wearing her out. "Maybe I should just call him up and explained what happened. I'll probably have to pull out of the competition, though, and repay them the money. I'll just work extra shifts at the diner and give him my paychecks and tips. I might as well quit. Even if I had the time and inspiration, I don't have the money to make it work. I've already used everything he gave me to buy supplies, and they're probably all destroyed, too. It's useless," she declared as she tossed her head against her pillow.

Marco pitied her. What a rotten way to see the future. Even in this fake world of theirs, her life seemed almost as rotten as how she'd described the real one in her application essay. It just didn't seem fair. If only they could help her.

"Hey! I have an idea that might work!" Marco announced excitedly. Karla stopped sobbing and lifted her eyes towards him slightly. "We all have some money saved up. Why don't we donate some of our savings to Karla to help her buy supplies?"

Drew frowned. Who was this guy, crowding in on his turf and now forcing him to give away his hard-earned money?

"Oh, no. I couldn't accept charity. I wouldn't feel comfortable," she protested.

Drew relaxed momentarily. He liked Karla but why should he help her out if she's only going to run into some other guy's arms?

"Marco, what a great idea!" April agreed. "We're only going to be here for a little while longer...."

Taylor interrupted with a cough, raised his eyebrows twice, and tossed his head in Drew's direction.

"...Here on this planet, that is," she attempted to correct her slip. "I mean...aren't we all supposed to help one another while we're here on this planet....alive?" She cringed her forehead, put on an awkward smile, and hoped that Drew wouldn't think too much about what she'd just said. "Come on Karla, why don't you let us help you a little?"

"I don't know..." she responded in a tone that indicated that she was at least giving it some consideration.

"You might as well," Taylor added. "It sounds like it's your only real hope."

Drew was growing increasingly annoyed with these guys. He needed to find some way to regain his ground and sidestep the money-lending issue. "Why are you all assuming everything's ruined? Isn't there a chance that some stuff survived? You guys are cops. Can't you at least check if any paintings survived? Maybe recover some so she could salvage them?"

Marco and Taylor looked at each other quizzically. Could they do that? "Well...er...um...sure....I guess we could try...we'd have to see...." They muttered and stammered together.

Karla perked up. "Would you? That would be a big relief to me to know. But I don't know if I feel right taking your money. You all work so hard for it."

"You can consider us your co-benefactors, if that makes you feel better." April said, taking control of the situation again. "Look, I know this is a big decision for you to make, especially in your weakened state. Why don't we leave and let you rest. I'll be in again to check on you. When you feel you've made a decision with which you can live, you let me know. In the meantime, these two can go inside your apartment and recover some of your belongings. OK?"

Karla nodded. She still wasn't sure if she should accept the money, but she figured this at least gave them time to accept her decision if she ultimately declined their offer. She liked the idea that someone would try to salvage her work for her. Most importantly, though, it took the pressure off her to be sociable when all she really wanted to do was rest. As she watched her visitors exit, she thanked them again. In less than a minute, Karla fell back into a deep sleep.

Chapter 13:
At Home

SimTime: January 20, New York

April entered her apartment, dropped her luggage, walked through the messy living room, tossed the week's worth of mail on the coffee table, went into the bedroom, kicked off her shoes, and collapsed on the bed. She could not believe how exhausted she felt, nor how crazy the past month had been. Just when she thought her life could not become even busier, people found new demands to place on her time. First it was substituting for other doctors who could not make their shifts. Then she became head of the ER. Some great deal that turned out to be. That just added lots of administrative tasks to her workload. In addition to taking care of all the hardest cases and supervising everyone else, she now handled inquiries from the administration and the media.

On top of that, she also had to sit on the search committee for a new ER doctor. About 5 weeks ago, McBain finally realized that, despite all his conniving, he was losing his bid for Chief of Emergency Medicine. Something inside of him snapped. The whole incident started innocently enough. He had just signed off on a patient and had strutted over to the board to see what he should do next. She remembered his cockiness clearly.

"All right," he had announced proudly, as he rubbed his hands. "Another victim saved by the miraculous hands of St. Vincent's speediest and most able doctor. What fascinating cases do we have for me now?"

"It's not your turn at the moment." April had responded. "You can go to the doctor's lounge and chill for a few minutes if you want."

"What's that supposed to mean?" he had barked. "You got a problem with me? Why are *you* trying to sideline *me* in *public*?" he shouted, as he poked her chest with his finger to emphasize his words.

April remembered how his green eyes glared at her. The whole room fell dead silent to see her reaction. Despite trembling on the inside, she had managed to hold herself together. She used her arm to sweep away his finger. "I'm not sidelining you," she had tried to explain calmly. "It's just that the administration approved our new rotation policy, effective this morning. You've got a few minutes now to relax before your name comes to the top of the list again."

McBain stood there dumbfounded for a minute. Apparently, he had not heard the news yet. He huffed and puffed and stammered, but ultimately turned around and walked away, muttering under his breath. She exhaled in relief that the whole situation had settled itself so easily. Actually, it had gone much smoother than what she had expected. Thinking back, though, April realized it was at that very moment that she made a critical mistake. Instead of returning to her business, she let her mouth get away from her brain. "I suggest you use this time to calm down," she scolded him.

Apparently, that broke the camel's back. McBain pivoted on his heels and charged at her. "Why, you stuck-up back-stabber…" he shouted as he lunged for her throat. "How dare you talk to me like that!" His hands grabbed her by the throat. "You're just barely my boss and you're definitely not my mother!" He shoved her against the wall and banged her head repeatedly against the concrete.

Two doctors and three security guards jumped on him and tried to wrestle him to the ground. Unfortunately, he held on to her like superglue. Time slowed to a crawl for her in those few minutes. She could still vividly recall that choking sensation, gasping for air, then feeling the force of six men come crashing down on her as she hit the tile floor with her back. She knew now how a mosquito must feel at the moment he's caught between a person's clapping hands. Oh, the shouting, the pulling, the clanging of shoved medical equipment trays. It made her tremble even now just thinking about it. Her world spun like a globe. Then, finally, calm returned. She remembered lying in a corner, coughing, gasping, trying to see straight. Several nurses tended to her while the guards dragged McBain away in handcuffs. Needless to say, that ended his work at the hospital.

Now, as she approached the end of her first career, April lay on the bed and took stock of her life. She considered some of the cases she had seen in the past several months: everything from beans stuffed up little kids' noses to gun shot wounds to drug overdoses to 5-car collision victims. Then, just when she thought she'd found a legitimate way to get away from it all for a few days, by attending a medical conference, someone asked her at the last minute to participate in a panel discussion. She had spent what little free time she had at the conference in Las Vegas working on her presentation. It had gone well and she received many compliments on it. However, now people were suggesting she rework her talk into an article for a medical journal. When would she have time to do that? Just as she deboarded the plane this morning, her pager beeped. Three doctors had called in sick, so she ended up going into work directly from the airport. Now, at 6:00 PM, she had finally made it home.

Home! For the first time in over three weeks, it looked like she would finally have a weekend to herself, even if it fell midweek. She had given specific instructions not to disturb her for the next 48 hours. The same doctor who always received praised for having her act together felt at the end of her rope. She felt exhausted and, on top of that, her place was a mess. The coffee table held a stack of bills that were at least three weeks old. Nothing hung in her closets, yet her laundry hamper overflowed. What little that remained in her refrigerator had so much mold, penicillin could be incubated in it. A layer of dust so thick you could write messages in it lined the bookshelves. Disgusting! April could not stand it anymore. Still, she felt way too tired to do anything about it right now. She only wanted to take a long, hot bubble-bath.

After a half-hour, April finally managed to peel

herself off the bed and move to the bathtub. As she examined her body while she soaked, she realized she was becoming increasingly pear-shaped. Unlike her thighs, which were gaining territory, her arms seemed to be shrinking. The nice muscle definition she had developed from years of weight-lifting in the alpha world had dwindled into large sacks of flabby skin, not unlike the gullet of a pelican. The thirties were not a gentle age on women, she decided.

Not only had her muscles become flabby, but they had also become tighter and tighter with tension. Her shoulders held so much stress that she imagined herself as hunched as Quasimoto. A massage wouldn't even begin to relax her at this point. Maybe she could just have a steam roller drive over her back to straighten it! When had she lost all her energy? Up until recently she thought she had an unending supply. Then it hit her: she hadn't exercised since the first week in September. No wonder her body was going to pot! As she often told her patients, if you don't take care of your body, it won't take care of you. Yet here she was, not even able to follow her own advice. How ironic. How pathetic, she corrected.

After almost an hour of soaking, April heard the phone ring in the other room. Her eyes popped open and she sat upright in the tub. *Rrriiinnnggg!* Who could be calling? The hospital knew better. *Rrriiinnnggg!* Could it be some of her friends? Would they want to ask her out? *Rrriiinnnggg!* Did she even have the energy to answer the phone, let alone go out? The phone stopped ringing. April was just as happy to have the answering machine take the message.

Looking at the prunes that her fingers had become, April concluded she'd been soaking long enough. She pulled her deadweight body out of the tub and wrapped herself in her favorite thick, terrycloth robe. Where to go now? She hated when she felt like this: even the smallest decisions seemed monumental. Should she try to find some edible food in her cabinets, order something for delivery, or just skip the meal altogether? Since her stomach wasn't crying for nourishment and her mouth and brain could not come to agreement on what taste they wanted, April resolved to skip the meal for now.

The telephone caught her eye as she left the kitchen. Who had called, she wondered? She glanced at the answering machine and couldn't believe what she saw: 14 messages awaited her. She knew that in order to hear that last message, she would need to listen to all the other ones. Did she have the energy to go through that right now? After several moments of debate with herself, she gave in to curiosity and hit the "Play" button. She would just listen to the messages, but not take notes. She would not erase them, so later, she could write anything important. For now it was good enough just to listen.

Fifteen minutes later the messages finally ended. Four were sales calls that just cluttered her tape with offers for supposedly free vacations, magazines, and other things for which she had neither the time nor the interest. Five different friends who either wanted to get together or fix her up with some nice guys they knew had called. Two calls were related to the conference she had attended last week. More requests for her to do things! Three, including the last call, came from mysterious but interesting sounding fellows asking her for dates. Not bad, she concluded with the first sign of a smile that she'd had in days.

Barely able to remain standing, April used the last of her energy to put some classical music on the stereo and head back to her bedroom. As she crawled into bed, her thoughts turned to her social life, dwindling though it may be. She hadn't seen her friends in so long that she could barely remember what they looked like. The Revolutionary War seemed more recent than her last date. When would she have time to meet all those handsome-sounding men on her answering machine? Certainly not now. The next two days were going to be dedicated to rest, recuperation, and, reorganization of her life. She scratched her head absentmindedly. Could this really be the life she wanted?

Chapter 14:
The Exam

SimTime: January 24, New York

"Turn here," Taylor indicated to Marco as they walked up Lexington Avenue. "If I'm right, the testing center should be within the next two blocks. Come on! Pick up the pace! We have less than ten minutes before exam time."

Marco straggled behind but made a faint attempt to catch up to Taylor. He could never understand how his partner could be so full of energy before 8:00 AM. What a stupid time of day to schedule a test! He could barely think at this hour.

"Here it is. Right where I thought we'd find it." Taylor announced. "You ready?" he asked cheerfully.

"I guess so," Marco mumbled.

Taylor shot his buddy an annoyed look.

Marco stopped outside the steps of the testing center. He felt a little bad about his less than enthusiastic response. "Before we go in, Taylor, I just want to say thanks for helping me with this and thanks for last night's cram session."

"It's nothing," Taylor responded as he patted his

friend on the back. "I was glad to do it. Do you think last night's session helped?"

"I don't know," answered Marco as they ascended the steps and entered the building. "In some ways, yes, because it helped remind me of lots of things. In other ways, though, I think it might have just made things worse."

"How so?"

"Now I realize just how much I don't know and it makes me even more nervous. I mean, how am I supposed to memorize all those facts? All those answers just start swimming in my head and I get so confused."

As they headed down the corridor towards the classroom, Taylor continued the conversation. "You know, you really don't need to memorize every detail. They're not really testing you on whether you can remember the legal codes for a particular crime. In reality, you can always find that information in the books. What they want to know is if you can think like a sergeant. In that area you should have no problem. Just think about what you would do if you were in the given situation and then find the answer that comes closest to your instinct. That's all there is to this test. I doubt it will be very hard at all."

As the two entered the classroom, Marco considered Taylor's words. Maybe he was right. After all, Taylor always passed every exam.

Twenty-eight people sat calmly in front of computers in the classroom. Only two empty places remained, each at opposite ends of the room. The two partners cased the joint, looked at each other, shrugged, and went to their respective corners. Let the games begin, Taylor announced to himself.

About a minute later, the proctor rose from his chair, pulled out a small pamphlet and began reading to the group:

"Good morning. In this room today we are offering the New York Police Department's Sergeant's Exam. If you are here to take any other exam, you are in the wrong place. Now would be the ideal time to leave."

As he paused, one person quickly grabbed his belongings and ran out of the room. The group laughed at the frantic departure and the tension in the room eased.

"You will notice a monitor on each of your desks," the proctor continued reading. "Today's exam will be given on the computer. You will not need to enter your answers into a booklet. Your answers will be scored as you enter them. At the end of the test, you will know your score. The test has been designed to ask progressively more difficult questions. If you answer correctly, your next question is likely to be more difficult. If you answer incorrectly, the next question will either be as difficult or a little easier. At times, however, even if you answer a question correctly, you may find the next one to be easier. Do not read too much into this. This combination of progression and random sampling ensures a more reliable and accurate score. Please note that once you enter your answer and hit the 'Accept' key, your answer will be calculated. Consequently, you will *not* be able to return to previous questions and change your answers.

"Before we begin, we must complete a few

administrative matters…"

At those words, Marco lost interest in what was being said and began worrying about what he just heard. A computerized test? Nobody had mentioned that! He was all prepared for a pencil-and-paper test. He hadn't formulated a strategy for this. Now he would not even be able to go back and check his work. At least the good old paper exams had given him the chance to fix some of his mistakes. Now he felt doomed.

"…Please take out a photo ID and your registration form for this exam. I will now come around and check them," the droning continued.

As the proctor walked around the room, Taylor reached in his wallet and pulled out his police ID. He couldn't wait to get started. Since the test focused on common sense, he was sure he could do it. Of course, the computer would make it a little more challenging. He'd read about this new method but had not yet tried it. He loved the idea that he would find out immediately how well he did. He always hated the agonizing wait for results. At least by the end of the day, he could quit worrying completely.

Mr. Exciting returned to the front of the room and continued reading his speech. "The computers have already been set to the first screen of the exam. When I tell you, you may turn on your monitor and begin. You will have four hours to complete this test. It is now 8:15. At 12:15 you must stop typing and turn off your monitor. You may now begin."

The room filled with the sound of clicks and whirrs

as 29 monitors came to life. Within seconds, the tap-tap-tapping of keyboards and the tick-tick-ticking of the clock on the wall were the only sounds of life.

9:15: Marco needed a break. He hated concentrating on one thing for so long. He was starting to get a headache. He also realized his bladder was bothering him. Bathroom! He had to go to the bathroom! He probably shouldn't have had the three cups of coffee before leaving the apartment, but he needed them to wake up. Now what would he do? If he left, he'd lose the time it took to relieve himself. If he didn't go, he'd explode. He decided he must go.

SCREEEECH went his chair as he backed away from his desk. Twenty-eight sets of eyes glared at him momentarily for disturbing their owners' concentration and then quickly returned to their screens. Marco quickly left the room to wander frantically in search of a men's room.

10:15: Taylor glanced at the clock and realized that half the allotted time had already passed. He could not believe how quickly the time was flying, nor could he judge whether he was half-way through the test yet. At least with the booklets, you could monitor your progress more easily, he thought. Other than that, it seemed to be going well. He quickly noticed a pattern in the selection of questions: Easy, moderate, difficult, easy. Once he figured out the method, he realized there was no point in trying to guess whether he had answered correctly. This helped relax him tremendously.

Thinking of relaxing, he suddenly wondered how his buddy was doing. He glanced across the room to a familiar sight: Marco hunched over his desk, running a hand through his already-disheveled hair, and sighing heavily. Taylor noticed that three minutes had already passed. No time to daydream, he reminded himself as he returned his attention to the matter at hand.

11:15: Marco's anxiety continued to grow. He only had an hour left and all his questions seemed equally difficult. He could not discern any progression like the proctor had said would happen. Of course, he also hadn't noticed any particularly easy questions, either. A momentary flash of hope struck him: Maybe he was doing so well he was stuck on the most advanced track. Not likely, he concluded. Needing another break, he picked his head up and looked around the room. A few other people were also stretching. Taylor, however, had the look of a tiger on the hunt: steady and calm but focused on the attack.

12:14: "You have one more minute. Please finish your current question and turn off your monitor," the proctor's voice boomed. An audible gasp of desperation floated through the room as everyone made one last attempt to squeeze in another answer. The proctor started walking around the room, checking that everyone was turning off the monitors.

"Congratulations. You have now finished the test. In a few minutes, I will instruct you on how to retrieve your scores. Before that, let's take a minute to stretch."

The room filled with the sound of squeaking chairs, yawns, and groans. Marco couldn't decide if he wanted to know the results. He had no idea how well he had done, and frankly, he didn't care. He only wanted to sleep. He had to be back at work in eight hours, and he would need to be alert for that. Besides, knowing what to do on the streets is more important than knowing what to do on an exam, Marco rationalized, and Marco knew he knew what to do when it really mattered.

For his part, Taylor could not wait to see the results. He figured this minute to stretch was someone's cruel idea of torture. Why not just tell the results immediately? The computer program should be designed to calculate scores on an on-going basis. If high-powered machines can calculate complex mathematical equations in less than thirty seconds, why would it take these computers two or three minutes to calculate a simple score? Clearly, this was a stall tactic designed to intimidate people, he reasoned.

"Please take your seats. I will now explain how to retrieve your scores," the proctor continued. "Before we print the results, please keep in mind that this is not a pass-fail test. Your score will show how many of the 100 questions you answered correctly. The top 2000 scores from all test sessions will be considered passing.

"This program has been designed to provide immediate results, protect your privacy, and ensure that you leave with a printed record of today's test. Please turn on your monitor now. You should now see a screen that displays the question, 'Print results?' Does everyone see that screen? If not, please raise your hand."

Nobody raised a hand.

"Click 'Yes.' Now you should see a dialog box asking you to enter your computer number. Enter the number pasted on the upper right side of your monitor. Click 'Enter'. Your exam results are now printing at my desk. When I call your computer number, you may come forward to pick up your exam and then leave. Thank you for coming. Have a good day."

As the proctor began calling numbers, Taylor caught Marco's eye and signaled for him to wait outside the building after he got his scores.

"Seventeen," called the proctor.

Marco gathered his belongings and picked up the piece of paper as he left.

Several minutes later, with everyone else leaving, the proctor finally called Taylor's number: thirty.

Taylor grabbed the piece of paper and practically ran out the door.

The partners met outside of the building, as arranged.

"So, how'd you do?" Taylor asked immediately.

"Not too bad, I guess: 75. How about you?"

"Not so great: Only 86."

Chapter 15:
The Diner Series

SimTime: January 31, New York

Karla pulled her bed sheets tight and dropped some throw pillows on top of the mattress. She looked at her watch: 11:30 AM. Sometime in the next half hour, Dr. Ping Ang would arrive to decide whether she wanted the commissioned works. Karla had been struggling for over three hours to give her studio just the right look for such an important visit. It needed to appear clean enough to show she should be taken seriously, yet disorganized enough to give the impression that here lived a true artist who was not confined by societal constraints on decorum.

Confident that she had finally achieved the desired affect, she plopped on the couch to await her visitors. What a relief to have a place to herself again, she thought as she surveyed the area. For most of the time since her two week hospital stay, she had been living off the kindness of friends while her apartment was being rebuilt. She had spent the first month at Drew's. That had started out OK until Drew grew more forward in his attempts to get her into his bed. It was a shame, really, she mused. They had started out as such nice friends and then he developed this crush on her. She'd played up her interest in Steve Ang to give him the hint, but he just didn't get it.

Later, he started putting his arm around her all the time in public and acting protective when other guys talked to her. She finally told him outright that she wasn't interested. Things had eased up for a few days, but then got really bad. It still gave her shudders just thinking about it. One night, they went out drinking like they usually did. Again, he had kept her out much too late.

"Time for bed," he had announced as they returned to his apartment. She remembered how he had grabbed her left hand and pulled her toward his bedroom.

"Why are you leading me in there?" she'd tried to ask coyly. "You know I sleep out here."

"I…uh…washed the sheets today but forgot to dry them," he'd replied. "Let's just make it easy on ourselves and share the one bed that has sheets." He tugged her towards the bedroom. "You can finish the laundry tomorrow."

She pulled her left arm, leg, and her head away from him. "That's OK. I'll just sleep on the couch, then."

"That's not necessary," he'd said as he picked her up and carried her into the room. "You're sleeping here tonight. End of discussion." He threw her on the bed and took a few steps back.

For a moment, Karla thought Drew was just being gallant, giving up his bed for her. Then he turned around, took a running leap, pounced on top of her, and began kissing her face. Karla turned her cheeks this way and that, struggling to avoid him.

"You don't know how long I've been waiting to do this," he whispered ferociously in between kisses. "Enough playing around, you know I want you."

Karla pulled her right arm free and broad-handed him across the face. "Get away, you bastard! Haven't I made it clear how I felt, too?"

As he reeled from the slap, she broke free and raced out the door. Too scared to look back, she ran for several blocks. Finally, she slowed down and looked behind her. Although relieved that he had not followed her, Karla felt overcome with new dread. Where would she stay now?

Not knowing where else to turn, she had headed to the police station and sought out Marco and Taylor. Boy, had they been kind.... Marco, especially. Since they were working the night shift, he offered to let her sleep at their place that night. The next day, the two of them invited her to stay with them for a while. They even escorted her to Drew's to collect her belongings. Luckily, Drew was working at the time, so they had avoided any incidents.

Karla stayed with the guys for about two weeks, but then she noticed that Taylor was growing increasingly short-tempered. Not wanting to cause any problems, she packed up her belongings and spent the next two weeks on the couches of various other friends.

About two weeks ago, she learned that her apartment was finally ready for her return. With the deadline closing in, and her being so far behind, she had taken off the last two weeks from work. She had worked non-stop to finish the paintings. She'd come pretty close, too. Now she only needed to impress Dr. Ang and then she could have it all: her paintings in a museum, money, and maybe Steve as a boyfriend or even husband. Wouldn't that be something wonderful, she dreamed.

At precisely 12:00, the doorbell rang to signal Dr. Ang's arrival. Karla ran down the stairs to meet her mysterious benefactor. Just be cool, she reminded herself before she opened the door.

"Dr. Ang, so nice to meet you! Please, come in." She smiled from ear to ear. "Steve, so good to see you again. I hope you don't mind walking. It's only three flights. I can't believe I'm finally getting to meet you. I've been looking forward to this day for quite some time now," Karla babbled nervously.

Dr. Ang shook hands politely and followed her up the stairs. When they arrived in the apartment, the doctor let out a heavy sigh and dabbed her forehead with her handkerchief to remove some small beads of sweat.

"Please, sit down on the couch. May I get you something to drink? Coffee? Tea? Soda?" Karla offered in her sweetest possible voice.

"Just some water would be fine, thank you."

Karla brought glasses for Dr. Ang and Steve then sat in a chair across from them. The three sat silently for several minutes. Karla could not help but stare at this mysterious woman and her son. Who was she anyway? She had pictured her patron as a tall, beautiful, refined Chinese woman who dressed in the most elegant fashions and always wore sunglasses to avoid being recognized in public. In reality, only the part about being Chinese and a woman turned out to be accurate. The doctor was short, about 40 pounds overweight, somewhere in her sixties, and a good ten years behind in her styles. Could this woman really be a power-broker in the New York art scene? It seemed hard to believe that so many influential museum curators would listen to her. Similarly, Dr. Ang used the guise of the drink to study this struggling new artist. She liked people who not only could do their craft well, but who would have the right mix of sophistication and artistic insolence to both impress and shock her friends. She did not like her artists to know her selection criteria because she wanted to discover the "real" person. So far, this one did not impress her that much. Yes, she was polite, but she seemed to be either very young and nervous or, worse yet, "perky."

As the two surveyed each other, Karla began to wonder if she should do something. She did not like extended silences and this one was really starting to bother her. She chided herself to stay calm, cool, and collected. When Dr. Ang was ready, she would know what to do. In the meantime, she would just sit there and look relaxed.

Finally, Dr. Ang put her glass on the table. "Forgive me. As you can see, I am neither young nor fit anymore. Those stairs tired me out. I hope you don't mind that Steve came with me. He has a wonderful eye for art and I value his opinion tremendously."

"Besides, she needs someone to drive her, and I'm her favorite chauffeur," he joked.

Karla grinned in response, maybe a little too largely for the remark. She couldn't help herself. Comments like that had made her fall for him in the first place. He was young, handsome, suave, and pleasantly disarming. She was very glad he had come, for he did much to ease the tension that his mother created.

Dr. Ang rose from the couch and headed towards the paintings that Karla had arranged sequentially on easels lining the other side of the room. "Are these the works you've made for me? Would you care to tell me a little about them?"

"Gladly. I call the series *Diner or Life?* I'm trying to show that all of life's ups and downs, and all types of city-dwellers, can be found in a typical diner during the course of a day. The diner acts as the great equalizer: everyone from the unemployed to wealthy party-goers eventually finds reason to be there. It's one of the few places in the city where this is true. The paintings occur at five distinct times of day and show not only the types of people, but also the moods that they bring with them. These moods give the eatery an ever-changing but still somehow constant atmosphere. I have tried to capture both the people and the mood through the use of lighting, textures, and some exaggeration of form."

"Un-humm," grunted Dr. Ang as she walked back and forth studying the works.

The patron stopped abruptly in front of the third in the series and stared hard. She looked at it from the left and then from the right. She peered at it from barely a nose length's distance. Then she marched to the far end of the room and looked at it from there. She walked back to the others and looked first up at the lights then out the window.

"This one here...what time of day is this?"

"Four in the morning. It is the time when the revellers are returning from their parties. They've had too much to drink. They are hungry but almost everything else is closed. They are tired but still too excited to go home. It is too late to be night but too early to be morning. The diner is their only choice. They must share this space with the homeless, who drink a slow cup of coffee to stay indoors as long as possible."

"I see...and how exactly did you get the lighting like that? I must say, I have never seen shading that is so...intense?"

"Yes, the shading." Karla's breathing started to shorten. "This was one of those serendipitous discoveries that occurred while I was trying to do something else." Karla hoped Dr. Ang would accept this explanation of the partially burned canvas. "I liked the way it looked, so I decided to keep it."

Dr. Ang continued her careful study of the works, walking from one easel to the next and saying very little to anyone. She could not understand why Karla had chosen to place them one slightly behind the next and so close together. It did little to show off each one's individual characteristics. She started to ask and then changed her mind, deciding it was just because this apartment was atrociously small.

As she walked to the last painting in the series, Karla crossed her fingers behind her back and chewed her lower lip nervously. "What's this?!" the shocked patron exclaimed. "Where is the rest of this painting? The right side is complete but the left side is blank! Did you think I would not notice? Is that why you hid it behind the other canvas? What do you take me for? A fool?! Is this your idea of a joke? If this is how you choose to operate, by tricking those who try to help you, then I will have none of this!"

"But wait! I can explain..." Karla attempted.

"I don't care. I only work with those I can trust. Come on Steve, let's go."

"Please, please...I swear I was not trying to trick you. I was just trying to make the best of a bad situation." Karla pleaded, following Dr. Ang across the studio. She turned desperately to Steve, grabbed his arm, looked him in the eyes and, with tears in her own, begged, "Please. You believe me, don't you? I'm not a fraud. Please, ask your mother at least to listen to what I have to say. Then, if she still doesn't believe me or if she doesn't care, you can both go without another word from me."

Steve looked at this young woman's eyes and saw in them both honesty and desperation. The look melted him, especially since he knew how callous his own mother could be. "Mother, maybe we should listen to what she has to say. We've already invested some money in her, and there seems to be some promise to what she has produced. What harm could it do to give her a few minutes to explain herself?"

She stopped in her tracks. Very seldom did her son contradict her decrees. When he did, he usually had a good reason. Besides, he made some good points. She turned around abruptly, looked at her watch, and said, "OK, speak. You have three minutes."

Karla breathed a sigh of relief. "Thank you. The truth is -- although I don't know why I'm starting with those words because I have not lied to you at all today -- but anyway, what really happened is that about three months ago I was just about finished with the first three paintings. Then one night a fire broke out in my apartment building. I didn't even know what happened. I fell asleep and when I woke up I was in the hospital recovering from second and third degree burns and smoke inhalation. You don't believe me? Take a look at my arms! They still bare the scars." She pushed up her sleeve and shoved the arm in Dr. Ang's face.

"I was in the hospital for two weeks. When I returned, my apartment was a mess. Two of the three paintings were destroyed beyond repair. The one whose shading you admired, that one was the only piece to survive. The interesting shades of night were the result of smoke and fire damage. I decided to turn the painting around to my advantage and changed the time of day to match the damage. So you see, it was serendipity.

"Anyway, I could not afford to move into a new apartment, so the landlord agreed to fix the damage for me. In the meantime, I spent the next two months sleeping on friends' couches. I borrowed money from some of them to buy new supplies, since the fire ruined everything I had purchased with the money you advanced me. I carried my easel from apartment to apartment so I wouldn't lose any time. I even took these last two weeks off from my paying job so I could deliver what I promised. In the past two months, I have not slept more than four hours per night. I have worked every waking minute and, as of last night, I was able to finish four and a half of them."

Karla gave her best puppy-dog look while she paused to see Dr. Ang's reaction. The lady returned a cold hard stare. Karla decided the pity approach wasn't working. Time to try Plan B. "Look," she said, lowering her voice half an octave and staring Dr. Ang squarely in the eyes. "I know we agreed that you would advance me some money and I would create five related pieces. I knew at that time, as did you, that I was taking a gamble: if you did not like the works, you would not have to buy them nor pay me the remaining amount. This deal, though, was also a gamble for you: You spent $3000 without knowing what you would get for the money. You could have paid me the money and I could have given you five canvases with a blue stripe painted on each of them. That would have been sufficient for me to make a pretty decent profit for a fairly small investment. You trusted that I would be fair with you, and I, in turn, hoped the same from you.

"From the way you were studying my paintings so carefully, I get the impression that, in fact, you do like them. I think I have shown my integrity, if that is your concern. I have given up sleep and income, invested my own money, and reworked completed pieces to deliver what I promised. Don't you think we could work out an arrangement whereby we both win a little? If you walk away from this right now, neither of us comes out ahead."

Dr. Ang uncrossed her arms and moved her hands to her hips. The hard core business approach seemed to be working, Karla noticed. She continued her pitch. "Of course, if you do not buy them, then I will be forced to sell them myself. You offered to pay me a total of $6000 for the five paintings. My other paintings are already fetching close to $1,000 a piece." That was a bit of a stretch, Karla realized, but it made the math easier. "I'm sure I could easily get close to $1,200 for each of these. If they were very well-received, the price could go even higher. Then you would have missed the opportunity to have discovered me and the chance to have bought the works for relatively cheap. Are you sure you are willing to take that chance? Are you sure four paintings wouldn't suffice?"

Karla looked imploringly at Dr. Ang, then at Steve, then at Dr. Ang. She was shaking from the emotion she was trying to control. Dr. Ang looked at her watch. "I'm impressed," she said flatly, "you said all that in 2 minutes and 53 seconds. Let me think about it. Steve! Come with me!" she ordered as she walked out the door.

Karla hardly knew what to think or do. She paced around the floor and nervously bit her fingernails waiting for some signal. She did not know whether the Angs would return. She had hoped to get along well with this woman, but clearly that wasn't happening. How had Steve developed such a nice personality after living with this woman, she wondered.

At long last the two knocked on the door. Karla ran across the apartment, opened the door, and invited them back in. Dr. Ang began abruptly, "You are lucky you have such an ardent admirer in my son. The quality of your art impressed him, as did the earnestness of your plea. It was he who convinced me to speak with you again."

Karla flashed this knight a modest look of gratitude.

"In my opinion, your art is not bad," Dr. Ang declared. "It needs polish, but at least you have good ideas. More importantly, I like the way you speak. You have a good way with words that will serve you well in life. That is important.

"You have caught me in a very good mood today. I tell you what I will do for you, although you are not to share the terms of this arrangement with anyone. I have a reputation to uphold, you know. The original deal was that you owed me five canvases and I owed you another $3000. You have only delivered 4/5 of your promise. How about I give you 4/5 of mine, or $2400?"

"Yes, thank you," Karla nodded. "I think that is immensely fair of you. Thank you! Oh! What about the fifth painting? Do you want that, too…when it is done?"

"I don't really care." Dr. Ang groused.

"Tell you what," Steve intervened again. "Why don't you give me a call when you finish it and I'll come take a look to see if we want it. I doubt we will offer as much as we would have paid had it been ready now, but at least we could have the complete series and your credibility with my mother would be restored. Would that work for both of you?"

Both women nodded, albeit one much more enthusiastically than the other.

"May I ask one more question?" Karla pressed. "Will you be displaying these at your holiday party?"

"Missy," gruffed Dr. Ang, "don't push your luck right now.

Chapter 16:
Return to Alpha

AlphaTime: February 1: New York City

"Are you sure this is going to work?" Mr. Auerbach asked as Lyle fiddled with LES' dials.

"It's worked in the past, hasn't it?" Lyle responded flippantly.

"Yeah, but now you're trying to bring back four people at once. How does it even know where they are?" Cheyenne wondered nervously.

"It's too complicated to explain. Let's just try it and see what happens. Now, everybody, clear the couch."

Within moments of this announcement, the lights in the apartment flickered and dimmed. LES' innards began to grumble and buzz as it returned to work. Mr. Auerbach and Cheyenne shot nervous looks between each other. They'd never heard LES strain so much. Would everything come out all right? Two minutes later LES belched electricity and spewed sparks that eventually formed a yellowish-white haze around the couch. The haze grew into a fog, then into a curtain of light so thick it blocked the entire couch from view. A two-inch metal coil sprang from the tray containing the old-fashioned TV antenna and landed by Lyle's feet. Lyle raised his right eyebrow and stroked his hairless chin. The machine fell deathly silent. Cheyenne looked wide-eyed at Lyle, who ignored her and stared, almost in prayer, at the couch. Slowly, the fog dissipated and revealed the images of Project 20/20's test subjects. Within seconds, the lights in the room returned to bull brightness and a bell on top of the simulator rang loudly   to   signal   the   end   of   the   task: *RRRRRRIIIINNNNGGGG!!!!!*

Lyle looked at his watch. "Five minutes," he remarked casually. "Not too bad." He bent down and picked up the coil. "I'll have to look into this, though," he added, fumbling with the still-hot metal.

The four participants shook their heads and blinked repeatedly as they tried to understand what had just happened. A chorus of "What the…?" "Where am I?" "What are you doing here?" broke forth from them.

"Welcome back to the Alpha world!" Cheyenne announced cheerfully. "Your first five months are finished and you're now back in Mr. Auerbach's apartment. Sorry to confuse any of you." She paused to let the information soak in while each of the participants stretched their fingers and felt their bodies to check for any missing parts. Finally, she added, "So?…What was it like? What happened to you? How were the transports?"

"Incredible," blurted Taylor. "I gotta hand it to you, Lyle: that's one heck of an invention you got there." He extended his right hand to Lyle while patting him on the shoulder with his left hand. "The transports were seamless and the knowledge infusions, if you don't mind me calling them that, are amazing. I never realized how much I could learn in so short a time! I bet you lots of people would be interested in paying you to take such trips. If you ever decide to make money off this, let me know. I'd love to come work with you."

"Thanks for the vote of confidence. I'll keep you in mind." Lyle accepted graciously. "Did anybody have any problems with the transports?"

They all shook their heads.

"What happens now?" April inquired.

"First, why don't you each update us on your lives? After that, you can tell us what you'd like to do for the rest of the experiment, okay?" Mr. Auerbach suggested.

One by one, the four subjects told their stories. They recounted their triumphs and disappointments. Throughout the discussion, the Project 20/20 board took copious notes. After over an hour of listening to the chronicles of their lives, Mr. Auerbach wanted to cut to the chase. "So did you feel you chose well? Was this career something you'd like to do for the rest of your life? More importantly, is this something to which you would like to return for the next five months? Marco, why don't we start with you?"

"Would I want to be a cop forever?" He shook his head emphatically. "No way. Sure I was pretty good at it, but...I don't know... the whole time I felt like I was just hassling people. I mean, it was good to fight crime, but at the same time, I didn't really like raining on others' parades. Besides, being a cop is dangerous. Why should I do something where I could risk my life?"

"So why did you choose this job in the first place, if that was your attitude? Surely, you knew being a police officer was risky business before you left?" Cheyenne asked.

"If I tell you the truth, you promise not to kick me out of the program?" Marco asked sheepishly.

The board members made eye contact with each other, then nodded their heads in agreement.

"I really only did it because I made a promise to Taylor. You see, we had a deal: he'd help me write my essay and, in return, we'd do the same first career so we could look after each other if needed."

"Why did you agree to that?" Lyle wondered.

"It seemed a pretty good deal for me. You see, I'm a lousy student. No matter how hard I try, I can never write a good essay...at least that's what my teachers think. Frankly, I hate school and can't wait to finish. I thought this would be a kind of interesting way to avoid the classroom for a year. I figured that since I stink at writing, if I wrote the essay myself, I'd never get picked. Taylor's smart, so I figured he could help me formulate my thoughts a little better."

"So do you feel like these past five months were just paying off a debt and nothing more?"

"No, not really. As it turned out, I got quite a bit out of it. For one thing, it gave me a little time to go to music clubs and to think about what I want to do with my life. I guess more importantly, I realized that maybe there are some things I can do well. It gave me some hope for the future."

"That's a good point," Mr. Auerbach confirmed. "Not everyone is suited for the academic life, but that doesn't mean you can't succeed at... shall we say... less academic endeavors. You know, it takes many people a lifetime of failed jobs to find the one area where they do excel. Others spend their whole lives not even trying to accomplish anything because they were told as a child that they would always be dumb or a failure. This just goes to show that success or failure in school does not necessarily predict success or failure in life. If you take that knowledge with you and use it to give you confidence, then that alone is a valuable outcome of this time."

"So, Taylor, you wanted Marco to share the thrills of police life with you. Was it worth it for you?" Lyle questioned.

"I guess so. As it turned out, being a cop wasn't as thrilling as I'd imagined. We spent most of the time just driving around the same several blocks over and over again. A lot of times about the only thing I could find to break the monotony was stopping people for traffic violations. If it weren't for Marco's amazing ability to spot trouble, I'd have been bored silly."

Taylor continued, "I gotta say, I never realized what eagle-eyes Marco has. He could spot a drug deal eight blocks away. Chasing the criminals was awesome, but the whole thing would be over just as it was getting going. The chases never seemed to last as long as they do on TV. So, mainly I spent 60% of my time patrolling, 10% of my time doing the cool cop stuff, and the remaining 30% dealing with all the paperwork associated with Marco's arrests."

"Aah, yes, reality does have a nasty way of interfering with fantasy," intoned Mr. Auerbach. "It sounds to me, though, that your real disappointment was not with the career but with yourself. Am I right?"

Taylor remained silent for more than a minute. "I suppose you're right. I always thought that I would be great in pressure situations. After all, test-taking is stressful, and I'm always calm there. What I found was that when push came to shove, even *Marco* did better than me." He turned to his friend, "No offence, man." Then turning back to Mr. Auerbach, he continued. "Frankly, even when it wasn't a stressful situation Marco outperformed me. I think that's the first time in our lives that's ever happened. I guess I'm just not used to not being the best."

"Maybe you should start getting used to it. Not everything in life will come as easily as school does," Mr. Auerbach advised with a somewhat fatherly tone. "Besides, one of the sad facts of life is that however good you are at something, there is always someone better. Even the best athletes remain on top only for a short time."

"Actually, I'm not sure being the best is all it's cracked up to be," contributed April, much to everyone's surprise. "Take me, for example. Clearly, I did well in my chosen career. I must say, I'm proud that I performed so well, not just technically, but also emotionally. As a doctor, I saw more gore than I could ever have imagined. I also saw so many sad and infuriating cases that made it hard to keep one's cool. I like to think I displayed a professional yet compassionate attitude at all times.

"Even though I enjoyed helping people and even though the hospital appreciated my work and rewarded me with a high position, at times I couldn't help wonder whether it was really worth it. I ended up with next to no time for myself or for my social life. My place was always a mess. The refrigerator was always empty and I was constantly tired. At times, I felt like the only person I wasn't helping was myself."

"It sounds like you need to learn to control your environment a little more instead of letting it control you," Mr. Auerbach observed.

"True, but I don't see how that's possible in an emergency room," April retorted.

"Well, at least you guys got to find out how successful you'd be. I never even got that chance," Karla whined.

"But you asked to be placed before you were at the height of your career. Surely you realized by the categories that you wouldn't see how successful you'd eventually be? If I remember correctly, you were more interested in seeing what an artist's life was like," Lyle reminded her.

"That's true." She paused as she considered her life. "I guess I've got mixed feelings. On the positive side, I loved being free to do whatever I wanted. I liked having a creative outlet with which to express myself.

"On the down side, though, I guess I never realized just how much work went into painting a really good piece of art, or, for that matter, into being a good waitress. I tell you, if I learned nothing else, I've learned the importance of always leaving a good tip!"

She paused again as she reflected. "I gotta admit that I'm disappointed to discover that I don't have the amount of artistic talent that I had hoped. I always imagined that beautiful images would come pouring out my hands. Instead, it took a while for me to even understand the works I had created before I arrived…and, it took forever to find inspiration. You know what else? Painting can be lonely. Even though I had friends, I had to spend so many hours by myself in order to complete my work. I never thought I would miss people's company so much."

The group breathed a collective sigh as they realized how off they had been in their choices. Seeing their glum faces, Mr. Auerbach attempted to lift their spirits. "My sad friends, look at it this way: You've just saved yourselves years of agony trying to fit into a job that wasn't meant for you. Better yet, you get a second chance. Have you given any thought to what you want to do next?"

"Well, I sure have," Marco declared. "I'd like to be a rock star."

Mr. Auerbach raised an eyebrow. "Are you sure this is how you want to use this opportunity?"

"Yes. You see," Marco explained, "Playing guitar has always been my one passion, and I haven't been able to do it as much as I would have liked for the past few months. I've heard so many neat sounds that I now have a ton of ideas in my head for new songs. Plus, I like being more in control of my time."

"OK. When you put it that way, it does seem to make sense. You've mapped out what's important to you and now you're trying to steer yourself down that road. Just remember to stay in control," Mr. Auerbach advised.

"Good. Then it's settled," Lyle stated. "And where would you like to call home?"

"Malibu always seemed like a cool place to live."

Lyle adjusted some more dials on the machine and typed on the keyboard.

"Right. Lastly, at what stage of your career would you like to be?"

"Might as well put me right at the height of my career."

"You got it. Now sit on the couch and prepare to go."

Lyle waited for Marco to seat himself and then flipped a big red switch. The machine buzzed and whirred again. As the cloud of electronic particles began to appear, Mr. Auerbach shouted, "Remember: Drive your future!"

With Marco now gone, the others could barely wait their turns. Taylor jumped on the couch. "I've learned my lesson," he continued without any prodding. "I'm giving up on the macho careers and sticking to something that requires a little more book smarts. I also want something that's going to pay really well. I'm sick of sharing my place and having to cook for myself! For my next career, I want to be head of a really big, successful company and have all the benefits that come with that. I want to be the one calling the shots for a change. Oh- and since I only have five months, could you place me at the height of my career? I don't feel like dealing with the scramble up the corporate ladder. After all, I'll have my whole life in the alpha world to do that. For now, I want to enjoy the sweet taste of success and living life at the top of the heap."

Lyle raised an eyebrow in amazement as he listened to Taylor. This guy is unbelievable, he thought as he began processing the request. What arrogance! How could Marco stand to room with him? Lyle entered the career choice. "And where would you like to live?" Lyle couldn't wait to get rid of him.

"I think I'd like to try a different city this time. Too many bad memories here, if you know what I mean. How 'bout Los Angeles? Lots of big companies headquartered out there."

Without another word, Lyle quickly flipped the red switch and watched as LES whisked him away.

"April, have you come up with a more suitable way to help others?" Mr. Auerbach inquired.

"As a matter of fact, I have. I would like to be a lawyer. They never have emergencies and they still can make a difference in people's lives."

"All right," said Lyle as he returned to LES' controls, "if that's what you want, that's what you shall be. At what point in your career would you like to be?"

"I like seeing how good I'll be at my best, so make me at the height of my career, please."

"Do you want to stay in New York City?" he asked.

"No. I missed the nice weather of my hometown. I'd like to be back in LA."

Once again, Lyle fumbled with the various knobs and then flipped the big red switch. As the haze began to envelop April, Mr. Auerbach shouted, "Remember: Drive your future!"

"That leaves only you, Karla. Have you decided what you want to do?" her friend asked. "If you want to see what happens, you'll have to stay as an artist for the rest of your time. If you want to change careers, you will never know whether all your hard work paid off."

Cheyenne practically could see the dark cloud returning to its normal position over Karla's head as she weighed her options. Poor Karla, Cheyenne thought, nothing is ever easy for her.

Karla raised her head and declared, "You know. I think I know how my pieces will fare. Frankly, I'm sick of the starving artist's life. I want to try something a little more exciting."

"Such as?" the three asked simultaneously.

"I know this is going to sound crazy, but I would like to be a songwriter. I think this may be a better outlet for me. Even Dr. Ang said I had a good way with words."

Everyone looked at her with surprise, but nobody said a word. Realizing that nobody was commenting, Lyle suddenly began typing. He resumed his normal professional stance of asking when in her career and where she wanted to call home. He entered the answers as he heard them: height of the career and Los Angeles. He then flipped the switch and watched as LES began the last transport.

"Remember!" Cheyenne shouted quickly as Karla started to fade from the couch, "Drive your future!"

Turning to the two men, she quipped, "I've been dying to say that!"

Chapter 17:
The Package

SimTime: February 1, Malibu Beach, CA

Marco blinked several times to bring the hands on the clock into focus: 1:15, he thought it said. Relieved that it was still the middle of the night, Marco rolled over and fell back into a peaceful slumber.   Even sub-consciously he was enjoying the fact that he did not soon have to wake up for another day of patrolling the beat. His dreams bore witness to his happiness: he saw cops in uniform lying by the beach. In another snippet, he saw himself riding a wave into the shore to be greeted by a bevy of California girls.

Just when they were about to shower him with kisses, the shrill chirping of the telephone shattered the night's calm.   Shocked and disappointed, Marco instinctively reached his arm in the direction of the noise. Who could be calling him at this hour, he wondered as he answered the phone.

"Marco! Glad I caught you...I wasn't sure you'd be there."

He did not recognize the voice at the other end of the phone. "Where else would I be? It's 2:30 in the morning! Who is this and why are you calling me? What's wrong?"

"Hey buddy! It's Lee…Lee Fong! Hey…wake up! Open your shades! It's 2:30 Sunday *afternoon*! I stopped by your place about two hours ago to drop off the stuff like you asked. I rang the bell, but nobody answered. I wasn't sure if you were sleeping or already out, so I just left the video and the package in your mailbox. Like I told you the other day, you really need to read through the papers. Our meeting is at 10:00 AM Tuesday, so I'll swing by and pick you up around 9:00, OK? Uh-oh—my other line is ringing. I gotta go. See you then!"

The dial tone sounded in Marco's ear for several seconds before he had digested enough of that lightning-fast monologue to realize he could now hang up the receiver. Sunday afternoon! Had he really slept away most of his free day? He pulled himself out of bed and headed toward the window. Gingerly, he lifted the curtain and peeked outside. Was he dreaming again? A beautiful sandy beach, an ocean with perfectly curling waves, and a bright blue sky stared him in the face.

Hello new life! If he had that view out his bedroom, he could not wait to see what the rest of his place looked like. What an eye-opening tour he took! His place contained four bedrooms, a living room, kitchen, dining room, den, and — his personal favorite — a small recording studio complete with cozy chairs, a big-screen TV, and four guitars.

Marco delayed his tour for a while to strum each of them. Carefully listening to the pitch and tone of each note as he played the guitars, Marco grew increasingly aware of a noise that seemed out of place. Unsure of the sound's origin, Marco's attention bounced back and forth between the two clashing sounds. Finally, he recognized the dissonance: his stomach was rumbling. He had been so excited by his new surroundings that he had totally forgotten about food. As he placed the guitars carefully in their stands, Marco tried to recall any other time in his life when he had forgotten to eat. Other than a few times when he was sick, nothing came to mind. Clearly, this was the beginning of something unusual.

On his way to the kitchen, Marco continued to look for clues of his new self. The remarkably clean house made him wonder if he were married. Certainly on his own, he would never keep a place so neat. The more he thought about it, though, the less he remembered seeing any tell-tale signs of women: no dresses in the closets, no flowers around the house, and no fashion magazines. Just to confirm his suspicion, he glanced quickly but carefully at his hand. What a relief: no signs of a ring! A wife would surely cramp the lifestyle he had planned for the next five months.

As he passed the front door on his way to the kitchen, he remembered what the guy on the phone had said about a package in his mailbox. Curiosity and excitement once again getting the better of hunger, he detoured momentarily to pick up a thick brown package that was, as promised, waiting in his mailbox. The box contained two items: a video with "January 12 – Richmond" written on it and a thick legal size envelope with lots of papers in it.

Back inside, Marco fixed himself a bowl of his favorite cereal, popped the video in the VCR, sat down on a soft leather couch, and ate his breakfast as he waited to see what would unfold.   The tape began in the middle of a concert scene: lots of screaming teenagers dancing to the music of some second-rate heavy metal band. Although the crowd seemed to enjoy it, Marco did not share the excitement. To him, they were loud and flamboyant, but their music didn't do much. After ten minutes, the show ended, much to Marco's relief. Clearly, an amateur had shot this tape: the camera shook and the editing was rough.

Marco didn't see the point. Eventually, the next group took the stage in a burst of song. The crowd went wild as the band reached its stride. Watching this show, at least he could understand the fans' excitement. This song rocked: it had a catchy tune, clever words, and fairly complex music. When the song ended and the lead singer began the next one, Marco gasped in surprise. He rubbed his eyes to fix his vision. There he was…watching himself on TV! Not only that, but he was good, too! His fingers flew across the guitar neck at lightning speed. His voice sounded clear as a bell and covered over 2 octaves. He connected with the audience in a way that made every person think he was singing directly to them. The audience loved him and the energy in the room was palpable even through the video tape.

Almost two hours later, the video ended. Marco decided to read the contents of the package while he watched the sun set over the Pacific. As he walked to the porch, he could not stop thinking about what he had just seen. How odd to see himself in a role he could not remember ever playing. Who had arranged to tape the performance? Did LES do that? Did that guy Lee do it? Had this earlier version of himself done it? Who cares, he decided.

He sat down on a lounge chair on his patio, kicked up his feet, crossed his arm behind his head, and watched the sun sparkle over a crystal ocean. Yup, this was the life! He glanced quickly at the manila envelope on the floor, frowned, looked back at the water, and smiled again. He dreaded opening that package. Anything that was over an inch thick with paper couldn't be good news. Just having to read through all of it would be torture. The package and he engaged in a staring contest for the next five minutes. Marco would ignore it, but it beckoned him. He'd stare at it, debating whether to read it or not. He'd look away, but the package never blinked. It kept looking him in the face.

Marco couldn't take it any more. He ripped open the envelope and pulled out the stack of papers. On top lay a long memo entitled "Centano versus Nordo". Marco didn't know who Nordo was, but he didn't like the sound of that title. Forgetting about the sunset, he focused on the document.

An hour later, Marco realized that the sun had already set. He headed back into the house, somewhat dumbfounded by what he had just read: Frankie Nordo, the lead singer from his opening act had stolen both property and songs. Lee Fong, Marco's manager, had canned the opening act as soon as he realized what was happening. The manager suggested they sue the singer. He wrote this memo to summarize the problem in preparation for a meeting on Tuesday with some high-powered lawyer Lee was hoping would take the case.

As he returned to the recording studio, Marco hoped this case would not consume all his efforts during the next five months. He just wanted to play his guitar and avoid all hassles. Now he wondered how much this lawsuit was going to get in the way of a good time. Marco sighed as he picked up a guitar. It had taken only one hour to melt the joy of his new life into a pool of troubles that he could already imagine would take quite some time to resolve. How much time, though, he could not even begin to imagine.

Chapter 18:
At the Office

SimTime: February 3, Los Angeles

"Mr. Centano, Mr. Fong? Please come this way. Ms. Hayes will be with you in a moment."

Marco and Lee entered the most impressive room that Marco could ever remember seeing. Clearly, this was an office of stature. It appealed strategically to whatever impressed people the most. The large, windowed office on the 40th floor of one of Los Angeles' most beautiful skyscrapers played to those who liked prestige. On a bright and sunny day like today, one could see the entire skyline and the Hollywood Hills. For those who wanted an attorney with proven brain-power, diplomas from Harvard and Stanford hung on the walls. Los Angeles being a town of star-power, the office also appealed to fame-seekers. The back wall contained rows of autographed photos of famous clients. The mahogany desk and red leather armchairs oozed power and control while the large arrangements of fresh exotic flowers appealed to those who wanted a woman still to be able to show her feminine side. Even the art world was represented: two large abstract paintings complete with detailed descriptions of the Los Angeles-based artists, filled the remaining wall space. Nothing in the room was left to chance, and the combination worked perfectly on Marco

"Good morning! I'm April Hayes. So nice to meet both of you. Thank you for coming in today. Please, sit down." In walked April, looking suave, sophisticated, and completely at ease in her new career.

"Thank you for finding time to meet with us today," began Lee. "May I introduce Marco Centano?"

Marco recognized her at once, and was pretty sure that she knew who he was, but both decided to play it as if this were their first meeting. The two shook hands and greeted each other.

"Nice to meet you, Marco. I heard one of your songs on the radio today as I drove into work. Nice sound," complimented April. "...and you are...?" April inquired of Lee.

"I'm Lee Fong, Marco's manager."

"It's my pleasure," April replied. "I understand you're having contract problems, is that correct?"

"Not exactly, although that is a part of the problem. Shall I tell you our side of the story?" Lee offered.

"Please," April accepted.

"It all started about six months ago. We were touring around the East Coast, playing a gig every few days. Galaxy Records, with whom Marco has his recording contract, had sponsored the tour as a way to promote their hottest new star. Since they were footing the entire bill, they had requested that we pair with a new heavy metal band that they were trying to promote."

"Heavy metal? Isn't that a little yesteryear?" April interrupted.

"True, but when the people with the purse strings make a request like that, it's pretty hard to say no, you know," Lee explained. "In my opinion, the grouping seemed odd. Right from the start, I doubted whether they'd get along, but what could I do? Anyway, we started touring with PastyLips...that's the band... and things were more or less okay.

"About two months into the tour, Marco and his band members started noticing that things kept disappearing from their dressing rooms. Nothing big, mind you, but annoyances nonetheless. At first it was stuff like drumsticks, extra guitar strings, and T-shirts. Over time, more expensive things disappeared: watches, a gold necklace, even some money out of wallets. Still, nobody thought too much of it. After all, backstage is a pretty crazy place. Everyone's in a hurry; it's not really that secure; and tons of strangers are always milling around. I kept telling the boys, 'Leave anything valuable at the hotel. You're a fool to bring it to the show.'

"One evening after a show, about half-way through the tour, Marco ran out of his room fairly frantic. He had started writing a song on the way to the show....You know how artistic inspiration is....After the concert, he wanted to continue working on it before he lost the idea. He looked all over his dressing room but could not find the paper anywhere. It must have been a really good piece, because I've never seen him so upset. Usually, he's a pretty mellow guy.

"Two weeks later, PastyLips added a new song to their set list. Marco told me that he thought it sounded a little like the piece he had started, but not enough to be obvious. We didn't think too much of it until about a week later. Now, you gotta understand how Marco operates. When he gets in a creative mood, the songs pretty much just pour out of him. He'll write several within a four-week period, then later come back and polish them up. When he's in that mood, his head flies off to a different place where songs fill the air and people can do no wrong. Part of my job is to protect him from himself...and others. When he told me that he'd lost another song that he'd been working on, I began to grow suspicious. I tried asking him not to write just before he was going to perform, but he refused. 'When inspiration hits'....and all that stuff." Lee made circular cloud motions with his hands to add a touch of sarcasm to his words.

"Since I couldn't convince Marco to stop writing at inconvenient times, I asked him to at least put his notes away safely before running out on stage. About a week later, another song turned up missing after a show. We retraced Marco's steps, and realized he'd left the music on a table in his dressing room. I chastised him about not securing his notes again, and this time he got the hint. First he'd put the music inside a book. Later, he put it inside his guitar case or suitcase. Now, I'll grant you these aren't the most secure places, but at least it was out of direct sight."

"Did that help?" April asked, caught up in the story.

"Not really," Lee continued. "Songs kept disappearing. This continued for almost a month. Marco would start a new song and hide it in progressively more secure places. Still, the music would disappear and then PastyLips miraculously would add a new song to its repertoire. Obviously, it doesn't take a genius to figure out what was happening. The problem was that we could not prove anything

"Then, about three weeks ago, Marco and the boys decided to vary the routine for the show. Five months of doing the same thing gets a bit boring, you know. So, in this new act, about midway through the show, Marco plays this really upbeat, rocking song that has him running and jumping across the stage. At the end of it, he talks to the audience and acts too tired to play anymore. In the end, he tells the crowd that he's going backstage for a short nap. While he's gone, the band will entertain them. He leaves the stage and the boys play a new song that features Kenny on the keyboards.

"The first night they tried this, Marco went back to his room to change into a clean shirt. He walked in the room and I don't know who was more surprised: Marco to find someone in his room or Frankie Nordo at being caught red-handed."

"And who exactly is Frankie Nordo?" asked the enraptured attorney.

"Frankie is the lead guitarist from PastyLips. There he stood, with the music sheets right in his hand. He tried to hide it, but he knew he had been caught. In his state of surprise, Marco could not help but shout. I happened to have been around the corner from the dressing room and heard him. I ran into the room to find the two guys yelling at each other. . Marco kept pointing to the hand behind Frankie's back. I ran over and grabbed the stuff right out of his hands. Luckily, Frankie's not a fighter. Sure enough, it was some sheet music in Marco's handwriting."

Something about that part of the story sounded suspicious to April. "How long did all this take? What happened to the rest of the concert?"

"It all happened very quickly. I mean, how long does it really take to walk backstage, enter your dressing room, find somebody in there, and shout? After I grabbed the music, Frankie started to try to talk his way out of a rather obvious and embarrassing situation. In the midst of his hemming and hawing, a stagehand came in to tell Marco he was due back on stage. I gotta hand it to Marco, he was thoroughly professional. He told me to deal with it, went back on stage and finished the set. He was so furious, though, that he refused to do an encore that night. So it turned out to be a bit of a bummer for our friends in Richmond."

That sounded plausible, April decided. "So what happened then? That was three weeks ago, wasn't it?"

"Yes, it was. We fired PastyLips on the spot. After all, who wants to travel with a bunch of thieves? We only had three weeks left on the tour, so Marco and the boys just finished up most of the remaining shows without an opening act. We returned to LA just last week, and this was the earliest appointment we could get with you. Marco still has two nights here in LA to do."

"That's some story. I can understand your anger, but what exactly are you hoping I can do?"

Now Marco chimed in. "We want to sue the pants off them. How dare they steal my music...not to mention all the other things!"

"You said you want to sue 'them'. Whom exactly do you want to sue?"

"Sue everybody that was involved with PastyLips. Sue Frankie, sue the band, and sue Galaxy," declared Marco, who was growing increasingly riled.

Lee cringed at the mention of Galaxy. He'd been trying to convince Marco not to go after a giant like the record company, but Marco wouldn't listen. It amazed Lee how upset Marco could get when he occasionally let things bother him. It's always the calm ones that explode, he thought to himself.

Meanwhile, April raised an eyebrow at the list of defendants. Putting on the voice of calm that she had mastered while a doctor, April tried to soothe her perspective client. "OK. If that's what you want to do, we can arrange that. However, I must tell you, I'm not sure I'm in complete agreement with your strategy. As I see it, you're absolutely right to go after Frankie. You've caught him red-handed stealing your music and, as Lee put it so succinctly, it doesn't take a genius to figure out he'd been stealing other songs. Of course, we don't have as much proof that he also stole the smaller items, but I think that's much less important. You're going to have more success going after him for theft of song than of guitar strings. As for the band, I suppose there is some legitimacy in going after them, too. It's going to be a tougher case: you're going to have to prove that they knew they were playing stolen music. I doubt that Frankie gave you any credit, so from their perspective, they thought they were just playing music that Frankie had written. It's still wrong, mind you, but it's a question of intent.

"Going after Galaxy is a different story, though. I think the case against them is the weakest. Do you really think they meant to set you up with a thief? I doubt it. That certainly, wouldn't be in their best interest. I'm sure they will say that they were just trying to promote two of their acts. They also probably will remind everyone how much it costs to put a group on tour for six months: the airfares, hotels, pre-pays on the venues, food, et cetera. If I were in their shoes, I'd be reminding you of how many musicians need to beg for funding from multiple corporations to finance them. Here they were coming to *you*, asking *you* to tour, and willing to pay for everything. If you involve them in a lawsuit, they'll put their best lawyers on the case and delay the whole trial until much of your money has run out. Remember, you're playing with the big guys here.

"I'm not saying that it's not worth it to go after a corporation if they have genuinely done something wrong. All I'm saying is that I think you need to consider carefully the consequences of biting the hand that feeds you when it did not mean to give you a spoiled apple. Not only will they bleed you with legal battles, but they'll never want to work with you again. You'll have to find a new recording label, and honestly, in this town, how many companies do you think are going to want to pick up an artist that sued his old label for something that probably was not their fault?"

April's words gave Marco pause. On the one hand, she had a point. This is a hard town in which to do business and much as nobody likes to admit it, good relations are key to everything. Besides, what she said sounded like what Lee had been saying. Clearly, the photos on the wall gave her a degree of credibility when it came to knowing how to deal with the powerful. Still, they got him into this mess. Shouldn't they be made to compensate him in some way?

April could tell that her words had made an impact. Marco seemed to be thinking things over. She hated to be the bearer of bad news, but suing the record company was just a big mistake. He was not her client yet, but he was, in a way, her friend from the alpha world. Sure, she could have just accepted the work and made lots of money, but that was not why she had wanted to be an attorney. For her, it was about helping people, not making the big bucks.

"Hey, I can see by the look on your face that you're not fully satisfied with letting Galaxy off the hook completely. Here's a suggestion: why don't you see if you can't work *with* Galaxy to jointly go after Frankie and the band?" April offered.

"Why would they want to do that if, like you say, they're really not guilty?" asked Marco.

"A couple of reasons," April explained authoritatively. "For one thing, your contract is about to expire. They might feel that helping you now will make you more willing to work with them when it comes time to renegotiating your contract. For another thing, in a way, they were robbed, too. They paid for the tour of this band of original music-makers, and now they learn that what they bought was a fraud. In a way, all the songs they stole from you, they also stole from Galaxy."

"I don't get it," Marco interrupted, "How did they steal from Galaxy if they were working for Galaxy?"

He can be so innocent at times, she thought. "Because," she explained, "if they recorded that song, they might have sold, say, 5,000 copies. If you had finished and recorded it, you might have sold twice that. This is all speculation, and there's no real proof to it, but the fact is that you are by far a bigger draw than they are. Chances are more people would buy your records."

"I really don't see how you could prove that in court," Lee interjected.

"True, you probably couldn't, but that's not the point. The point is to use this line of reasoning to convince Galaxy that it's in their best interest to work with you on this matter. From their perspective, it's just good publicity. You know: 'We more than represent your music; we represent you.' That kind of thing."

Both men nodded in understanding and agreement. Lee grew increasingly impressed with this attorney. He had seen many good ones in his day and this one seemed to be living up to her reputation as one of the shrewdest lawyers in LA.

"So you think the two of us should make an appointment with someone in Galaxy's legal department?" prodded Lee, hoping this would bring the attorney around to representing them.

"You can if you want, but frankly, I think you're

wasting your time. A company that big has a large legal department so it can stall pending lawsuits as much as possible. My theory is go to the top."

"To the top?" asked an incredulous Lee, who now felt like he might be in over his head. "I don't know if I have that kind of pull."

"You don't need to. I'll arrange it for you. I have a way of opening doors in this town."

"Does this mean you'll take our case and represent us?" Marco asked excitedly, as he sat forward in his chair.

April Hayes smiled from across the big mahogany table. "It would be my honor."

All three stood up and shook hands, happy with the new arrangement. Lee felt relieved that someone with more experience and pull would now be in charge. April was excited at the challenge she was about to face, and how it could enhance her standing in the firm. Marco felt comforted by having someone he trusted on his side.

Chapter 19:
The Negotiation

SimTime: February 7, Los Angeles

Taylor's head bobbed to the rhythm of the music playing on the CD player as he pulled his Mercedes into the parking spot reserved for the CEO of Galaxy Records. He had received the CD during the lunch meeting from which he was now returning. Galaxy had a policy that the CEO must approve all new artists before signing any contracts. So far, Taylor had come to enjoy this aspect of the job the most. He relished people treating him with the respect and deference that comes from knowing that their fates lie ultimately in his hands. This had been the third and best of these lunches this week. This artist was really clever and his music had a unique sound. He kept replaying that last song in his head as he headed toward the elevator. If Taylor had been leaning towards signing this guy by the end of the lunch, hearing his demo on the way back to the office had convinced him completely.

Riding up the elevator, Taylor wondered how much longer he could continue this tradition. Galaxy was a multi-billion dollar company, but compared to other record companies, it was still a fairly small player. True, it was probably the largest company in its class, but that only made it a big fish in a little pond. Taylor wanted to be, and wanted the company to be, something more. Just yesterday he had attended a meeting with some of Galaxy's lawyers and bankers about a deal to purchase Cloud9 Records. Like Galaxy, Cloud9 was a big fish in a small pond; however, Galaxy was clearly the larger fish. If the two companies could be combined, the new organization would move into a whole new class and would be poised to play with the big boys. Taylor had set a goal for himself: Finish the take-over of Cloud9 before leaving this simworld.

"Good afternoon, Mr. Washington," his secretary chirped as he strode past her into his office.

"Good afternoon, Mrs. Pelingham. Any messages?"

"Of course! You have about twenty. Here are the message slips. Don't forget: you have an appointment with Marco Centano and April Hayes at 2:30. I believe Mr. Gossett briefed you about this yesterday evening before he left."

"Oh, right. Thanks," Taylor acknowledged as he sat behind his desk. "By the way, is Gossett still around? I'd like to talk to him briefly."

"No, sir. Remember? You let him take the day off for family matters."

"Oh, right," Taylor remarked dejectedly. Between the martini at lunch, the cool conversation, and everything that occurred that morning, Taylor had forgotten why April and Marco were coming to visit. He assumed they wanted to check in with him now that they had been in their new careers for about a week. Well, he'd just have to wing it, he decided.

At exactly 2:30 Mrs. Pelingham brought in his guests. Although a little miffed that she had shown them into his office without giving him prior notice of their arrival, Taylor realized the importance of not showing how little things like that annoyed him. Instead, he bounced up from his chair, walked purposefully around to the door, plastered a gracious smile on his face, and welcomed the visitors.

"April! Marco! How nice to see you again," he greeted as he shook their hands. Taylor noticed another man, unknown to him, entering behind Marco. Sensing the awkwardness of the situation, April quickly volunteered the missing information.

"Taylor, I'm not sure if you ever met my client's manager. This is Lee Fong."

"Lee...so nice to finally see you," Taylor replied with all the hospitality of a southern gentleman. He hoped that line would cover him just in case the two had met sometime in the past. "Please, won't you all have a seat?"

As Taylor took his seat behind his mahogany desk, he realized that this was not going to be a social visit. He could tell by April's tone that this was official business. "So...what can I do for you today? Is it contract renewal time already?"

"No, not just yet...although that's not too far around the corner," April responded in a manner that indicated clearly she would be controlling the conversation on that side of the desk. "We wanted to talk to you about the PastyLips situation."

PastyLips....Taylor had to think back through everything he had heard and read in the past week to remember what exactly that meant. He vaguely remembered reading a memo about a band being fired from the tour, but he couldn't remember why.

"What exactly do you have in mind?" he ventured, hoping something in the conversation would fill in the gaps.

"To cut right to the chase, we think Galaxy should compensate Marco for the losses," April declared.

"You want us to pay Marco for losses related to PastyLips?" reflected the slightly confused CEO. "Why would we want to do that?"

"For one thing," began April as she mounted her soapbox, " it would be the decent thing to do. After all, it wasn't Marco's idea to tour with PastyLips. Galaxy put the tour together and appointed PastyLips the opening act. What was Marco going to do? Say 'no' to the people who bankroll him? So what does Marco get for being the good team player? He gets stuck with a second-rate band that engages in both petty crimes and intellectual property theft."

Now that Taylor understood a little bit better what was at stake here, he felt more like he could properly defend his company.

"Look, if Marco wasn't careful enough to properly protect his property, we shouldn't be responsible for paying him back. If we started down that road, how long do you think it would take before all our acts started "suffering theft" while on tour? We'd start bleeding money, believe you me," Taylor responded, meeting April on a nearby soapbox. "Besides, it's routine for record labels to pair their big tickets with up-and-comers on tour. It helps promote the newer act."

April stood momentarily shocked. She had not expected to run into this much difficulty. She assumed that because they were all friends, that this would be an open-and-shut case. Now she was being forced to actually represent her client's best interests.

"Still," April countered, "you should have at least done a background check or something."

Taylor let out a condescending laugh. "Please! If we only represented artists that had no skeletons in their closets, the world would be listening to Pat Boone! Come on! These people are artists. By their very nature, they're often bound to rebel against society's norms. Most have something in their background of which they are not particularly proud. This industry isn't interested in their pasts. We're only interested in whether they perform to the audience's liking."

"Understood, but, according to the contract, you, as the sponsor, are responsible for covering any expenses incurred while on the tour. In this case, that includes the cost of stolen goods and, more importantly, plagiarized songs," the lawyer retorted.

Taylor thought about this for a moment. He was not familiar enough with the law to know if this were true. Unfortunately, he didn't have any of his lawyers in the room to verify that point. Besides, he could see that April was much more prepared to discuss this issue than he was. Rather than continue this debate, which he could see he was going to lose, he figured he might as well keep the tone of the meeting positive and hear what they really wanted.

"OK. Let's cut to the chase: What amount would make you happy, Marco?"

"Five million dollars," replied the singer's spokesperson.

"Five million?!" gasped the surprised CEO. "How much money do you carry in your wallet? How many guitars did they steal?!"

"As we've mentioned," April explained, "it's not the petty thievery we're after. It's the lost revenue from the stolen songs."

"How do you figure?"

"According to Lee, about 90% of Marco's songs have made it into the top 100, and 10% have made it into the Top-10. Marco figures approximately 10 songs were stolen. Therefore, nine would have made it into the top 10 and there's a good chance that one of those nine would have been another Top-10 song. You do the math."

"But there's no guarantee that they would have followed suit," Taylor countered.

"True. That's why we're only asking for five million dollars and not more."

"And if we don't pay?"

"Then when Marco's contract is up, which is in less than three months, he might look elsewhere."

Taylor considered these words and tried to assess whether she was bluffing. He looked at Marco for about a minute.   For once, Marco maintained the perfect poker face.

"OK.   Let me think about it.   May I call you back with my answer?"

"Sure.   I know you'll do what's right for our client."

On that note April rose, signaling the end of the meeting.

Taylor saw his guests to the elevator, then returned to his office to ponder the situation.   For the first time in his life, he had been outmaneuvered.   Either April really was one heck of a lawyer, or he needed to prepare better for his meetings.

Preferring not to think about the matter any longer, Taylor turned to other business. He pulled from his briefcase the proposed contract from his lunch meeting and began reviewing it for final approval.   Reading the document was a long and difficult process for a non-lawyer like himself. He pondered each sentence carefully, looking for anything that could eventually come back to haunt Galaxy Records. The offered amount seemed awfully high.

Curious to compare this offer to established acts, Taylor asked Mrs. Pelingham to bring him a few other contracts. She returned with Marco's contract on top of the pile.   Scanning his friend's contract confirmed his suspicion that Galaxy was about to overpay its newest talent.   Marco's contract gave him substantially less. Reading through other contracts, however, shook Taylor's confidence in his original assessment. As it turned out, the new artist's contract was no more than most of the others. In fact, Marco's was the one that was out of line.

This realization gave Taylor pause: A proven success like Marco was earning a smaller percentage per song than was being promised to less well-known and less successful acts. Taylor looked at Marco's contract again. Just as April had said, the contract was up for renewal in May. Taylor thought some more. At long last, he determined the proper course of action: He would approve the contract for the new guy and prepare to negotiate a settlement with April for the damages. He hoped that, by acting like the good guy, he could prevent a known producer from leaving the fold and limit the percentage increase that would be demanded during the contract negotiations.

Taylor asked Mrs. Pelingham to call April for him. A few minutes later, he picked up the line and began talking. "April? Taylor here. I've been thinking about our discussion earlier today and I think we might be able to work a deal. What do you say?"

"Go ahead. I'm listening," she replied cautiously.

"Galaxy values Marco as a member or our family. As such, we recognize we might be partially responsible for the losses he has suffered. The problem is that coughing up five million dollars at once is going to hurt our cash flow. We'd prefer to spread the payment out over time. How about we renegotiate his contract so he'll get 3% more on sales? If his sales keep going as is, by the end of next year, he could have gained more than the $5 million from a settlement?"

"Hmmm…interesting idea," April considered. "Of course, the flip side is that if Marco doesn't produce as many hits, then he never gets his full recovery. Look, I understand your situation about the lump sum payment, but I think Marco needs a little bit more protection."

"What do you have in mind?" Taylor asked, trying to hide his fear that she might out-think him again.

"How about $2 million up front with the rest coming out as you proposed."

"Do-able!" agreed Taylor. "Do we have a deal?"

"Not quite. There's one more thing. Frankie Nordo seems to have gone into hiding. We've been trying to track him down so we can sue him. Unfortunately, he seems to be better at hiding himself than at making music. Could Galaxy lend detective and legal support so we could find him? Otherwise, all the money Marco wins is going to go into paying for lawyers and detectives?"

"I think we could manage that. After all, we want to protect those whom we represent."

"Well, then, Mr. Washington, it looks like we have a deal. "It's a pleasure doing business with you," chirped the proud lawyer.

"Likewise," replied the satisfied CEO.

Chapter 20:
The Encounter

SimTime: February 13, Los Angeles

"What'll it be tonight?" asked the bartender.

"Gimme a beer, please," Karla answered somewhat sullenly.

"Don't beat yourself up. It was a tough crowd out there tonight. You did a good job."

Karla appreciated the words of support. By now the bartender knew her pretty well. She'd sung at this club several times already in the past two weeks. Whenever she felt her show had gone well, she ordered a soda or water to calm down afterwards. On nights where she didn't quite connect with the audience, she consoled herself in a beer. Not exactly the healthiest solace, she recognized, but it worked for her.

"Thanks, but it wasn't the crowd," she responded. "They were all over that blues band that went on before me. They were great. What a tight horn section …and that singer's voice! They were a hard act to follow."

The bartender nodded. He didn't want to hurt her feelings, but he had to admit she was right. The lineup for the night had been all wrong. The early crowd heard the rowdier music. The later crowd got the mellower stuff. He had tried to tell his boss, the owner of the club, to switch the order, but the man had not listened. As a result, the early crowd left after the first act, the club sold less drinks, he had received fewer tips, and another new singer got lost in the shuffle.

A good-looking young man sidled up to the bar beside Karla and ordered a beer. Recognizing his new neighbor as the last act, he attempted a conversation.

"Hey, weren't you just up there?"

"Yeah, that was me, " she admitted without looking up.

"You new around here?" he ventured. "I don't recall seeing you perform here before."

"Apparently, you don't come here very often," she remarked snidely. "I've been here every other day for the past two weeks."

The man shrugged his shoulders. "Hmm. Maybe I've just come at times when you weren't on. It could happen, you know."

"I suppose," she responded non-committally.

Something about Karla's aloof attitude attracted the man. He found her something of a challenge. "So you play here all the time. How did you get this gig? I hear it's pretty hard to get a steady job here."

"It's not too difficult, I guess. I saw they had an open-mic night here a few weeks ago, so I decided to try it. I figured it was at least somewhere to begin. After I was done, the club owner asked me if I wanted to play here a few nights a week. He pays me a little, and it gives me a chance to perform some of my songs." Karla wasn't really sure why she was telling all this to the guy. Maybe the alcohol was relaxing her.

"So you're new to the area, then" he inquired curiously. The more she talked, the more he felt a connection. He felt oddly comfortable with her, like somehow he already knew her. He was determined to keep this conversation going.

"Yeah, I guess you could say that," Karla mumbled. She hid her cheek in her right hand, blocking her face from his view. She did not like the direction this conversation was turning and didn't want to have to come up with a story to explain her life's history. She hoped the guy would take the hint.

He did. Not willing to walk away from this yet, though, he tried a different tack. "So how many songs did you perform? I got here in the middle of your act and so only heard three."

"Actually, you didn't miss much. I only played five tonight. The boss said they were running late or something, and asked me to only play for half an hour. He doesn't pay me much, but he does control the stage."

"I never heard any of those songs before. They were really good."

"Thanks," she smiled. "I wrote them myself."

"So you're a singer and songwriter," he mused aloud. "Very cool. How many songs have you written so far? Any of them been played on the radio?"

"I've got a bunch. I usually use part of each day for writing. Unfortunately, I haven't had much luck getting airplay for them."

"Yeah, it's pretty tough to get anyone to listen. I remember how that was."

Now Karla's ears perked up. "Oh? Are you a songwriter too?"

"Yeah, you could say that." Now it was his turn to play it coy.

"Do I know any of your songs?" she pried.

"Oh, I don't know. Probably not. You probably listen to different radio stations than where I'd be played."

Now Karla was confused. Just a few minutes ago, this guy was hitting on her. Now that she was finally getting interested in him, he was clamming up. Maybe he thought she was just interested in him because he was on the radio. True, that might have had something to do with it, but, crazy as it seemed, she felt comfortable around him. Now that she had pulled her eyes up from her beer mug and actually looked at him, she was surprised to see what a handsome guy was paying attention to her. He had classic Latin looks: tall, dark, nice build, wavy hair, brown eyes. She could not help but smile and sit up.

"Gee, you know, when you smile, it really lights up your whole face," he complimented, sensing she was finally starting to take his bait.

Karla blushed.

"You mind if I give you a little professional advice?" he offered.

Karla stepped back into her protective shell as she steeled herself for criticism. She really didn't want to hear this guy's advice, but she knew if she said no, he would walk away. "What?" she mustered.

"You know what would improve your performance a bit? You should try talking to your audience. Look at them a bit more. Show them that pretty smile of yours. Don't just look at the floor or your guitar. You need to connect with them. If you make the connection, you won't lose their interest. They'll stick with you all the way to the end."

"Is that so? What makes you think I didn't have their attention?" she asked defensively.

The man was taken aback by this attitude. He had come over to make friends and to help a fellow musician. Instead of just graciously accepting his thoughts, this woman went on the defensive. This did not look very promising. Still, her music and her looks intrigued him enough to make him press on.

"You forget: I was in the audience. Believe me, I can tell when a crowd is with you."

Karla was not sure she liked his cockiness. More accurately, she realized, she didn't like his brutal honesty. She knew full well that she had lost the crowd tonight; she was just hoping nobody else had noticed.

The man interpreted her silence as disagreement. Sensing he was about to lose her, he tried to explain. "Hey, you don't need to listen to me. I just call them like I see 'em. But I do have some experience in these matters. You see, I play gigs all across the country. Whenever I'm home, I like to check out the new local talent. I've got a good ear for what's hot and what's not. I've seen enough audiences to know who's in charge of a concert. Which brings me to a second piece of advice for you: When someone offers you advice, at least act like you care. This is a tough town and you never know who can help you or who can hurt you."

Karla got the point. She had come across a little more stand-offish than she had intended. This guy was right. She needed to learn to control her mouth a little better. Now that she realized this guy might be somebody, she also realized how much she needed to back-peddle and try to re-sell herself as a nice person.

"I'm sorry. I didn't mean that to come out the way it did. I do appreciate the advice and I will try to work on it…looking up, that is. I guess I'm still just suffering some post-performance nerves."

The two sat silently for several moments and drank their drinks. Karla took a big swallow as she thought about what an awful night this was turning into: first a bad show, then she accidentally blows off a cute guy that might be a record producer or something.

For his part, the guy could not figure out what to do. On the one hand, this woman, and her music, interested him. He had hit on her in hopes of getting to know her better. He even offered her some sagely advice. Still, she did not seem to be falling for his lure. Maybe he should just cut bait and go elsewhere. If it were meant to be, it would go easier than this. He paid for his drink and stood up to leave. Sensing her eyes following him, he realized that all might not be lost. He paused for a second as he debated asking her out on a date. Deciding it wasn't worth all the trouble, he started heading for the door. In a rare moment of clumsiness, he tripped on the guitar that lay on the ground behind Karla's chair. Something in the jolt reminded him of his other reason for wanting to talk with her.

"Look," he began again after several awkward minutes. "I was really impressed with your music tonight. I think you have potential. The thing is this: I'm just finishing up my current national tour. We've played some pretty decent size houses. It sounds pretty grueling, but it was also pretty fun…."

Karla could see where this was going. This guy probably had a girl in every port and was just looking for someone in this town. Either that, or he was already nicely blowing her off. He probably was going to ask her out, but then when she came across so brusquely, he changed his mind. Well, she was ready for that. She knew what to say and how to react. She'd just let him go through his whole speech before casually thanking him and saying goodnight. After all, who needed either of those two problems?

"…Anyway, so even though we're a bit different, I think it would be fun and it might even help you a little," he continued, "So, if you're interested, why don't you call my manager and he'll take care of the arrangements?"

Huh? she wondered. What was he talking about? Karla now understood what her mother had meant about her not listening when people speak. Now she had to figure out a way to find out what he had in mind without looking stupid. What a night!

"So you want me to call your manager to handle the details? Isn't that a little…unusual? Can't you just make your own plans?" she inquired.

"I suppose I could, but he likes to get involved in these things. That's part of his job, after all."

Karla shook her head in amazement. She'd heard strange stories about Los Angeles and rock stars, and now she was beginning to understand why. What kind of guy can't make his own plans for a date? And exactly how involved did this manager like to be in his dating?

He looked at his watch. "Hey, it's getting late. I really need to leave. So what do you say? Are you interested in pursuing this? You know, I gotta say, you're definitely different. Very few people would hesitate at the chance to make a guest appearance and sing a couple of songs on the closing nights of a national tour. Should I give you my manager's number or not?"

"OH! Er...um....Yeah!" Karla finally exclaimed enthusiastically, now that she understood the question. "Definitely. I'd love to talk with your manager. Thanks."

"OK, here's his card," he said as he put it in her hands. "Call him tomorrow afternoon and tell him that you're the one that Marco mentioned."

Chapter 21:
The Offer

SimTime: February 20, Los Angeles

April lifted her head momentarily from her law books and noticed a fist floating halfway up the doorway. In the time it took her to take off her reading glasses, the body attached to the fist made its way into the doorway. There stood Martin Hufington, the senior partner at the law firm, smiling inquisitively as he rotated his thumb upwards and downwards. "Well?" he ventured, "How did we do?"

April smiled broadly. "We got 'em!" she responded proudly.

"Atta girl! I knew if anyone could land Hollywood's hottest new motion picture studio it would be you! I'm telling you, you've got what it takes…and we here at Hufington, Cabash, & Chow are darn happy we've got you on our side!" With that, Hufington turned on his heels and let April return to her work.

Frankly, April was relieved that he had left so quickly. Normally, one of his visits would take an hour of her time, and today was one of those increasingly common days when time was scarcer than men in a lingerie store. In order to seal the deal with Hot Rock Pictures, the star lawyer had spent over two hours and five hundred dollars with their team at yet another of those swank LA lunch spots.

Exhausted from all the schmoozing she had done, she returned to her office and the waiting stack of books. A new pile of papers needing her review sat on top of those books. Deciding she needed the comfort of research, she moved the papers to the back credenza until tomorrow. Unfortunately, she had done the same thing yesterday, so the pile of papers behind her now looked like a small mountain. She had been reading for only 15 minutes when her boss had interrupted her. Now she closed the door to her office and returned to her reading.

Thirty minutes later the phone rang. April threw down her glasses, shook her head in annoyance, and answered the phone.

"April? Morrison McDean here. How's tricks?"

"Oh, just fine," she responded coolly. April could not stand Morrison. He was abrasive, unrefined, and halfway competent at best. She couldn't believe that of all the private detectives in the greater Los Angeles area, Galaxy had chosen this one to look for Frankie Nordo. What were they thinking, she always wondered whenever she spoke with him. Did they just pick his name from the phone book without interviewing him? "So, are you calling to tell me you found our man?"

"Well, you're not too far off. As you know, I tracked him down to Arizona. Unfortunately, by the time I got here, he'd already beat feet. I think someone must have tipped him off or something. Anyway, I've got a really good suspicion of where he's heading next."

"And where might that be?" April could hardly wait to hear. This was the third time he'd come close to finding Frankie only to miss him by a day or two.

"I've got a hot tip that he's headed to Cabo San Lucas, Mexico."

"Uh-huh." April could not help wonder if Morrison even knew for whom he was searching. Maybe he thought he was looking for Carmen Sandiego!

"So, anyway, April. I was calling to find out if you wanted me to go all the way down there and look for him."

"Look. Here's the deal. We need to find Frankie Nordo in order to sue him, so as far as I'm concerned you can go ahead. However, I'm not paying your bills. I would suggest you call Taylor Washington at Galaxy and get his approval before continuing your jaunt."

"Jaunt?! You think this is fun for me? This is serious work, lady," he rebuked. "Why don't you call Galaxy and get back in touch with me. It's a local call for you."

This annoyed April even more. "Morrison, I'm too busy to deal with this. You know the deal: we'll cover your expenses during the search, but if you want the big bucks, you need to deliver for us. That means *you* need to do whatever it takes to find him…including dealing with Taylor. I've got a client coming in now, so I have to go. Good bye."

Desperately wanting to finish the research before the day's end, April called her assistant. "Jeremy? Please hold all calls and visitors for the rest of the day. I don't want to talk to anybody unless they're calling to tell me I've won the lottery. Is that clear? Thank you."

April glanced at the clock: 3:00. She could see where this was going to be another long day at the office. She guessed she had a good three hours worth of reading to do, which meant another 12-hour workday.

Accepting her fate, she put on her glasses and dove into her reading. Hours passed, the pages moved from right to left, pencils shrank in size, and the stack of note cards grew. Work progressed slowly but steadily. Although she was forced to think hard, the chance to concentrate on only one thing for uninterrupted hours seemed like a mini-vacation to her. She could barely remember a day in this job where she had worked on only one or two projects for an extended period. She was not begrudging her lot. Just as when she was a doctor, she saw that the more successful you are at your work, the more you are asked to do.

Her mini-vacation ended abruptly when the phone rang. By the number of rings, she could tell that her assistant was calling.

"Jeremy, is Ed McMahon outside my office?"

"No, ma'am."

"Then why are you disturbing me?"

"I know you told me not to forward any calls, but I think you might want to take this one."

That piqued April's curiosity. "Is that Morrison calling to say he actually found Frankie?"

"Ma'am, that's less likely than Ed McMahon! No, I have Diana Krakovits on the phone and she wants to speak to you about, as she put it, 'an opportunity you won't want to miss.'"

"Who's Diana Krakovits and why do you think I'd want to talk to her right now?" Although April had a terrible memory for names, she knew that her assistant remembered everybody who was anybody.

"Who's Diana Krakovits?! Why, she's just the publisher of *Style & Substance* magazine and one of the most influential news publishers around. You *have* read the magazine haven't you? It's the one that explores current events from both sides of the political spectrum, launches many a poet's career, and also publishes the annual list of the 200 most influential people."

"Ooh…right. Now I remember," April attempted to say convincingly, as if she had really read the journal. "Ok, I guess I do have to take this call."

Jeremy transferred the call. "Good afternoon, this is April Hayes."

"Hello, Ms. Hayes," resounded a totally charming voice. "I'm so glad I managed to catch you with a free moment. I'm sure they are quite rare for you these days."

"Indeed they are, as I'm sure you also know well." April appreciated the sympathy and was already starting to enjoy this conversation with another female professional.

"Listen, darling, I don't want to keep you too long so I'll come right to the point. We're adding a new feature to our magazine. We thought our readers might find it interesting to get an inside view of the lives of people who are tops in their fields. Of course, countless journalists have done similar interviews, so we wanted a fresh approach. Then we came up with the brainstorm of having these successful people try their own hand at a completely different endeavor: fiction. Wouldn't it be fascinating to see how well, or how poorly, a Wall Street genius does when he is taken out of his element of numbers and thrown into the world of words? Get the picture?

"Anyway, as my editors were mulling over whom to choose, your name came across our radar screen. You certainly have been involved in some big cases of late and we know that you've also been bringing in many high profile clients to your firm. So, what I'm trying to say, in a rather long-winded fashion, is that we want to extend to you the invitation to write a short story based on your work experiences. What do you think? Does this interest you at all? Could we convince you to do this for us?"

"Goodness. This certainly comes as a surprise," sputtered the attorney. "How long would this need to be?"

"Oh, not too long at all. Actually, we can be rather flexible for you. I would say somewhere between 3,000 and 4,000 words. After all, you need some space to build a good story. Still, we need to remember that this is for a magazine not a book."

"When would you need it?"

"We'd like to run your piece as the first in the series. Do you think you could get it to us by the middle of April?"

"April? Gee, that's awfully tight. I have several cases pending."

"Don't worry. We're not asking for a donation of your precious time. We'll pay you for your story….well, I might add!"

April considered the offer. It might be fun to try something a bit different. Still, it would make her life even more pressured. On the other hand, it would be some great exposure. Not wanting to waste anyone's time on the phone, April made a proposition. "I'll tell you what. Why don't you send over the contract for me to review. By the time it gets here, I will have thought about this more fully. If I feel I have time and if the offer looks good, you'll have yourself a deal. How about that?"

"Splendid! I can certainly understand your desire to think a little more about making such a commitment. We'll send the paperwork immediately. I'm sure you'll find it acceptable. "Thank you so much! I'm sure the article will be smashing! Ta-ta!"

Chapter 22:
The Boxing Match

SimTime: March 20, Los Angeles

"Will you get serious?" Karla shouted in exasperation as she threw her pencil on the table.

"I am serious!" replied Marco as he followed her out of his studio and into the kitchen. "You're just unhappy because I want to write an upbeat tune." They'd been through this argument at least ten times since they began trying to collaborate about three weeks ago.

He was beginning to wonder why he had even suggested the idea of co-writing a song. At the time, it sounded like a good idea. He'd already warmed her up by letting her sing two of her songs at both of his LA performances. Sure, she had been nervous playing in front of thousands of people. What new performer wouldn't be? The crowds had been nothing if not polite to her.

After the last show, she looked so disappointed that he felt he needed to do something to cheer her up. He also needed to act quickly to come up with a reason to see her again. Collaboration sounded like the perfect excuse. She jumped at that chance, saying she had the perfect song in mind. She'd written the words the previous day, but still hadn't come up with the music. He was starting to regret agreeing to work on that song. If she weren't so darn cute, he would've given up on this weeks ago.

"That's only because you're missing the point of the whole song," Karla complained, snapping Marco's attention back to the argument of the hour. "It's supposed to be a slow, thoughtful, meditative piece about how people wander in and out of each other's lives and how things are so curiously interwoven. How are you supposed to convey contemplation when the beat says party?! Contrary to what you might think, not everything is about having fun."

"What's wrong with thinking that happily? Why does everything have to be sulky? In case you hadn't noticed, sulky doesn't sell as well as happy."

"That's fine if all you're interested in is making money. But what about the artistry in what you do?"

"There is artistry. Look," he said trying to switch the topic, "If it's going to be a big hassle to write together, maybe we should just forget about it." Half of him desperately wanted Karla to call it quits, but the other half hoped she'd be her usual stubborn self. He hated to admit it, but he found these arguments simultaneously frustrating yet stimulating.

Hearing these words made Karla realize she was in danger of pushing her partner away permanently. She backed off immediately. "No, that's not what I want. I guess we can find some way to compromise." She thought for a moment. "Maybe we can start slow and end fast?"

Marco mulled the idea in his head. "It might work," he agreed. He tossed her a beer as a peace offering. Both sat quietly for a moment to calm down. He guzzled his beer in hopes of finding the courage to start a completely different conversation. "What's up with you anyway? Lately, you seem so...on edge."

"I have things on my mind," she answered bluntly, hoping he would drop the whole subject.

"You don't even come out with us anymore. Why is that?"

"I don't know," she muttered as she walked away from the kitchen table and back towards the studio.

He grabbed her arm and pulled her towards him. Looking deep into her eyes, he implored, "Talk to me. If we don't communicate, how will we ever know what we're thinking? Isn't that how the line in one of your songs goes?"

Ouch! She hated when somebody used her own words against her. "Yeah. Ok. Truth is... I heard a rumor the other day."

"So?"

"So," she began, a little sheepishly, "...it was about us."

"Oh yeah? What was it?" His curiosity piqued now.

"They were talking about how I've been spotted out together with you and the band so many times lately that I must be your latest conquest."

"So?"

Men can be so dense, Karla thought. "So it's not true!"

"So what?" He loved egging her on like this. It was the only way to hear what she was really thinking.

"So I don't like being the subject of rumors," she answered matter-of-factly.

"So you're not coming out with us because you don't want to supply any more fodder for the rumor mill?"

"Pretty much."

"What's wrong with them thinking we're dating?" he explored.

"We're not."

"So? Who cares what they think? Besides, would it be so horrible if that were true?" he asked, now holding both her arms so she couldn't escape.

"But it's not."

"Yeah, but if it were, would that be so terrible?"

"I don't know. I guess I never thought about it," she lied.

"Oh come on. You never thought about it? Ever? Every other girl seems to! Come on, admit it: it wouldn't be so bad." He sensed her discomfort with the conversation.

"With that ego, I'm not so sure it wouldn't be!" she retorted defensively.

"Come on, am I that awful a guy? At least admit to me that you might not find it so repulsive to date me."

Marco was enjoying this more than he thought he would. It was like a boxing match, and he sensed that he was starting to have his opponent cornered. Now he would move in for the knockout punch.

"Can't we get back to work?" she asked as she tried to pull away from him.

He smiled, seeing her dance around the issue like

this. It confirmed what he had suspected for a while.

"Not until you admit it," he declared as he held her firmly but gently.

They looked at each other for several silent minutes. Karla did not know what to do. Was he just trying to put himself in a dominant position in the relationship? Did he just want to have his ego stroked? Was he trying to tell her something...something of which she had been afraid to even dream? If she admitted her true feelings, would it ruin their friendship and business partnership? She looked in his eyes. She saw no malice, but she could not be sure. She looked again. She saw a determination to find the answer to the until-now-unspoken question between them. She needed to say something soon, as the silence was becoming awkward. She needed to say something that would allow her to keep all options open...just in case.

"Ok. It might not be horrible," she finally declared flatly.

Marco smiled smugly. He knew what that tone meant. He'd heard it before from her. "Now say it like you mean it," he cajoled.

"It would not be so horrible to date you. There, are you satisfied now?"

"See? That wasn't so hard." Relieved that his instincts had been on target, he now began plotting the next steps in winning her. "Come on," he added gently, "Let's get back to work. Let's see if we can't turn this into your first top-10 hit."

Chapter 23: The Lunch

SimTime: April 15, Los Angeles

Talapia was one of LA's new hot spots. Just big enough to hold a good lunch or dinnertime crowd and still small enough to be intimate and exclusive, it drew customers from the top of all walks of Hollywood. The restaurant had garnered quite the reputation both for star-gazing and fine dining. Karla sat with Lee Fong in the far corner, behind two fichus trees and in front of a wall-length waterfall waiting for her partner and his client, one of the nation's top singing sensations.

Karla still could not believe that Lee had even agreed to represent her temporarily. He was one of the top managers in the music industry. He did everything from arranging gigs to advising clients. Musicians knew they had arrived when he agreed to work with them and when they could afford to pay his fees. Since they both knew that she could not really afford him, she understood that this arrangement was mainly a means to get through to Marco. In the months since she and Marco had been working together, she had watched his alcohol consumption increase considerably. Since they started dating, she also had noticed a marked change in Marco's spirit, cleanliness, and reliability. She knew he used other drugs, too, although he'd been smart enough never to light up in front of her. Although she couldn't understand why, she kept feeling that somehow all this was her fault. In desperation to save her boyfriend and ease her guilt, she had turned to Lee for advice. It was he who had concocted this plan, yet again, she felt guilty.

Karla sat across from Lee, nervously checking her watch and fixing her hair. "Do you really think we should go through with this?" she inquired nervously. She could not understand where Marco was. Everyone knew that if Lee invited people to lunch here, it meant he had big news to share. No one in his right mind would dare decline his offer or show up late. No one, that is, except Marco.

"Definitely," confirmed Lee, as he took another bite of his steak. "Look, I've been in this business a long time, and I've seen this happen to a lot of people. What Marco needs right now is a good wake-up slap in the face."

"I guess so," Karla accepted. "It just seems so ... harsh."

"Hey, you were the one who brought this to my attention, and you were absolutely right to do so. Don't second-guess yourself so much."

Karla picked nervously at her salad.

Five minutes later, the demure hostess delivered the missing guest to the table before quietly returning to her post guarding the privacy of the rich and famous.

"Hey, Lee. Sorry I'm late. I see you started lunch without me. That's cool. Things kind of got out of hand. Sorry." Turning to take his seat, he noticed Karla sitting there with her pretty, nervous smile. "Hey, Babe! I didn't know you were going to be here, too!" He leaned over and kissed her with genuine affection. She, in return, did her best not to recoil at his stench.

After ordering a burger, Marco turned to Lee and asked, "So, what's the big news? You said you had some new plans brewing? What are we going to do next?"

"Well," Lee began tentatively, "I've decided to make some changes to my client list. As you know, I only take on a limited number of clients, so I can provide them with superior service."

Marco knew this and wondered why Lee was giving his sales pitch. Marco already trusted Lee completely. His reputation for protecting his clients was well-deserved, despite the high prices he charged.

"I've decided to take on a new talent. Someone that hasn't quite made it big yet, but that I think has a lot of potential. With my help, she could make it big. I'm sure of it. I believe in her because she has the right attitude and drive." He paused momentarily. "That someone, in case you were wondering, is Karla."

Happily surprised for his girlfriend, he put his arm around her and gave her a congratulatory hug. "That's great! Good for you, Babe! See, I told you you'd make it!"

The waitress brought Marco his hamburger and disappeared quickly. Marco chomped away happily. Life continued to treat him well. The food had come quickly, his girlfriend had landed a big-time manager, and Lee didn't even complain about his late arrival. As he delighted in the taste of his juicy burger, he couldn't help wondering why he had bothered wasting his first months being a cop. This was definitely the life!

Lee cleared his throat to signal he had more to say. Marco returned to the conversation at hand. "Right now, however," Lee continued, "my plate is full. I really can't take Karla on without dropping one of my existing clients, so I'm considering letting go of someone who doesn't seem to want my help anymore."

"Well, if that's what you gotta do, it's what you gotta do, right?" Marco gulped some soda.

The three sat there silently for several minutes. Karla looked at Marco, then at Lee. Lee stared at Marco, then shrugged in amazement at Karla. Marco dunked his french fries in ketchup and popped them in his mouth. Finally, Marco's laid-back attitude got the better of Karla, who could no longer contain herself. "Aren't you even curious to know who he's going to drop?" she prodded.

"Is it really any of my business?" he responded.

"Actually, it is," Lee interrupted. "Marco, I'm thinking it's probably going to be you."

"ME??!!" Marco shouted, a half-chewed fry flying from his mouth. "Why me?! What did I do? I thought we were buddies? How could you do this to me?"

Karla put her hand on his leg to calm him. "Shhh! Keep your voice down! Remember: we're in public!" she scolded him.

"Simple. It's a matter of business and personal pride. I like to represent people who have both the talent and the drive to make it big and to stay big. You seem to have lost that drive lately."

"Whaddya mean?" Marco asked, dumbfounded.

"You know what I mean. You used to be very hard-working. I remember how, before the tour, you used to come to me every few weeks with a bunch of new songs, and they were all really good. In the past few months since the tour ended, you've written two new songs, which, frankly, have very little potential."

Marco felt like an iceberg had just hit his ship. Like a survivor on the Titanic, he feared all he could do was struggle to keep his head above water for just a little while longer. "Hey! I've written at least two since then," he said in his own defence. "...And not every song can be a hit, you know. Even I can lose my inspiration momentarily. But I'll get it back. Don't you worry."

"Not if you keep partying the way you do," Lee responded sternly. "You're up half the night drinking and smoking, and you sleep through a good part of the day. That lifestyle is more acceptable on the road, but it doesn't play so well afterwards. You have to learn how to return to a more normal life."

"My lifestyle is fine. Tell him, Karla!" he prodded her with his elbow. "I'm just resting and relaxing from the gruelling tour circuit." He wiped some spit from his face with a napkin.

"Well you're doing a little too much relaxing. Meanwhile, you have a contract that says you're supposed to cut an album in another two months and you haven't done anything for it. You're constantly late for appointments and you're health is deteriorating. You've got bags under your eyes, your face is puffy, and you've probably put on 20 pounds in the past month." He lowered his voice to signal he was about to talk man-to-man. "Work aside, how do you intend to get –er, um, keep – any girls looking like that?"

That hurt Marco where he lived. He looked down at his growing belly, and had to admit that this man, whom he was paying to look out for his best interests, might indeed have a point. He glanced shamefully at Karla. Karla crossed her arms and tried not to show any emotion.

Just then, the waitress came over and quietly left the bill for the meal. She put the paper on the table, gave him a quick once-over, and walked away. Marco didn't know whether to be flattered that he was being eyed by an attractive female or embarrassed that this lady might think that he was not as good-looking as she had imagined him to be.

"Well, at least that caught your attention," Lee continued. "Listen to me. I'm telling you this as a friend: you're starting to have serious drug and alcohol problems. You need to do something about it fast before you bring about your own ruin. Personally, if you can't bother to care for yourself, then I see no reason why I should bother, either."

"Oh, come on! I'm ok, really."

Lee was not surprised by this reaction; in fact, he had expected it. After all, it wasn't just because he had a great network that Lee was considered one of the best managers in town. He had been in this business a long time and had dealt with many different problems. Marco's was one of the most insidious, but also the most common. The lure of popularity and success had ensnarled yet another victim. Still, Lee had been through this disentangling routine many times before and knew how to hold this "you need help" conversation. He had convinced many a more stubborn man than Marco to straighten up.

The worst had yet to be said. Stiffening his spine, he leaned in to Marco and stated sternly, " Oh yes, it is getting in the way. In fact, let me tell you something as your manager: I'm not here to be your babysitter or your drug counsellor. I'm sick of covering up for your inexcusable absences. I'm here to help you make as much money as you can with your talent and to make some money for myself along the way. Unfortunately, I can't do it alone. This is a partnership. If you aren't going to hold up your part of the bargain, then I don't have time to waste on you. There's plenty of other talent who could use my help."

Marco felt like a wave had just broken over his head. "Come on! You can't be serious. I'm not that bad. Tell him, Karla! You're with me more than anyone. Tell him how hard I've been working lately."

Karla looked at him painfully and shook her head. "Frankly, I'm with Lee on this one. You're getting out of hand. The last five times we were supposed to get together to work on the album, you showed up late and stoned each time. Even today…look at yourself! You stink of pot and beer again! I thought it was pretty lousy when you stood me up, but to show up 45 minutes late to meeting with Lee…well…you know better than to do that."

Marco felt caught between a crab's pincers. "So what are *you* trying to say?"

Karla took a deep breath and stiffened herself. She was not sure if she had the resolve to do this, but she knew she had to. "Look, I've had it with your nonsense, too. Here's what I've decided: I can't afford to waste this opportunity. If you don't want to work with me, fine. I'll do it on my own. If I find that you either miss one more date – either social or business -- or arrive not in your full mind, we're through. Do you understand me? Through."

"Through? You mean no more collaborating or no more dating?"

"Both. I'll stop writing songs for you and will prevent you from singing those that I've written. And as for us, I want a boyfriend whom I can trust. If you can't do that for me, then we shouldn't be together. The one thing I don't need is more troubles in my life."

"But even you said we made such a good couple. You really want to give that up?"

"It won't be me who will have given up on us; it'll be you. I'm just protecting myself," she explained matter-of-factly.

"Wow. You're really serious."

"Yes. I am." She handed him a large manila envelope.

"What's this?" he asked.

"This is your last chance. I've written the lyrics to three new songs. I'd suggest that over the next two weeks you take a look at it and see if you can't come up with some appropriate and good quality music to accompany it.

I'll come over in a few days and we can work on it, ok?"

"I suppose I don't have much choice," he responded dejectedly.

"Sure you do. You can blow this off and kiss our relationship good-bye. Your choice."

Marco felt dazed. He'd arrived in such a good mood and then been blind-sided. He never imagined that his girl and his manager would double-team him. He looked first at Lee's stern face, then at Karla's, then again at Lee's. Feeling trapped between unfriendly faces, anger, and a public setting, he didn't know what to do. Desperately wanting not to cause a public scene as his emotions erupted, he threw his napkin on his seat and stormed out of the restaurant.

Chapter 24:
The Dinner

SimTime: April 15, Los Angeles

April slammed the door, turned on the ignition, and flew out of her driveway. She had 20 minutes to meet Taylor for dinner, and she did not want to be late. April hated being late; it made her look unprofessional. She was not really sure why they were meeting, but she assumed it had something to do with finding Frankie Nordo. Well, she had plenty to say to Taylor on that subject! Now maybe she would get the chance. Still, she reminded herself to be professional, even if she was not happy with the situation.

Professional. The word carried so much meaning for her. It was more than just a descriptor; it was an entire attitude. She always tried to "be professional" rather than just to "act professional." In her mind, it was the difference between being an adult and a kid. She saw professionalism as a form of respect to others, to issues, and to oneself, and she attributed a large part of her success to it. To her, professionalism included having the skills and talent to do the job at hand but still preparing ahead of time. She had to admit, though, that she had hardly given this meeting the attention it deserved.

She couldn't help it, though, she rationalized. She had a more pressing deadline to meet: she had to write her story. She had finished it just in the knick of time. It had taken so long to find a good topic and get her writing groove that she didn't want to stop until she was done. Now she would pay the price, as Taylor would have the upper hand in this meeting. That pained her. Taylor, more than anybody else she knew, brought out the worst of her competitive side. To give him the advantage in anything rubbed her the wrong way.

Arriving at the restaurant, April parked the car and rushed inside. Seeing him sitting with just a water glass, she felt relieved that she hadn't arrived too late. She took a deep breath then confidently and calmly walked over to his table.

"Taylor? I hope I haven't kept you waiting long," she ventured.

"Not at all. I just got here myself. Please, sit down." He offered her a chair. "Glad you could join me tonight. I'm sure you're pretty busy these days."

"You have no idea!" she half-joked in reply.

The two continued their small talk through a round of drinks and appetizers, all the while April wondering what was the point of this meeting. After the waiter had brought their entrées, the young lawyer could no longer contain her curiosity. "So," she began, "what do you hear from our intrepid investigator? Has he finally managed to catch up with your former star or is he still off frolicking somewhere?"

"Oh, who cares!" Taylor sighed with exasperation.

"Who cares??" she repeated in amazement. "Who cares?! I can't believe you just said that…although I guess it really doesn't surprise me altogether either. Honestly!"

"Whoa! Relax!" he cried, using his hands like stop signals. "That's not what I meant. Of course I care. Marco is part of our happy Galaxy family and, more importantly, he's a good friend. I just meant I didn't want to talk about work right now. It's Sunday night and I just felt like enjoying a pleasant dinner without thinking about work for a few hours. That's all. Tomorrow I'll care again, I promise."

April bit her tongue after realizing that Taylor was speaking truthfully. Why did she always suspect the worst of him? April scrunched and unscrunched the napkin in her lap. Taylor had managed to unnerve her in less than thirty minutes. Why did she always felt like a cat with her back arched when they were together? What was his angle tonight? Could this really be just a social engagement? She found that hard to believe. More and more, she wished she had simply declined his invitation. She could handle him when they were in a business setting. Take her out of that environment and she felt completely ill-at-ease with him. Still, she realized, she couldn't back out now. "Well," she grumbled at last, "you sure have a weird way of expressing yourself. You should be more careful what you say."

Both took a sip of their drinks. Taylor could not believe how much she had overreacted. Really, that was a bit extreme, he thought to himself. For her part, April just kept looking for the silver lining. The more she thought about what he'd said, the more she admired Taylor's ability to separate himself from his work. She didn't know how he did it, but she certainly would like to learn.

"So if this isn't about Frankie or work, what is this about?" she broached.

"This? You mean this dinner?" he clarified.

"Yes."

"It's for pleasure. Don't you ever just go somewhere for fun?"

"Not lately," she responded softly, as she tried to remember the last time she had been out with a friend.

"What do you do all the time? Just work and sleep?"

"No," she declared defensively. "I do other things with my time. For your information, I just finished a four-day weekend. "

"Really?" he asked with genuine interest. "What did you do with your time off? Go to the mountains? Have you checked out Tahoe yet? It's really beautiful up there. I went there a few weekends ago…did lots of hiking and biking."

"No." she hesitated. "Actually, I wrote a short story."

"You took two days off from work just to write a short story?" he laughed. "Why would you do that? Didn't you get your fill of writing stories when you were in elementary school?! Now, why would someone as busy as you take vacation just to write? That hardly seems like a vacation for someone who probably spends a majority of her time in front of a computer or at least at her desk. What kind of fantastic story is this anyhow?" he asked sarcastically, sensing she was withholding information.

Although annoyed at his tone, April couldn't help being impressed by his deductive reasoning skills. "If you must know, it was about being a lawyer."

"So you took time off from work to sit at a desk and think about work?" He paused as he digested the information. "Nope." He shook his head. "It still doesn't make sense." He squinted his eyes and leaned across the table toward her. "What are you up to?"

"Why do you care so much?" she retorted. With others, she would have been happy to share her news, but his haughty attitude irritated her. The more he talked, the less she felt like telling him.

"Don't you remember what we said in our last simworld?" he asked, softening his tone as he realized she wasn't responding well to his sarcasm. "We said that we should try to make more of an effort to catch up with each other throughout the months. That way we could check up on each other and at least have three friends in this world. If you must know, that was the real reason I asked you to dinner."

That stopped April in her tracks. Over the months, she had come to expect many things of Taylor, but a show of genuine friendship was not among them. She viewed him as extremely clever, but also arrogant and devious. Still, she reasoned, a kind turn must never be snubbed. If he were turning over a new leaf, or even just showing a different side of himself, she should probably go along with it, if for nothing else than to reward good behavior.

Deciding to take a leap of faith with him, she finally opened up and explained what she had been doing.

"Ok, you got me," she said, loosening up a bit. "My two days off really weren't a vacation. I just needed some time to think without interruptions. You see, a few months ago *Style & Substance* magazine asked me to write a fictional account of my life as a lawyer. I figured it might be fun, and it probably would be good for business. It took me several weeks to come up with an angle that would work. It was tougher than I thought. I had to find a hook that would be interesting, loosely based on reality but still fictionalized enough not to be too recognizable. You know how things are in this town: people can sniff out a story like bloodhounds."

"Tell me about it," Taylor concurred. "So what happened? What did you come up with?"

"About three weeks ago, I finally figured out how to get around this problem: I invented a divorce case that incorporated the elements from two different cases. I tried to write after work, but I was so tired that I just couldn't put myself in front of a computer. Then I tried to write during lunch or at other points in the day, but I just couldn't get enough quiet time. On Monday, I looked at the calendar and realized that I only had a week left before the deadline. I decided to clear the rest of my week and just crank it out. Lucky for me, I work well under pressure."

"So it came out ok?"

"I think so, but I haven't had the chance to reread it again yet. I only finished writing it a few minutes before I left to come here. I gotta say, though, that once I felt comfortable with the idea, writing was actually a lot of fun. I loved the sound of the keyboard tapping as I got on a roll. The rhythm actually encouraged me to continue. For four days I was master of my own universe."

Finally feeling more comfortable with each other, the conversation flowed more freely.

"That's cool," Taylor responded. "But have you had much chance to check out the real world you're in? I mean fantasy's fine and all that, but don't lose sight of what's around you."

"Oh, believe me. I haven't lost sight of what's happening in this world. I've been working 12 hour days trying to keep up with it." April slouched in her chair a little. She'd meant this to sound like she was successfully busy becoming a success, but it came out sounding like her work consumed her. Taylor immediately picked up on that.

"I'm not talking about work. I mean the rest of life. You have to explore your surroundings, too." Taylor began to wonder if he had misjudged her intelligence. He wasn't trying to explain rocket science. Why was she having such a hard time understanding him? "Take me, for instance. Sure, I've got tons of work to do between running the business, signing new talent, and lately trying to pull off a merger. I'd tell you more about that, but it's very hush-hush. Still, I take some time out of every weekend for fun."

"Like what?" April inquired, happy to have the spotlight off her momentarily.

"Different things. I've taken some surf lessons, checked out Tijuana, done some mountain-biking, eaten at fancy restaurants like this. I tell you, it makes a difference. I feel great…like I could conquer the world."

April smirked. Conquering the world came as second-nature to Taylor. She shoved a forkful of meat in her mouth before she accidentally let that thought tumble out of her mouth. Taylor took the opportunity to eat some more, too. As she sat there chewing her food, she thought about what he'd said. Certainly, he must be busy as CEO. Yet, somehow, he did look healthier than she. His skin had color, unlike her pasty whiteness. He didn't have huge bags under his eyes like she did. He still had tons of energy, whereas hers had faded months ago.

Her shoulders began to get tense. Why was he doing this to her? Why did he have to show off that he could handle adult life better than she could? Why did everything become a competition between them? More importantly, why couldn't she get it right? Why couldn't she find that perfect balance? She shoved some food into her mouth, but could no longer taste it. Her breathing became shallow. "I'll be right back…have to go to the bathroom," she stammered as she walked away from the table.

Taylor followed her with his eyes until she turned a corner. What happened, he wondered. One minute they were having a perfectly nice conversation and the next she looked like she was about to cry. Had he said something wrong again? He shook his head. Women…, he thought, …they're all the same: way too sensitive. He'd expected more from April, but he guessed that leopards just couldn't change their spots after all. Now he'd have to work at finding a suitable topic that wouldn't upset her so much. He sighed. He had looked forward to a nice, relaxing meal; now he'd have to work at conversation. Ugh.

April returned to the table a few minutes later looking much more composed. "Sorry about that. I had something...in my eye," she flubbed. The two finished the remainder of their entrées then ordered dessert.

"So what do you think? Are you enjoying being a lawyer?" he inquired after several minutes of awkward silence.

She thought about the question for a few minutes. "It's certainly been an interesting experience so far. The work is wonderfully stimulating intellectually. I love doing the research to prepare for the cases. Negotiating with the opposition is like playing a game of human chess. Standing in front of a courtroom and delivering the closing arguments makes me feel like Daniel Webster. The issues that arise also provide excellent materials at social events."

"But?" he sensed.

"But although my brain loves it, my heart and gut aren't fully in agreement. One part of me wants to be as successful as possible; another part of me keeps nagging that the whole reason I got into this field was to help others."

"So where's the problem?"

"The problem is that I spend most of my days helping rich companies get richer or protecting the money of the wealthy."

"So? What's the problem?" he repeated. "You're helping people protect themselves from potentially bad schemes."

"Yeah, but I'm just not sure if that's really what I want to do. I always pictured myself helping the poor, the misrepresented, and the unjustly accused. I don't get to do any of that. Those people couldn't even afford my rates."

April blinked twice. She suddenly felt like a rock had been lifted off her shoulders. She couldn't believe she'd just confided in Taylor, of all people. More curiously, she couldn't believe how good it felt to get that off her chest.

"So why not lower your rates and help some of those people?" Taylor asked, still not grasping the complexity of April's conundrum.

"Because if I want to succeed within the firm, then I need to bring in more money. The only way to do that is to go after the rich clients. The poor won't help me."

"I think you need to put this in perspective. How important is it that you become partner? You need to ask yourself what is more important to you: helping others or helping yourself." Taylor counseled.

"That's exactly my point. I never thought that I would ever have any trouble prioritizing, and now I am disappointed in myself that this has become such a big issue."

"You could always take steps to change your situation."

"Whaddya mean?"

"Since you can't take on different clients while working for your firm, why don't you take them on after-hours?"

"How?"

"Volunteer for organizations or clinics that help the poor. There's plenty of people that need legal help but can't afford it. You'd be doing charity work, and I really find it hard to believe that your firm would fault you for that."

Taylor's words gave April pause. For once, she could not spot any hidden agenda ...and his idea made a lot of sense. That could be the solution to the problem. Of course, it would mean re-arranging her work schedule, but if it meant being happier, then maybe she should do it.

The arrival of the check cut their conversation short, much to Taylor's relief. He never did like playing psychiatrist to others. It always made him feel like a nosy-body. Grateful for the interruption, he reached for the bill.

"Allow me," he offered, making a grand show of his generosity.

"Oh, no. Please let me. It's the least I can do to thank you for your good advice," April countered politely.

"That's not necessary," he responded, all too familiar with this dance.

"Can we at least split the bill?" she offered. She always felt uncomfortable when men paid for her meals.

"No, really. I'd like to pay. After all, I invited you." Taylor always hated this part. He could never understand why girls make such a fuss over splitting the bill. Why did every girl seem to think that if he paid for her meal, he must want something more? Couldn't he just pay to be nice, he wondered.

Sensing his growing frustration, April quickly backed off. She did not want to offend him any more than she might have already done.

"Thank you," she finally relented. "That's very kind of you."

Heading home along the coastal road, April pulled into the first parking lot she found. She jumped out of the car, stumbled to the sand, and put her head between her knees. She felt dizzy. The dinner had forced her to stand all her assumptions on end: Was she really happy? Did she really control her life or was her life controlling her? Could life be fulfilling outside of work? Was Taylor right? Had he beaten her to finding the secret of happiness? Was Taylor a decent fellow after all? Why did she care about that, anyway? She sank into the sand, frightened at the possibilities.

Chapter 25:
Writer's Block

SimTime: April 21, Los Angeles

Marco reclined on a lounge chair under the noontime sun. Although the ocean might have been pacific, he most certainly was not. He tore off another sheet of paper from the pad on his lap, crinkled it up, and tossed it behind him. It landed just inches from the trash can, amidst a pile of tossed shards of ideas from the past hour. Frustrated, he reached under his chair for his beer bottle.

He needed that drink. It cooled his body and calmed his insides. He really didn't know what had come over him. Time was, he could write a song in as little as fifteen minutes, and it would rock. Now, he couldn't come up with a single decent riff for the life of him. He'd been trying for almost a week, but all he could manage was dribble.

Marco swallowed the last bit and laid the bottle to rest. He stared at Karla's song sheet again. Writer's block. Nothing. Nada. Maybe he just needed a different inspiration. He reached to his left and picked up his guitar. This old, acoustic guitar was his favorite. It sounded pure, untainted by the lure of electricity. The instrument's body fit comfortably against his own. The curves suited his arms perfectly. He knew exactly where to touch the neck to make it do just what he wanted. If he touched the strings lightly, it would whisper delicately to him. If he strummed with just the right mix of force and gentleness, its sound took him on a musical journey the way few others could. Still, it was a guitar like any other guitar: touched incorrectly or treated poorly, it would respond in kind, screeching a wake-up siren in his ear. This was the magic of any guitar, but for some reason, this simple one appealed to him more than any of the fancier ones in his collection.

He half-heartedly strummed the strings, hoping it would inspire him. Instead, it just kind of whined. Frustrated, he tossed the guitar on the ground and decided to stretch his legs. He walked directly to the refrigerator and grabbed another bottle of beer. Marco took another swig and stared at the five empty bottles under his chair. The bottles reminded him of the how his life had turned upside down in a single day.

It all started when his buddies from the recording studio decided the practice wasn't working. They figured some brews would help them relax enough to get their groove back. Now feeling in a more creative mood, they returned to the recording studio. After a while, Dirk, the bassist, got hungry and disappeared for a while. He returned with a tray of his special brownies that he had baked the previous night. Once everyone had enjoyed the delights of the brownies, the music really got interesting. After a while, it seemed like a natural progression to start lighting up. Time floated by and before he knew it, it was already 1:30. Then he remembered he was supposed to meet Lee for lunch at 1:00. He knew better than to drive himself, so Dirk raced him over to the restaurant. After all, better to show up late than not at all.

As he returned to his seat on the porch, Marco considered the fallout from that meeting. He still couldn't understand why Lee would drop him. That was bad enough, but Karla's ultimatum was just plain old humiliating. What kind of nonsense was that, wanting to break up with him? Most girls would give their right arm to be his girlfriend and she wanted to throw the whole thing away. The nerve! After all his hard work to woo her! He had to practically throw himself at her. It was almost insulting to him, considering how few guys chased her and how many girls chased him. And now she wants to break up with him? Amazing.

Marco decided to stop thinking about that. He needed to write these songs if he were to have any hope of keeping her. She'd be here in about two hours and if he didn't have anything to show her, she'd kill him. He grabbed the lyrics and read them again. Blah! They were just so boring and whiny! Why couldn't she ever just be happy and carefree? Maybe that was the cause of his block: maybe he was just being forced to write about things that were meaningless to him. Maybe her moodiness had rubbed off on him and that's why his music was becoming dull. Maybe he'd do better just going solo again. He could continue writing songs about parties and having fun. Those always sell. He could write the next great party anthem, and teenagers throughout all time would know the words to his song. He could be the next KISS!

That made Marco stop and shudder. He needed to clear his head and stretch his body. He put down everything, ran across the beach, and dove into an oncoming wave. The breaking water crackled in his ear. The cool temperature slapped him in the face. He broke the surface like a porpoise bounding through the ocean. He tingled as the warm breeze blew lightly against the water drops on his skin. Blood coursed through his veins as he swam against the current. The waves washed over him and carried away all his worries and frustrations. The pistons in his brain began to fire. Nothing woke him up better than a dip in the ocean! How lucky he was to live on the beach!

Returning to his patio fifteen minutes later, he felt like a new man. He towelled himself dry and grabbed his guitar again. "Come on," he whispered lovingly to it, "let's make some beautiful music together." He picked at the strings, then scribbled notes on paper. Finally, progress. He played some more, then wrote some more. The music flowed out of his head. Yeah, this would do just fine. Wouldn't Karla be surprised? This sounded awesome. She'd dig it. He'd show Lee that he still had more good tunes inside him. He wrote some more, then stopped. He read his music and played back what he had composed so far. Light, bouncy, not too heavy. You could throw any sappy words on this tune and it would work. Karla would definitely love it.

Marco rested the guitar on his lap and folded his arms behind his head. His mind began to drift again. Yup, he thought smugly, he still had what it took. What were they talking about? The sun's rays felt like a loving blanket over his body. A nap would feel so great right now. He shook his head vigorously. No, he must finish this song. Karla would be here soon. He forced open his eyes and hummed the tune in his head to help him figure out the next part of the song. The musical faucet in his brain slowed to a trickle. Uh-oh…it was happening again. He'd lost his inspiration. He couldn't think of anything else to add. He drummed his fingers on the guitar and listened to the rhythm of the tapping. Come on…come on! He coaxed himself. Don't stop now. Nuts! Too late. The well had run dry. No new ideas. What would he do now? Could he sweet-talk Karla into accepting only one verse and a chorus?

He needed more. If he could just calm down, the groove would return. Marco went back inside the house and rummaged through one of the kitchen drawers. Finding his stash, he returned outside and lit up. The large breath of sweet-tasting grass started working its magic. His muscles started to loosen. Karla's frown faded from his mind. Yeah… this felt better. He took another puff.

An idea finally hit him: He could just repeat the tune for each of the verses and choruses. It was a cheap trick, but others had pulled off similar stunts. He decided to chalk this song up to bubble-gum pop rather than hard rock and let it go at that. His work now complete, he drifted into dreamland.

****

Marco saw himself as a multi-colored fish happily swimming about in a psychedelic ocean. He was busy darting in and out of kaleidoscope-colored whirlpools when he saw a delicious-looking, chocolate-covered worm directly in front of him. Hungry, he scooped it up in is mouth. The sweet worm melted on his tongue. Just as he came to the middle of his treat, something sharp poked him in the mouth and started pulling him where he didn't want to go. He fought with it for several minutes: he exerted all the energy he could muster to escape and return to where he'd been, but the overwhelming force pulled him thither and yon until he could no longer resist. He saw a bright light growing larger and stronger. He knew the end was near. He broke the surface of the water and heard bells ringing. The bell grew louder and louder until Marco finally opened his eyes. The bell continued to ring. Marco blinked several times until he remembered where and who he really was. The doorbell rang non-stop, as if someone were leaning on it just to annoy him. He jumped out of his seat, and rant to the front door, tripping over the empty beer bottles along the way.

Karla stood there in the doorway with guitar in hand. "It's about time you answered. I've been ringing the bell for the past ten minutes." Karla invited herself in and headed straight for the patio. "How's the writing coming?"

Marco followed behind her, knowing he was powerless to do anything else. "I was just working on that," he responded.

"Great! Let's hear what you've got," the fearless songstress requested as she parked herself on a chair.

"Here's the thing," he began hemming and hawing. "I've been working on this for days but I've been having a hard time coming up with anything good." He could tell by the look in her eyes that she didn't believe one word he had said. "Honestly," he continued, "I have been working. I swear!" He pointed to the corner of the porch, "See? All those papers are song ideas that didn't go anywhere. You don't believe me? Read for yourself!" He grabbed a couple of balls of paper and tossed them at her. He didn't know why he felt the need to defend himself so strongly.

"I believe you," she said with feigned indifference. "I just think you might have more success if you worked with a clear head." Her voice rose in indignation as she surveyed the mess under his chair. "It's only 2:00 p.m. and already you've killed a six-pack and smoked a joint. Geez! What's wrong with you lately? You never used to be like this."

"Get off my case!" he snapped at her. He was sick of her whining. "It's not that much. And besides, they're not the problem. The real problem is that your songs are just too depressing for my type of music."

"That's not so!" Karla countered. "In fact, if you had bothered to read the words, you'd see that two are about happy topics. One's about being in love and the other's about travelling."

"As a matter of fact, I did read your songs. I know what they're about. And if you'd have just let me finish talking before jumping all over my back, you'd have heard me say that today, I finally came up with something that will work. It's more pop than I normally would write, so you should find it acceptable," Marco replied indignantly.

"Oh," Karla answered with surprise and

embarrassment for having sounded so nasty. "In that case, let's see it."

Marco handed her the music and waited while she reviewed it. She hummed it as she read it. She cupped her chin in her hand as she considered it. Something about it seemed wrong, but she couldn't figure out what. "Hand me the guitar, will you," she said to Marco.

Marco obliged and she began to play his tune. She played through it once, paused, then played through it again. "Then what?" she asked. "Where's the rest of it?"

"That's it," he explained. "It's pretty much the same for each of the verses. You see: it's simple, but easy to remember." He smiled uneasily.

"Uh-huh," she acknowledged. "Remember"...the word stuck in her head. She snapped her fingers. That's what kept bothering her about this tune! She already knew it. She played it again on the guitar, then pursed her lips in annoyance and nodded her head.

"Of course it's easy to remember," Karla began. "Don't you remember it?" she asked snidely.

"Of course I do," Marco replied. "I just wrote it!" What kind of stupid question was she asking?

"No, you didn't," she replied flatly

"Yes, I did."

"No, you didn't," she answered louder.

"Are you trying to tell me I don't remember what I just did an hour ago? Of course I did!" he shouted at her.

"No, you didn't!" she responded emphatically. "You wrote that a month ago for our first song." She slapped her hand on the table for emphasis.

Marco fell onto his chair dumbfounded. No wonder it had come so easily. He didn't know how to respond to that.

Karla took his silence as apathy. She cut the air with her hand. "That does it!" she shouted. "You know what? You don't need to worry about it anymore. You can go back to writing your trivial little party songs because we're through!" Karla's voice shook as she announced this. "You couldn't even keep your promise to me to be sober the next time we got together, could you? Well, now you won't have to worry about it because I'm out of here. Do whatever you want. I don't care any more!" Karla grabbed her music and left through the back gate, slamming it good and hard as she exited.

Marco watched her leave. Not knowing what else to do, he lit another joint, shook his head, and sighed in disbelief and anger, "Women."

Chapter 26
In a New York Minute

SimTime: April 30, Newark Airport

"Attention in the terminal: Flight 73 to Los Angeles, which was scheduled to depart at 5:30 PM has been delayed. The new departure time is currently estimated at 6:15 PM."

Taylor sighed in frustration as he watched his chances of celebrating in LA disappear with the passing time. More importantly, though, Taylor knew that the delay meant he wouldn't get any dinner for at least another two hours. He knew how these airlines worked. First they start you with a 45-minute delay, then they continue to expand it 15 minutes at a time. Still, he had had too good a day to let this inconvenience ruin his mood. He decided to get some food and just be patient.

He headed into the nearest lounge and dropped his bags beside him at the bar.

"What'll it be?" asked the bartender.

"Just nachos and a cola, please."

Several minutes later, the bartender returned with the order. Just as he put the plate down in front of the customer, something on the TV behind Taylor's head caught the bartender's eye. He stared at it, then looked at Taylor, then looked at the TV again.

"Hey- that's you, isn't it? Hey, buddy, I think you're on TV."

Taylor turned around to see his face plastered on the screen as the anchorwoman introduced the next story. The bartender grabbed the remote control and turned up the volume just in time to hear the report:

> "That's Taylor Washington, CEO of Galaxy Records, opening trading on the New York Stock Exchange this morning, following a press conference to formally announce the beginning of operations for the new and improved Galaxy Records.
>
> Just last night he signed the papers to acquire Cloud9 Records. Cloud9, which began operations in 1979, has been a medium-sized recording company with contracts for a number of today's hot acts, including Melodie Postriso, the Shrubs, and Da-Bom. Despite their list of acts, Cloud9 has suffered in the past two years from poor management. Galaxy, the larger of the two, boasts this year's hottest act, Marco Centano.
>
> Industry experts have reacted favorably to the news. The combined talent list puts the new Galaxy onto the same playing field as big boys Arista and Columbia. Galaxy's much stronger management group, led by

Washington, is bound to turn around Cloud9's sagging numbers.

This acquisition not only brings the new company into the spotlight, but also its young CEO. Hailed throughout the industry as a whiz with numbers, Washington is known to run a tight ship. This differs significantly from Cloud9's more relaxed family-style of operations. Analysts are waiting to see how well these two cultures will blend. Galaxy shares rose 3 percent in the first day of trading.

Back to you, Kurt and Emily...."

"Hey, Mister, congratulations! Sounds like a cause for celebration. Care for a drink on the house?"

"Thanks, but no," Taylor declined. "I don't like to drink alcohol when I'm flying. Dries you out, you know."

"Hmm...I'm impressed," interrupted the voluptuous woman who had been sitting next to Taylor. "A businessman who knows how to take care of his own body."

"I do what I can," answered Taylor meekly, surprised that such a beautiful woman would start talking to him.

"Is that so?" she whispered flirtatiously. "So, what was it like to ring that bell? Pretty exciting, huh?"

"I gotta admit, it was pretty darn cool. I mean, think about it: There I was giving the signal to start the day's trading. Everybody was waiting for me so they could begin their work."

"When you put it that way, that does make you sound so…powerful," she purred.

"Ringing the bell really is only symbolic. The real thrill was in putting the whole deal together. I mean, it was because of me, my vision, my persuasion, and my hard work that the whole deal came together. Can you imagine what it feels like to bring two bodies together?"

"Oh, I can imagine," she cooed as she moved in closer to him. "You must really know how to call the right shots," she said, stroking his ego as well as his hand.

Taylor began to blush. He grabbed his water with the hand the beautiful lady had just touched. "I'd like to think so," he blurted. He tried to maintain his cool exterior. "It took a lot of salesmanship and political skills on my part to convince the boards of both companies that this was the way to go. Sure, I've always been able to convince some people to do whatever I wanted, but this time I had to convince smart people to see things my way. It really made me stretch the limits of my skills, but in the end, I won."

"You must be quite the leader of people," the woman responded.

"I am, but I didn't just talk a lot. I actually did a lot of hard work. I mean, I can't even count the number of days I was up until 3:00 in the morning studying the financial statements and the terms of the contracts. Sure, I've got professionals to do that for me, but you can never be too careful. If you don't mind the store, something's bound to go missing."

"Fascinating," she commented with markedly less

enthusiasm.

"Still," Taylor continued, unsure of how to handle himself with this kind of woman, "even though the days seemed long, the weeks flew by, especially when I was working the numbers. It's fascinating to discover the stories the numbers tell. Whether I was examining how well Cloud9 had done or looking at projections for future growth, I felt like I was unraveling a mystery. Of course, the story grew better and better with time."

Taylor gulped some water nervously. He found it too good to be true that such a beautiful woman would actually hit on him first. In his view, men should do the initiating. He loosened his tie. Anything to keep this woman from touching him. He didn't know anything about her, nor did he want to. What was the point? He was about to get in an airplane and fly across the country. He presumed she had similar plans.

Giving it one more try, the woman inquired, "So now that you're done with all the hard work, your life should get pretty interesting, huh? Plenty of parties and social obligations, I would imagine. Ever consider bringing someone with you to them?"

"Parties? Nah, too many other things to do. Come Monday, we're going to begin working on our new combined strategy and reorganizing the entire company. Then there are all the personnel issues to be settled. Everyone thinks the CEO doesn't get involved in personnel matters. Well, I don't know how it works at other companies, but I can tell you that this CEO pays attention...."

Something caught Taylor's eye. He jumped out of his seat, ran to the entrance, craned his neck around the corner, and peered through the crowd of people. That couldn't be, he thought to himself. But it sure looked like…. But that didn't make sense, unless of course, they were….But why would they be so stupid as to get together here?

Taylor ran back inside, grabbed his belongings, and tossed some money on the counter. "Nice talking to you, m'am," he said dismissively to the woman. "Bye."

Taylor bounded down the concourse, zig-zagging between fellow business travelers and vacationers with children, his eyes looking over and beyond everyone's heads. Past the restrooms, past the newsstands, Taylor ran like a lion on the chase. He had seen them, he was sure of it.

Eventually, he arrived at a crossroads: turn left towards gates 71-80 or go straight towards gates 81-90. Which way to go? He came to a dead stop, his bags hitting him in the side. He looked around him: normalcy in all directions. On his left, businesspeople made their way to their respective gates. Ahead, a few stray passengers straggled between construction workers and airport employees. But where did *they* go? He had lost sight of them. Standing there, catching his breath, he gave up the hunt for now.

Chapter 27:
The Phone Call

SimTime: May 20, Los Angeles

Karla threw open the door to her apartment, dropped her guitar and backpack on the ground, and bounded for the ringing telephone.

"Hello?!" she cried breathlessly as she grabbed the phone on the fourth ring.

"Karla! Lee here. You okay? You sound funny."

"Yeah. I just need to catch my breath. You caught me just as I walked in the door. What's up?"

"I was just calling to check in. How did your day go?" he inquired.

"Yeah, the gig at the Arts Festival was fine," she responded flatly.

"You don't sound so enthused. What's up?"

"It was okay. I think performing is not really my thing, though. I definitely prefer writing the songs and letting someone else sing them."

"Yeah, but all the money is in performing."

"I know, but my heart isn't all there."

"I understand, but here's another way to look at it: people are more likely to buy your songs if they know who you are. If you only focus on creating, then nobody will know your masterpieces. You need to promote yourself."

Karla plopped herself on her couch. "I thought that's why I hired you," she remarked dejectedly.

"I can only get you so far. I can make the connections but it's up to you to convince others of your talents."

Karla could not argue that point. At some level, she knew he spoke the truth. She just didn't like the truth.

Taking her silence as agreement, her manager continued his investigation of her activities. "So did you go to the lunch I told you about?"

At this Karla's spirits picked up. "Yes, I did...and I want to thank you for wrangling me an invitation. It was great! Just to sit down to a relaxed lunch with some of the biggest female singers would have been enough of a treat, but – man! – I learned so much from them. They were so friendly and giving with their advice."

Lee grinned knowingly, "And what exactly did you learn?"

"It's kind of like you said. Most of them aren't that interested in buying other people's songs. They have enough of their own ideas not to need to buy from others. They also told me about some good clubs and labels that target women artists."

"Great!" Lee responded. "Glad you felt it was worthwhile."

Karla decided it was time to turn the questioning around. "So what about you? What have you learned lately? Were you able to pass around my demo tape?"

"Yes, I did shop it around a bit, and I've got good news and bad news. Which would you like first?"

"Give me the bad news, I guess."

"OK. The bad news is that most of the people who listened to it thought your style is...how can I say this delicately?... indistinctive. The songs sound pretty much like those of all the other female singers with whom you had lunch today. They thought the songs were a good beginning, but recommended you go back to the drawing board and try to create something a little more...unique. However...and here's the good news...I did find two people who were interested in hiring you for your lyrics. Both thought you were pretty clever with your wording."

Talking to Lee was always a roller coaster, Karla thought to herself. He always couched bad news with good news so she wouldn't feel too dejected. But, he also always managed to say something to prevent her from getting too hopeful about any good news. As he always reminded her, nothing is certain until it is done. "That's great!" she responded with all the enthusiasm she could muster. "Who are they? Which songs do they want?"

Lee took a deep breath before continuing. "I want you to remember that it's not easy making it as a songwriter. Sure, Burt Bacharach did it, but how many more do you know by name? Very few, I'd venture to say. So you have to keep in mind that it's really important to get your name out there in whatever way you can."

Karla's suspicions grew. Why was it taking him so long to answer her question? It really wasn't that difficult. "Right, right. I know that. You've told me that before. So, who's interested?"

"I've got two options for you, which I think is pretty darned good. The first is as a songwriter for advertisements...a jingle-writer, if you will." Before she could get a word out, he continued quickly, "The other is for a new music game show that a pal of mine is trying to pitch. The idea is that contestants are judged on how quickly and how creatively they can finish a new but incomplete song."

"And he wants me to be a contestant?"

"No, silly! He wants you to write the songs that the contestants will finish."

Karla crinkled her nose in disgust. This was the best he could do? Both were so crass and commercial. "Look, Lee, I didn't decide to go into songwriting so I could write nonsense. I'm an artist. I have stories to tell, and songs are my way to express myself. I want to leave a meaningful mark on the world. What kind of mark am I going to leave by accepting either of these jobs?"

Lee was now growing weary of telling Karla the same thing over and over. He gave one more impassioned plea. "You know how many times I've heard that? You know how many budding stars didn't make it because of attitudes like that? It's great that you want to leave your mark on the world, but be realistic. Even Barry Manilow, one of the few other successful songwriters known to most people, got his start in advertising. What is the mark that you're trying to leave: I didn't give up my principles, but I never achieved my goals either? Wouldn't it be better at the end of your life to be able to say 'I knew what I wanted;

I went after it with a sensible plan; and I accomplished my mission in life'? To me, that would truly be a meaningful mark, even more than just finding fame and fortune. Think what an inspiration you would be to all aspiring artists. You would be a reminder that they do not need to starve themselves to death for their art." Lee stood up from his desk and began pacing around his office. Now she'd done it! Every time he heard this stupid artsy-fartsy attitude, it got him going.

Lee continued, "What honor is there in living the life of the poor starving artist, anyway? You can neither take care of yourself nor express yourself appropriately. You end up counting every penny or maybe even living off the generosity of others, and nobody ends up listening to or even hearing your most important message. Isn't it better to find a way to be self-reliant, to earn an honest living, and still pursue one's craft? Just because you're working doesn't mean you can't follow your dreams on the side. To me, true success comes from balancing pragmatism with idealism."

It was hard to argue with such eloquence, so Karla did not bother. She tossed her head back against the couch pillows in frustration. "How much time do I have to decide?"

Lee sighed with relief that his words had not been wasted. He sat back down and spoke more calmly. "The jingle writing gig is open-ended. They're always looking for new talent. The game show has about a month or so before going into production, so you only have a few weeks to decide."

"I don't know what to tell you, Lee," Karla sighed. "I guess I need to think some more about what's really important to me. Can I call you back within the week with my answer?"

"Sure, take your time. But remember, lots of other people are also competing for the same jobs. I can't guarantee that the opening will still be there."

"In that case, keep shopping around my demo tape, OK?"

The manager and the songwriter ended their conversation and hung up the phone. Each frustrated by the other, neither was quite sure what to make of the call. In the privacy of their own rooms, both shook their heads and wondered why people never listened to them.

Chapter 28:
The Skinny

SimTime: May 30, Los Angeles

"Come in, come in," greeted Taylor Washington, as he shut the door to his office. "Glad you could make it on such short notice."

"What's up? Your message sounded pretty urgent. Is everyone OK?" April asked.

"Yeah, yeah. Everybody's fine." He swept away the worry with his hand, then paused as he decided what to say next. He wanted to come to the heart of the matter, but decided maybe he should try to act like he was interested in other people's business. Ever since the merger he'd had to learn the fine art of diplomacy. As he walked April over to his conference table, his mind drifted to his current pet peeve.

Taylor couldn't believe how distracted everyone at his new company suddenly seemed. The Cloud9 executives, in particular, acted more concerned with their own careers than with the future of the new company. He had promised them that they would keep their jobs. Wasn't his word worth anything? Apparently, not that much.

Taylor   stared   out   the   window,   momentarily

forgetting about his guest. People had become much more sensitive lately. Before the merger, the group had managed to work together well and seemed to understand each other. Now, as if the ringing of that bell at the stock exchange a month ago had signaled an instant loss of communication skills, the executive team constantly bickered. Taylor couldn't say anything without causing a storm of controversy. Even the most benign statements in meetings would bring torrents of debates. Taylor had gotten to the point of thinking twice about every word that came out of his mouth. Not only was this incredibly tiring, but it made him respond twice as slowly to every statement. How was he supposed to look like a decisive leader if it took him five minutes to figure out how to answer so as not to offend someone, upset apple carts, or undo the last hour's worth of progress? Things were so much easier when he was playing with the figures. Numbers never cry when you change your mind, he mused.

April, feeling uncomfortable with the prolonged silence, finally broke the ice. She knocked on the glass conference table to grab his attention. "Well, then, what's up?"

Taylor returned to the moment. "I saw your article in last month's magazine. Very interesting. I was duly impressed. I hear you're going to write some more articles for them. That true?"

April nodded. "That's true. I enjoyed writing the article and the readers seemed to like my style. I figure I can write articles based on the cases I'm seeing at the Legal Aid Society where I'm now volunteering. Besides, it's a good way to gain some more publicity for me."

"That's great, if you can manage it all," he cautioned her. Taylor paused again.

April held her breath. How she hoped he was not about to ask her out to dinner again. She knew she didn't want to go through that again.

Enough small talk, Taylor decided. He turned around and faced her, "I thought you might be interested in some inside information."

April exhaled with relief. "Frankie Nordo?" she ventured.

"You got it."

"Morrison actually found him?" she asked somewhat surprised.

"Yup…and a lot sooner than he let on to us."

"Whaddya mean?" April asked, her curiosity piqued.

Taylor loved when he could grab someone's attention like that. "You're not the only one that's picked up a job-related hobby, you know. I've been using my off-time to do a little investigating. You see, just after the merger, I thought I spotted Morrison and Frankie together in Newark Airport. I chased after them, but they disappeared.

"The whole plane ride back I kept stewing on what I thought I'd seen. I'm not one to hallucinate, so I was pretty sure it had to be them. I thought about Morrison's complete inability to track down this guy. It just didn't make sense. He might not be the world's best detective, but Frankie is hardly the world's smartest crook. If I could spot him in an airport, then surely Morrison must have been able to find him, too.

"When I got back to work the next day, I asked Accounting to send up Morrison's file. I decided to take a few days off, ostensibly to recover from the merger. During that time, I got out a map, his notes to me, and his receipts. You know what I learned?"

"That Morrison couldn't find his way out of a paper bag?" April hazarded sarcastically, as she sat down in one of the burgundy leather conference chairs.

"Initially, that's what I thought. After all, he'd gone to Aspen, San Diego, Mexico, Toronto, Miami, and London and always seemed to be just a day or two behind Frankie. Then I decided to approach this from a different angle. You know, maybe things weren't quite as they appeared. I decided to go to the last two locations to see if I could discover any patterns and get any hints about where he might be going next."

"But didn't you have work to do?"

"Sure, but I scheduled some business trips to those cities and left my Number Two to deal with the meetings here."

"And did you?"

"Did I what?" Taylor asked, momentarily distracted again.

"Did you find any patterns?"

"As a matter of fact, yes. It turns out that in both cities, Morrison stayed at places within two blocks of Frankie's hotel. Yet nobody seemed to see them together."

"How do you know this?" April questioned, the

mystery-lover in her becoming aroused.

"I did some old-fashioned footwork: I went around to hotels and restaurants in the area and asked people if they recognized either of them. Although some had seen one or the other, no one had seen the two together."

"That's odd," April remarked.

Taylor was glad to see that he was successfully luring April into the story. He continued confidently, "I was taking another look at Morrison's submitted charges when it hit me: he never submitted actual receipts; just his own invoices with expenses listed individually." He shook his head in disgust. "Why our accounting people didn't catch that is beyond me. If I had been in charge of finances, that never would have happened. Important to have tight financial policies, otherwise people rip you off. Everybody knows that..."

April sensed the start of one of Taylor's famous digressions into the wonders of math and finance. Hoping to nip it in the bud, she interjected impatiently, "Anyway....?"

"Right!" Taylor's mind bounced back to the subject like a yo-yo on the uptake. "I checked with Morrison's hotels, and it seems that he actually paid anywhere from two to four times less for the rooms than what he was invoicing. He was also doing the same with the airfares. Can you believe the nerve of that guy?! He was trying to suck my company dry! He'd buy discounted tickets and then make a hefty profit off Galaxy...and he paid in cash! I then checked out Frankie's rates and learned he also was paying discounted rates." Just the thought that someone could get away with such chicanery at a company over his watch made Taylor's blood boil. He liked to think he was smarter than most people, and here was a clear example to the contrary.

Once again, April sensed Taylor was likely to get off track. He'd do so much better if he could just stay focused, she thought to herself.

"I also found out that Frankie would travel under assumed names. Usually some version of Harlan McFay or McFox or McFaux."

"Is that his real name? Who would make up such an awful name?"

"I don't know. I haven't tried to figure that one out yet. I did notice, though, that Frankie would always write as his registration address some bogus street address but the city and state where he was next planning on visiting."

"Why would he do that?" she wondered aloud.

Taylor shrugged off the question casually. "Who knows? But the guy isn't that bright or he wouldn't have had to steal other people's tunes in the first place!"

"Well he can't be that dumb either if he's been able to steal so much money from your company without getting caught," April reminded him.

Taylor crossed his arms and continued, "Here's the clincher: I think he had some help in that endeavor from our dear friend Mr. McDean." With his arms still folded, he pointed his index finger toward the sky. "I think the two of them must have met at some point and realized that they could continue this jet-set lifestyle by keeping up the charade that Morrison was searching for him. Meanwhile,

Galaxy was actually funding the whole venture and fattening their bank accounts, to boot." Taylor threw his head back and brushed his hands through his hair. "How could I have been so stupid? I guess I was so busy with the merger that I ran out of time to keep a close eye on this matter."

Poor Taylor. He really did feel bad about not doing a perfect job as CEO, April realized. She knew that feeling; she had undergone the same guilt attacks whenever her patients had died on her. "Don't be so hard on yourself," she offered supportively. "You can't keep a close eye on everything. That's why you have people who work for you. You're job is to be the leader and visionary, which you do well."

April paused. "So what now? Do you have any idea where they're going next?"

"I think I might. In the evenings, I've been researching different cities on the Internet. I think I know how they could meet and never be seen."

Now she was beginning to get annoyed at the way he would break right before every critical piece of information just to make her beg for it. Why couldn't he just tell a story plain and simple? Unfortunately, he had her hooked. She couldn't help but prod, "Go ahead."

The new detective, evidently proud of his sound reasoning ability, returned to his usual confident tone as he explained his logic. "Obviously, going to meals together in public restaurants would eventually get them spotted, as I'm sure Morrison realized. However, they could meet somewhere either where they were alone or where there were so many people that no one or two individuals would stand out.   As I did my research, I realized that in every city they visited, there happened to be a music or arts festival at the same time.   I think they hooked up in the middle of these crowds. Frankie loves music, so this would appeal to him."

The lawyer nodded at the soundness of this deduction. "Makes sense. Have you checked with his old band members to see if he's been back to visit them?"

"But of course!   Unfortunately, either he hasn't visited or they're covering up for him. They keep saying that they haven't seen him."

"So where do you think he'll go next?"

"I have a hunch he'll be in the Bay Area before long.   It looks like the Monterey Blues Festival is about to start. I wouldn't be surprised if they turned up there."

Taylor paused for dramatic effect.   Then, in a slightly lower voice, he looked the attorney straight in the eye and announced, "Which brings me to why I asked you here."

"Oh?"

"What do I need to do, legally, to nab him? Do I have to get a subpoena to have him appear in court?"

"You could go that route, but I wouldn't recommend it. Although legally you need to appear in court if you are subpoenaed, you're still under your own free will until the court date. Considering how neither Morrison nor Frankie are too big on following the law, I think they'd just skip town anyway. I'd recommend that you get warrants for both of their arrests. At a minimum, you could get them for theft and fraud. You'd need to have a cop actually arrest them, but at least they wouldn't be able to get away again." She paused as something struck her. "But why don't you just ask your legal department?"

"Frankly. I'm a little embarrassed to. You see, nobody knows I've been doing this. I mean, how would it look if the CEO of a newly public company was discovered to be spending all his brain-power playing detective? Besides, I don't want anyone to know how Morrison swindled us."

That made sense. "I'll tell you what," April volunteered. "When you feel more confident in their exact whereabouts, let me know and I'll arrange for the arrest through some of my contacts. In the meantime, if you give me copies of your evidence, I'll arrange to get the warrants. OK?"

Taylor was pleased with her reaction. "Thanks, April, I knew I could count on you."

She responded with an approving smile in kind. "Anything to help out a friend." Looking at her watch, she jumped from her seat. "Goodness! It's late! I need to go down to the clinic now. Thanks for keeping me informed."

With that word of praise, April rushed from the office. As April shut the door behind her, Taylor kicked his feet up on the desk, leaned back with his arms behind his head, and basked in the contentment of a perfectly run meeting.

Chapter 29:
The Show

SimTime: May 30, Los Angeles

Karla found herself surrounded by hoards of teenage boys and girls. The surrounding crowd undulated in unison to the rhythm of the drums pulsating from the stage. The guitar turned almost human in its emotional range as the solo climaxed. It shrieked in the strain of the moment; it exploded in fits of ecstasy; and it hummed in joyous release. Boys in the audience played their air guitars while the girls twisted their bodies to the strains of the gut-wrenching solo. Karla had heard this song before, but never from this vantage point. The energy level in the room could have lit a small town for a week. Until now, she had never realized exactly what made the difference between a good performer and a superstar. She finally felt the total devotion, the total offering of oneself, that the singer gave to his fans, and they to him.

The crowd surged forward as Marco finished his last song. The girls were going crazy, trying to rush the stage so that maybe the superstar would grace their hands with a touch, or even something more. Karla wondered how many of them had fantasized about kissing or dating this man. The girls weren't the only ones rushing the stage. Boys raised their hands in hopes of catching one of the guitar picks that Marco would throw at the end of the show. Would their new acquisition raise their status of "cool" among their buddies? Would it help them impress the girls after whom they lusted?

The magic of Marco was not lost on Karla; however, neither was the reality. She used this opportunity to take a final look at him from afar and then quickly exited the building before the tide of people flowed back. Walking out the door, she had to admit that Marco looked and sounded better than he had in months. She figured that his transformation must have been why Lee told her to go see the show. Spotting the stage door she decided that she should at least congratulate him on a good performance.

She waited at the door for about five minutes, then changed her mind and walked away. Three steps later, Karla stopped. She looked longingly over her shoulder at the door, hesitated, then jerked her head forward and continued walking. Although one side of her felt the need to let him know of her presence, the other side didn't quite want to talk with him. It would be awkward for both of them, she reasoned, and she was not sure she wanted to put herself through such an emotional strain. Karla twisted her hair nervously between her fingers as she slowed her pace. Still, if he had cleaned up his act, maybe they could handle working together again. She slapped her hands against her thighs in a fit of exasperation, then turned around and marched back towards the stage door. She had asked to be sent to this simworld at the height of her career; she now realized that in order to reach her definition of success, she needed his help.

About half an hour later Marco finally left the building. Spotting her in the corner of his eye, he instinctively headed towards her. "Hey!" he greeted as casually he could. "What are you doing here?"

"I was in the neighborhood and managed to catch your show," she responded with as much fake coolness as he had displayed. "You sounded good." She hesitated. "Listen…I was wondering…would you like to get something to eat?"

"Sure," he smiled.

****

The former partners sat across from each other in a booth at a little diner a few blocks away from the theater. Just like before, Marco ordered a cheeseburger with fries and Karla a plate of lasagna. Both couldn't help thinking about earlier, happier times. Even though they were eating the same foods, the atmosphere felt completely different. Back then, things were easy between them. They joked, they talked, they laughed. Now both sat there not knowing how to act.

Karla realized it was up to her, as the host, to say something. She ventured, "You sounded really good out there."

"Thanks…. You mentioned that earlier. So, what brings you 'round? Scouting out the place for a future gig or just bored?"

"Neither. Actually, Lee suggested I come. He said I'd be in for a surprise."

"Was he right?" he asked knowingly.

"Yes," She responded honestly. "Not only do you sound as good as you did when I first met you, but you look better than the last time I saw you. Looks like your eyes are less red and puffy, too."

Marco dropped some of his smug attitude. "Thanks for noticing. I've been working real hard lately." He paused and gently touched her hand that was resting on the table. "You know, your little stunt with Lee really worked. It took me a while, but I finally gave up the drugs altogether."

"What finally did it for you?"

"Frankly...it was you. You see, after I left you guys that day, I was really mad...like I've never been in my life. I felt like I'd been double-crossed and played like a fool. I went to the first bar I could find and downed a whole bottle of vodka to forget about what had just happened. Unfortunately, it didn't work. I just turned into a really nasty drunk and got into a fight with a biker guy. I don't even remember what it was about. Actually, I didn't really care. I just felt like beating on somebody and I guess having them beat on me. After all, what was a little physical pain to what you guys had just put me through?

"When I got home, I was still too upset to go to sleep, so I smoked a few joints until I finally crashed. I slept most of the next day away. When I woke up, I was sore all over. I mean, I've never been hung over like that before. It felt like every drop of air was a nail being hammered into my head. I couldn't move without groaning...and you should have seen the bruises that biker left on me. On top of all that, I'd wasted the whole day. I'd really planned to use that time to write some new songs, and now I was in such bad shape that I couldn't even use what was left of the day to do anything productive. I was lucky to make it to the couch. I guess that's when I started to realize I couldn't go on like this anymore."

Karla shook her head in dismay at hearing what Marco had gone through. "You poor thing," she said sincerely, "but I guess if that's what it took to get you to quit, then it was worth it."

Marco looked down dejectedly at his food. "Actually, that didn't convince me to quit. That just convinced me to cut back."

"What do you mean?"

"Well, after I healed, I was still really hurt and angry by what you'd done. At first, I decided I didn't need you. After all, plenty of other girls are willing to go out with me. I took advantage of my new-found freedom..."

"Hey! I never tied a rope around your neck..." Karla interrupted indignantly.

Marco made a stop sign with his hand to cut her off. "Just listen, OK? This is hard enough. Don't make it worse."

"Sorry," Karla mumbled as she slouched in her seat.

"Anyway, I decided to date a different girl every night. At first, it was fun...and great for my ego. Believe me, I had no trouble finding girls. You should've seen these chicks, I mean they were hot...I mean they were *really HOT*! They could melt ice with their looks, they were so hot. Girls who never would've spoken to me in the real world were going crazy over me in this simworld…and most of them were more than happy to tell me how wonderful I was. It was fun like you couldn't believe, and I needed the pick-me-up after your rejection. I felt on top of the world again, like I could make it on my own after all and didn't need Lee or you to tell me what to do. I started to relax and began partying more again."

Marco noticed Karla sitting there silently with her arms crossed, glowering at him, and realized he should probably get to the point of this story before he screwed things up with her again.

"Toward the end of the second week, though, I began to feel like something was missing. Then it hit me: none of these girls, or even any of the guys from the band, ever really challenged me. They all just agreed with whatever I said. It felt weird to realize that I was suddenly in charge. I'm not used to that. Usually, Taylor forces me to get off my butt and do something or even just to think more. I then realized that when you and I were dating, you always challenged me. You never just accepted what I said. You always forced me to do more, or do it better. I guess I started doing the drugs in part because that was annoying me. I wanted to just chill and have fun in this simworld, and you refused to let me do that.

"Once I'd had a few weeks of that life, though, I realized it wasn't as great as I thought it would be. I missed the stimulation. At first, I didn't know what to do. I didn't feel comfortable going to Taylor, I couldn't talk to Lee, and you were out of the question."

"Why couldn't you talk to Taylor?" Karla

interrupted. "He's your best friend."

"In the real world, yes. But here, he's my boss. We're about to go into contract negotiations with him, so letting him know about my drug problem didn't seem like such a good idea. Besides, he spent a good chunk of our time in the first simworld trying to convince me not to choose this career. What was I going to do? Go to him and admit he was right…again?"

Karla tilted her head noncommittally. "What about April?"

"She wouldn't understand," he said dismissively. "As I was saying, at first I didn't know what to do, but then it hit me. I needed to talk to you."

"So, I was last choice?" she asked indignantly.

"No," he responded with exasperation. "Don't you get it? I missed you. I needed you…I mean I need you. You understand me and you challenge me. I need that."

Karla didn't know how to react to what she was hearing. "So you want me to be your substitute mother…or worse, your substitute Taylor? I don't think so."

Marco grabbed her hands in his and lightly banged them on the table. "No! Don't you get it? I'm not looking for a substitute anything. I'm looking for you. You make me want to do more, to be better, to show you the ultimate I can be. I want to please you. You challenge me and stimulate me…both creatively and ….uh…otherwise." He shot her one of his seductive smiles. She blushed.

"Once I realized this," he continued, "I knew what I had to do. I knew I had to win you back, no matter what it took. I quit smoking that day…cold-turkey! The next day

I started a diet to lose the "munchie weight" and began going to the gym again.

Karla's heart leapt at this revelation, but her head remained cautious. "What about the drinking?"

"That's been a bit harder. I'm still working on cutting down."

"Mmmm," Karla responded coolly. She was doing everything she could to control herself. Part of her wanted to jump for joy. After all, how many women get to hear such an amazing declaration from a man, especially one as special as Marco? Still, she found it hard to believe that he could have come so far in just a few weeks. "Why didn't you just cut them both out at the same time?"

"Jeez, give me a break, will you? It's not that easy, you know. There's the whole social aspect: everyone drinks. I still feel like a loser if I'm the only one in the group with soda."

Karla shook her head with pity. She could understand why he thought like that, but it annoyed her that he still hadn't figured out that the real loser is the one who does things just to seem cool. He had so much charisma and such a devoted following that if he just stood his ground and abstained, he'd soon make drinking soda seem cool.

Marco could tell by her silence that Karla was judging him again. He didn't need that right now. Why couldn't she see that he was trying really hard? What more could he do? Still, he didn't want to ruin the reunion. He decided to shut up and let her digest the news, so he bit into his burger.

Karla quietly ate her lasagna. She was afraid to open her mouth. She obviously had already offended him twice. She feared three times might be the charm that sends him away for good.

No longer able to take the tension, Marco gave in and broke the silence. As lightheartedly as he could, he asked, "So, that's what's up with me. How have you been doing?"

"OK," she responded glumly. "I put together enough new songs for a demo which Lee and I have been shopping around. Not too many bites, yet, though."

"Sorry to hear that, babe," he answered softly.

"But I do have a new gig lined up to begin on Monday," she announced optimistically.

"Oh yeah? That's great! What is it?"

"I'm going to be a songwriter for a new game show with a music theme. Every week I'll write the start of a bunch of new songs. The contestants have to come up with the ending. They've written the contract so that any song I start for them, I can also finish and use under my own name. I can't take somebody else's ending, though."

Marco was impressed, and happy for his friend. "That's a great deal! It will force you to write on a regular basis, you can explore all different musical styles, and you don't even have to finish the songs to get paid. Way to go! Plus, it will get your songs out to a wide audience. Best part is, you'll have a decent regular income so you can also write for your own pleasure. It sounds like the perfect job for you."

Karla couldn't help but smile. That was so typical

of him, she thought. He always managed to find the bright side of every situation. He was like his old self: he knew exactly what to say to make her feel good. She missed that support.

Her smile made Marco feel better. He could see that she was becoming more at ease again. Maybe the ice was finally melting. He felt good about the current détente and thought the time might be right to take another bold step towards reconciliation. "Say, I just remembered something! We still have four more weeks before our recording deadline. Now that I've straightened myself out, I bet we could knock out those songs in no time. Whaddya say? You want to give it another shot and see if we can do it?"

"The album?" she mused coyly. "Gee, I don't know, Marco. I'm not sure if I really want to go through all that again. I've already written most of the songs. If we try to collaborate again, we'll just end up in all the old arguments about rewrites. I don't know if I have the energy for that. Besides, it's only been a month. That's hardly a track record. Frankly, I'm not sure if I can trust you yet. Like you said, I've got a good gig about to start. Why should I bother with the collaboration again?"

Marco reached across the table and grabbed her hands again. "Why not?" he urged. "For one thing, you've got very little to lose. If it doesn't work out, you still have all the songs anyway. If it does work out, together we might come up with a better album." He paused to let her think about this. Seeing that she wasn't changing her expression, he added, "You're amazing. I'll tell you what:

If you don't like the way I'm behaving, you can back out again and I won't even hold it against you."

"Well, you sure better not!" she reacted indignantly. "If this falls apart because you're smoking again, you'll have no one to blame but yourself."

"Does that mean yes?"

"Ok. But I mean it: one joint and our joint album is over."

Chapter 30:
The Stakeout

SimTime: June 20, Monterey

Blue sunny skies and temperatures in the low 80's added to the festive air surrounding the annual music festival. Thousands of people flocked to the town of Carmel, California, to hear the biggest names in rhythm and blues music. Despite the numbers, the crowd was surprisingly orderly. People milled about with hot dogs in one hand, and children on the other. Police stood everywhere, but their presence was understated. No need to cause alarm when trying to preserve the peace. Everyone seemed content to live and let live.

Everyone, that is, except for a trailer-full of people surreptitiously parked just across from one of the entrances to the festival grounds. Inside, five men peered back and forth between multiple surveillance screens as thousands of unsuspecting visitors passed in front of their cameras. In their attempt not to arouse suspicion, they had agreed to keep the door closed. Inside, two fans blew hot air on the sweaty men.

The rising temperature inside the trailer did not compare to the rising heat of impatience boiling inside one man. Taylor had taken three days of vacation to participate in this stake-out. On the first day, he found the prospect of nabbing his prey in public exciting. He felt just like one of those TV detectives. By the second day, he began to think that the whole effort might be futile. He had as much chance of finding Frankie in this crowd as he did of finding the proverbial needle. By the third day, today, he was sitting there mainly out of a sense of responsibility and respect to April, who had gone through a lot of trouble to arrange this.

Worse than the agony of the wait, Taylor felt frustrated that he couldn't even go into the festival and enjoy the events, lest someone see him and figure out what was going on. The lieutenant explained that people might recognize a music executive and somehow tip off their suspects. Begrudgingly, Taylor accepted this point. For the first time since entering this simworld, he actually regretted his fame and fortune.

Sitting still staring at nothing never interested Taylor. He didn't mind sitting if it were connected with something useful, like studying or planning. He found just waiting to be an exercise in futility. In his mind, the only time things happen is when they have a jumpstart. Three days of watching crowds only added to his belief that he needed to force the issue.

"Are you sure I can't go outside and just wander through the crowd?" he asked the lieutenant for the fifth time in three days.

"No," the exasperated officer responded tersely.

"I'll keep on sunglasses so nobody will recognize

me. I'll just look around and see if I can spot him."

"No."

"I promise, I won't do anything stupid. If you want, you can hook a mic to me and I'll just mention his coordinates to you. You can even place a camera on me to check."

The officer took off his glasses and said in as calm a voice as he could muster, "Look, Mr. Washington, I appreciate you wanting to help. We all do. But what your suggesting isn't going to help. It's just going to cause more problems and take resources away from our central focus. I know this is hard for you to understand, but there's a reason why stakeouts are done by police. We're professional at this."

"Trust me, I know," Taylor responded. "It's not like I never did this before. I ...." He cut himself off just before he blurted out about his prior simworld experience.

"Yes, sir. You did a wonderful job of tracking him down. Someday, when you give up on the entertainment industry, you could slum and become a detective. In the meantime, let us do our job. In fact, if you really want to help, why don't you go back to your hotel and we'll call you when we've nabbed him."

Out of the question, decided Taylor, as he sat down determinedly in his chair. He had gotten them this far; there was no way he was backing out now. He'd sit there quietly—somehow—if that's what it took to participate in that grand moment when they nab those thieves.

For the next half hour, Taylor didn't say a word out loud. Internally, he groused about the stakeout. Recalling his times in his first simworld, he wondered if acting like a jerk was one of the required skills of all lieutenants. That had certainly been his experience. In between complaining quietly, he kept praying that something would happen soon. He didn't know how much longer he could keep quiet, or how much longer the lieutenant would let him stay in the trailer.

As if the gods had finally heard his pleas for activity, a voice broke the silence over the airwaves. One of the undercover cops saw someone that looked like Frankie. Lt. Carmody pushed Taylor out of the way to get a closer look at the monitor. Taylor looked over his shoulder to see a shaky image coming into focus on the screen. "That's him, all right!" Taylor confirmed excitedly. The lieutenant pushed a button to begin recording the events. "Camera Two, we've got positive ID on the subject," advised the officer into the microphone. "Whatever you do, stay with him and keep the camera locked on him at all times. Wait for my signal before closing in on him."

The sun started to break through the clouds of Taylor's world. He had found half the team. He was sure that since Frankie was there, Morrison couldn't be too far behind. He peered carefully at the monitor, looking to see if anyone to the sides of the suspect was the elusive detective. For more than fifteen minutes, Taylor paid close attention. Now he understood how Frankie could hide so well despite his fame. Walking around in dark shades, a tie-dye shirt, cut-off jeans, and Birkenstocks, he looked just like everyone else. He bought food, checked out the stands, and sat in the sun.

Fifteen minutes later, and the radio crackled again. "Camera Three thinks he might have Morrison," announced the lieutenant. "Wanna take a look and see if we've got the right guy?"

Camera Three's picture was jumpier than Camera Two's. It took Taylor a few minutes even to find the focal point. He examined the image carefully. Finally, Taylor shook his head. "Nope. It's close, but that's not him. This guy's a little too young." The lieutenant, wondering whether Taylor would even recognize the guy, finally passed the word to continue the search.

The men in the trailer continued to look at all the screens simultaneously. Taylor was sure that Morrison would be there. He could feel it in his bones. If they just kept following Frankie, eventually he would lead them directly to his partner in crime.

Taylor looked at Camera One's monitor. As he watched the people pass by his window on the world, he reflected on the popularity of this event. The young parents with kids made him realize just how many activities were planned for children of all ages. A couple walking arm-in-arm made him contemplate how this was the perfect date: lots to do with various levels of talking required. The groups of high school students flirting with each other also rang a familiar chord. They loved events like this, where they could hear live bands and hang with their friends in a safe environment. Even singles would like it, he supposed as he noticed a lone person sitting on a bench, if they were either true music lovers or .... The more he thought about it, the less he could understand why anyone would come to this event alone. He quickly spoke into the mic, "Camera One, can you go back and take another look at the people sitting on the benches, please?"

"What's up?" asked the lieutenant, a little annoyed that the guest was now giving orders into the microphones without permission.

"Something struck me as strange. I want to check it out."

The lieutenant took control of the microphone as Taylor studied the benches carefully. "What do you see?"

"Nothing here. Can you ask him to walk back to the bench before that?"

A minute or two later, Taylor saw the bench come into focus. The detective jumped up and pointed at the screen. "There! There! You see him? There's five people on that bench. The two on the left and the two on the right are couples. The guy in the middle. He's alone."

"So?"

"So?" Taylor mimicked with impatience. "Doesn't it seem odd to you for a single, middle-aged man to be sitting by himself in the middle of a music festival? Wouldn't it make more sense if he were with somebody: a date, a friend, or something?"

"Maybe he is. Maybe he's just waiting to meet somebody."

"Exactly my thought! Can you ask the camera man to get a close-up of him?"

With nothing better to do, Lt. Carmody obliged.

"I knew it!" shouted Taylor. "That's him! That's

definitely Morrison! No doubt about it!"

Carmody passed the word to the cameraman to continue focusing on this suspect until he, too, heard the signal.

Now things were becoming interesting. Taylor couldn't wait to see how the two would meet. He watched the two cameras with intense curiosity. In between, he plotted their movements on a map. At 4:20 pm, Morrison glanced at his watch and finally left his bench. Weaving a path through the different venues, he eventually made his way to a far corner of the fairgrounds. The entire walk took about 25 minutes. Taylor wondered if this were part of Morrison's normal ritual or if he suspected that he was being followed.

Meanwhile, Frankie had walked over to the same corner of the grounds in about five minutes. Having noticed that it was only 4:25, he had decided to throw a blanket on the ground and take a nap in the late afternoon sun.

Taylor traced their paths on the map and realized that they were within a five-minute walk of the trailer. He could hardly contain his giddiness. All the work he had done in his spare time was finally paying off. He knew he could figure it out! He knew there was a connection! Now the animal was about to enter the trap. He wanted to pull the string. Taylor asked the lieutenant if he could leave the trailer and participate in the arrest. Carmody refused, telling him to leave the arrests to the professionals. The officer ordered him to just sit tight and be patient. Patience, Taylor grunted to himself, was not his strong suit.

Resigned to the fact that he could not participate in the arrest, Taylor parked himself in front of the two monitors to watch the events unfold. There, in front of his very eyes, he saw Morrison come over and casually kick Frankie's foot. Frankie sat up and shook hands with his partner. The two walked together to a different location a little further into the crowd. The cameramen did their best to keep photographing the events while avoiding being seen. Reality TV at its finest, thought Taylor.

The two sat on the grass near a puppet show. Odd location, he mused. Perhaps they wanted to be somewhere where there was less chance of Frankie's fans spotting him. What teenager would go to a puppet show? As the two sat together and talked, Taylor grew more impatient. "Why don't you give the signal? What are you waiting for?" he asked the lieutenant urgently. "They're not going to watch the whole show, you know. They're probably going to have a short meeting, exchange information, and then disappear again. We're going to miss our chance!"

"Relax," answered the policeman. "We've done this before. We know how these things work. We're not going to let them go. We just want to record as much of their conversation as we can to make for a stronger case. Here....listen to this." The officer fiddled with some dials. He turned up the volume on the two cameras so Taylor could hear. Next, he pushed some knobs up and down to filter out background noise. A few more twists and pulls and his top-notch surveillance equipment had zeroed in on the conversation of the two subjects:

"So what's the plan this time?" Frankie

asked.

"I was thinking, we're already on the West Coast, and we've done a lot of this part of the country. If we stay here much longer, people are going to start to recognize us. You know what I mean?"

"Yeah," nodded Frankie.

"So I was thinking, why not head over to the land down under?"

"Where?"

"Australia, Frankie, Australia."

"Australia? That sounds cool. Will we be safe there?"

"Probably. Did you ever sell any records down there?"

"Uh…I don't think so. I don't remember seeing any fan mail from Australia. But I don't really know. I left those details to those dweebs at Galaxy."

"Well, lucky for us, those dweebs don't bother too much with details either!"

"Ain't that the truth! So, you got everything ready?"

Morrison leaned in and handed him a fat envelope. "You know it. Here's the plane ticket and your share of the money. You got the dope?"

Frankie kicked the pillow on his blanket. "I wasn't just lying on this for my health, you know. I picked it up just before we met, just like you said." He tossed it to Morrison. "Here, you take it."

"Good going." Morrison responded as he caught the bag. "I'll meet you at our regular airport location in two days, ok?"

"Unbelievable," the officer declared. "Right there in the open." He pushed on the microphones. "Let's go, boys! Let's get them before they split! Go! Now! Now!" Turning back to Taylor, he instructed, "Now the fun begins. Watch Camera Three."

Just after he said this, a 20-something year old man in a PastyLips T-shirt swaggered in front of the camera and headed towards the pair.

"What the...? Who's this idiot messing things up?" Taylor exclaimed.

Carmody put a hand on Taylor's shoulder, smiled, and said, "Just watch."

"Hey!" cried the man, pointing at Frankie. "I know you. Aren't you Frankie Nordo?" The man looked down at his shirt, then back at Frankie. "Yeah, man, you definitely are! Dude! I'm a big PastyLips fan! Hey, can I shake your hand?" Frankie, loving the attention, extended his hand warmly.

"Oh man, am I interrupting something? I didn't know you were talking to someone. Who's your buddy? Is he in the band, too?" The man studied the faces on the shirt.

"No, uh, this is Morrison. He's my

manager." Frankie introduced innocently.

Morrison cringed slightly at Frankie's honesty.

"Wow! A real musician's manager! Cool! Hey, can I tell you guys something?"

Frankie shrugged his shoulders openly. "Sure, I guess. What is it?"

The man held onto Frankie's arm and brought him in close to tell a secret. "You...you're...you're under arrest. Anything you say can and will be used against you in a court of law..."

From the trailer, Taylor watched as a swarm of police officers flashed badges and handcuffed the two. He couldn't help but laugh at the totally unsuspecting looks on Morrison's and Frankie's faces. He turned to Lt. Carmody and gave him a high-five. "Excellent! That was fantastic! Did you see their faces? That was brilliant!"

Lt. Carmody patted his guest on the back and enjoyed the moment, too. "Yeah. Tony is one of our best undercover cops. He loves making those kinds of arrests. I think he wanted to be an actor at one time. Congratulations, sir, you've got your man."

Chapter 31:
The Ax

SimTime: June 25, Los Angeles

April parked her car and took the elevator to the law firm of Hufington, Cabash, & Chow. She glanced at her watch nervously. For the first time in her life, April worried that she'd made a bad decision. She corrected herself: not a bad decision, but a really bad career move.

She stepped off the elevator and headed directly to the private conference room in the back. Her heart thumped with every step. She knew she was going to get an earful when Mr. Cabash himself called her up and asked her to meet with a few of the partners in that room.

Although the law firm was outfitted in mostly open spaces and glass walls, one conference room had been kept in the old hardwood panel style. Since nobody could see inside this room, it was almost always used for personnel issues. Mr. Cabash had refused to give her many details about the meeting, stating only that they wanted to discuss recent developments with her. April, however, had a strong suspicion about the real issue at hand.

As she walked down the hall, she took a hard look at the surroundings. Although avoiding eye contact with everyone, she had the strange sensation that every set of eyes was glaring at her. When she did look up, she noticed people averting their eyes. She suddenly felt as welcome as a germ in a hospital.

Mr. Cabash sat in the conference room with his two senior partners, re-reading the latest edition of *Style & Substance* magazine while he waited for April to arrive. Holding the journal in his left hand, he slapped it with his right. "Unbelievable," he roared. "Where does she come off with this? Just listen to the way she closed this last article:

> *And so, like untold others living outside the mainstream of color and money in this country, Mr. Turnbull found himself yet another victim of this country's judicial hypocrisy: Those with bulging bank accounts are presumed innocent until proven guilty while those who struggle to survive are viewed as guilty until proven innocent.*
>
> *Yet, the hypocrisy lies not only within the judicial system. For even when a competent lawyer salvaged the malpractice of the public defender, and cleared the man of all charges, Mr. Turnbull returned to society a marked man, kicked to the curb by both his landlord and his employer, forced forever more to wear the scarlet A for Accused.*

April knocked lightly on the door and let herself in. She entered the room to find Messrs. Hufington, Cabash, and Chow sitting at the big conference table. "Please come in, April," Mr. Hufington invited.

"Thank you," April answered as she took a seat.

Hufington engaged her in polite conversation for about five minutes until Cabash's face had lost its blush of anger. Everyone knew they needed to be on their best behavior. Eventually, Mr. Cabash regained his composure and got to the heart of the matter.

"Have you been enjoying your extra-curriculars, April?" he began.

"Oh, most definitely. I really can't thank you enough for letting me cut back on my hours. I want you to know that I have been putting that time to very good use."

Ever since taking Taylor's advice to volunteer at the Legal Aid Society, April had been limiting the time she spent in her own office. At first, she cut down from 70 hours per week to about 50. Then, when the magazine had offered her the chance to freelance, she cut back to 30 per week. It was the only way she could do all three activities and not kill herself in the process.

Sure, the partners weren't so keen on her new activities, but they really didn't have much choice. April had some of the highest profile clients and brought in lots of money. Besides, how would it look if they penalized her for doing charitable legal work? Not to mention the good publicity her articles were bringing.

"Oh, we know that," he confirmed. "Your work at the Legal Aid Society has been all over the news. It's not every day that someone of your caliber volunteers there.

"And isn't that a shame?" she replied passionately. "Imagine if more top-tier lawyers helped those on the bottom rung of society's ladder? Think how much better those people's lives would be. You can't believe how much shoddy legal work I've seen since I've started there. Not that I'm knocking the other volunteers. Usually, their work is fine. Mostly it's the lawyers that these poor people had previously paid to represent them who did the bad job. They practically stole the money from these poor souls. Then the defendants end up in worse condition than when they started. Out of desperation, they finally come to us for some decent help."

April loved this topic and could not stop herself from continuing. "And imagine what would happen if other professions more actively helped the less fortunate. Imagine if more doctors volunteered their time to treat those who couldn't afford proper medical care. I'm not even talking about the poor on other continents. Just look in our own back yard. Thousands of people need help; yet so many of our best practitioners are more concerned about making money for themselves than they are in healing."

"That's very admirable of you to think that way, April," Mr. Hufington commended. "And we're happy to see that you are doing more than just dreaming about a better way. We admire people who put their money where their mouth is."

"However," added Mr. Cabash, playing "bad cop" to Hufington's "good cop," "we're a little concerned over the way you're...spreading your gospel, as it were."

"What do you mean?" asked April.

"As you know, our clients are among the wealthiest and most powerful in Hollywood...and probably in the country," Mr. Chow began to explain, trying to find the middle ground between his two partners. "For many of them, prestige is critical to their image. Many count exclusivity among the ways they measure their success. They fly private jets to avoid dealing with the masses, they eat in only the most exclusive restaurants where most people can neither afford the food nor even get a table. For better or worse, they love the idea that they have special privileges, and everything they do is aimed at maintaining that separation and that image."

April knew exactly what he meant. What they viewed as privilege, she viewed as snobbishness.

"When they look for someone to represent them, they want the best, and to them, that means someone that is not available to just anyone," Chow continued. "When they come to us, they do so because they feel confident that we are in that same inner circle. Do you see where I'm going with this?" he asked her.

She nodded but said nothing. She was not sure where this was headed and wanted to avoid saying the wrong thing.

Cabash took the floor back from Chow, impatient with his platitudes. "Frankly, April, your work there has caused some of our clients to raise concerns over whether we are an exclusive enough firm for them."

"Are you saying that clients are considering leaving simply because of my work? They don't want a lawyer with a good soul who is willing to help others?" she rebuked.

"Not exactly. They definitely want a good lawyer with a good soul. Some of them, however, don't seem to want to share," Chow attempted to explain.

"But isn't that their problem, not mine?" she asked.

"It becomes your problem if we start losing business because of your actions," Cabash declared as he poked the table with his index finger.

"So you want me to stop volunteering because some clients are selfish?" she asked incredulously.

"Not at all," Hufington intervened. "We value what you are doing and support you in that endeavor. That's why we're willing to accept fewer hours from you."

"So what is it then?" April asked, now confused.

"We can explain away the pro bono work very easily," said Chow the mediator. "We start having more concern when you use your magazine as a soapbox to rail against the whole profession. It just doesn't help our cause any."

"When you started writing for *Style & Substance*, we thought it would be an excellent way to gain more exposure for the firm. We figured you'd continue to represent us in a positive light. However, your stories have grown more and more cynical and critical of the profession as a whole. You are coming across sounding more liberal than we care to be portrayed. Even though you are doing this independently of us, everyone knows that you work in this firm. It reflects badly on us, you see," Cabash finished.

April nodded knowingly. Cabash was right that she

had grown more cynical. Her *pro bono* work had opened her eyes to a whole other world, and she was shocked by what she had seen. The more time she spent writing and working at the Legal Aid Society, the more disillusioned and stressed she felt with her current work environment.

The partners stared at her as she sat their silently digesting the conversation.

"So, what exactly are you saying?" she ventured, "That I have to choose between my work here and at the Legal Aid Society?"

"No, not that exactly," drawled Hufington.

"That I should stop writing for the magazine?"

"You're getting warmer," Chow encouraged.

April feared this day might come. She doubted her current lifestyle could survive the pressures of the high-stakes world of entertainment law. Still, she could not choose. To stop writing would remove her only hobby. To continue writing, but to moderate to the point of harmlessness took the fun out of the articles. To stop working at the Legal Aid Society would remove her from the very reason she had decided to become an attorney. To stop working for the firm would be a blessing and a curse. Free from the pressures of looking for business and trying to conform to others' standards, April could do as she wanted. However, she would lose the safety net that the firm provided. Would she be willing to go it alone, even if it meant a less luxurious lifestyle?

Cabash slammed his hand on the table. "Enough of this nonsense! Don't play coy with us April. We know you know what we're trying to say. So now you're going to make us come right out and say it, eh? OK, then. I'll do it.

"You know we want you to return to being the rainmaker you used to be and to stop writing these types of articles. It's clear by your hesitation that you don't have the guts to do that, or maybe you just lost your stomach for this work. Whatever the reason, we can't afford to wait as you slowly come to terms with your conscience. We've had too many clients call to complain about this article and your shenanigans. So I'll make it simple for you: Follow your heart. Go work for the poor and rail against the system. Just don't do it here."

Chapter 32:
Success

SimTime: June 30, Los Angeles

The door burst open and broke the peace that had surrounded the house for the past three days. Lifted by the wings of an optimistic energy never before experienced by either of them, the two songwriters bounded through the doorway and practically twirled their way to the living room before flinging themselves onto the couch in a mix of energy and exhaustion.

"I still can't believe we did it!" Karla declared with a sigh of relief. "I can't believe we managed to get the whole album recorded on time!"

"I know! And did you hear what Lee said? He thinks this is likely to go gold!" Marco added before giving her a high-five.

"What an intense month! I can't believe how hard we worked, especially the last three days. It was almost non-stop in the studio. Did we even sleep?"

"I don't remember! All I know is that I've never worked so hard for anything I've wanted so much before. What a feeling! I'm not even tired yet!" Marco bounced up from the couch and placed his hands squarely on Karla's shoulders. "Wait here!" he announced. "I'll be right back."

Karla was in no mood to argue, so she shrugged her shoulders and reveled in her memories of the past month. Moments later, the superstar reappeared with two glasses and a bottle of Don Perignon champagne in his hands.

"I bought this bottle as an incentive when we decided to work together again," he explained as he unwrapped the cork. "I told myself that if we finished, I'd open it up with you to celebrate. If we weren't able to make it, I'd have to cut out alcohol all together."

"Aha!" joked Karla. "Now I see your true incentive! And all this time I thought it was me!" Becoming a little more serious, she added in a low voice, "Do you think it makes sense for you to drink it?"

"Yeah, I'm ok. I can handle this now. I promise."

He poured the champagne carefully into the two glasses, and, making quite everything of the occasion, presented his partner with her glass. Seating himself next to her on the couch, he put one arm around her and lifted his glass with his other hand. "To the woman who saved me," he toasted romantically. The two clinked glasses and savored the sweet, dry taste.

Karla was impressed by his current graciousness, not to mention the remarkable transformation he had made. She swallowed her drink, then commented humbly in response, "Thanks, but you know, I really didn't do anything to save you. You saved yourself."

"Yeah, but I wouldn't have changed my ways if you hadn't given me that good kick in the pants," he explained as he tasseled her hair.

"As I remember it," she countered somewhat sarcastically, "a number of other people suggested the same thing I did."

"Yeah. But you were my inspiration."

Karla stuck her finger in her open mouth with mock disgust. "Oh please!!" Now this sudden sentimentality was becoming a bit too much for her taste. "You were the one who kicked the drug habit cold turkey. You were the one who started working out regularly at the gym. You were the one who cut back on your alcohol consumption, and you were the one that suggested we try collaborating again. And then, when we started working together, you were the one who re-wrote the music to twelve songs in less than three weeks. It was inspiring to watch such a creativity flash."

Marco had to admit that he, too, was pretty impressed by what he had done. "Yeah, it was pretty intense. You know, working those long days for so many weeks and living on adrenaline for so long was like a drug high in itself...only better. I felt that I was finally working to achieve a dream. I wasn't just following the crowd and I wasn't just handed something. I had this amazing sense of … what's the word I'm looking for?...purpose!…and it was so neat to see the creativity in myself. When I was on the drugs, it felt great, too, don't get me wrong. But it was empty. It was like I was escaping into a magical land. When I came down, though, I felt more depressed and empty because I knew I was just wasting my time and talent. Despite that, I got into a spiral and had a hard time getting out of it."

Karla was proud of her guy. She wanted to savor the happiness the two of them were feeling. Nuzzling in close to him, she whispered softly, "Well, I'm glad I was able to play some small role in helping you help yourself. You know," she paused, smiled, and looked him directly in the eyes. "I'm very proud of you."

Enjoying the elation of their accomplishment, the champagne, and her full approval, Marco shot her a flirtatious look and asked smugly, "Oh yeah? Just how proud of me are you?"

Also caught up in the moment, she responded with equal parts smugness and flirtation, ""Well, let me see if I can show you...." With that she flashed a teasing smile, grabbed him, and planted a long, wet kiss squarely on his gorgeous lips. "Does that show you?" she joked after they finished.

Marco slowly stood up and stretched casually. In one fell swoop, he reached over and swept her up in his arms. Karla did not resist. Making his way up the stairs with her, he responded sarcastically, "It's a good start!"

Chapter 33:
Wrap-Up

AlphaTime: July 1, New York

"Clear the area! Here they come" shouted Lyle as LES screamed into action. Like before, LES first enveloped the staging area in a curtain of electric fog. Behind the curtain lights flashed and a variety of sounds masked the activities. When all was ready, LES drew back the curtain to reveal the players in this grand experiment, on stage for their final curtain call. The small audience applauded their triumphant return while the test subjects scanned the environment and adjusted to their new surroundings.

"Welcome back!" Cheyenne cheered. "Congratulations! You have just completed the toughest part of the experiment. Judging by the looks of you, I'd say you all fared well."

Mr. Auerbach and Lyle applauded then shook hands with everyone.

"Is it really over already?" Marco questioned. "It all went so quickly...almost like a dream. What day is it?"

"Yes, it's really over," Cheyenne confirmed cheerily. "It's 10:00 AM on Sunday, July 1. To celebrate your return we have arranged a nice brunch for you. Please go into Mr. Auerbach's kitchen and help yourselves to breakfast. Once you have chosen your food, we'd like you to come back out here so we can hear all about your experiences."

One by one, they filtered into the kitchen. As Cheyenne surveyed the spread, she felt proud that she had thought to ask Mr. Auerbach for help. Not only had he been instrumental in convincing the adults that this was a worthwhile program, and had also given Lyle and her lots of good advice, but he was also kind enough to have arranged this brunch. The selection impressed everyone. One counter held bagels, croissants, and a variety of muffins. Another counter had scrambled eggs and huevos rancheros. The group milled back and forth between the different stands for several minutes before choosing their food and returning to the living room.

When everyone had slowed from wolfing down their food to picking at the remains, Mr. Auerbach decided it was time to begin the final stage of the experiment. "Well," he ventured as he finished swallowing a sip of coffee, "I hope you have found this experiment to be worthwhile?"

Everyone smiled and nodded enthusiastically.

"I know everyone is probably tired and anxious to return to their friends and family. We have airplane tickets waiting for you and we'll take you to the airport in just a little bit. Before you go, though, we'd like to hear your final assessment of the experiment. No long speeches are necessary. Just a few sentences will do. What did you learn from this time? Were you happy with your career choices? Was participating in this experiment a good idea? Would you recommend this to others? Who wants to go first?"

The four subjects glanced at each other, caught between being very excited to share their tales and wanting to be polite and proper. Assuming that everyone else was afraid to go first, Taylor stepped to the plate. Speaking with his customary air of authority, he began, "Well, if no one else is going to speak, I'll go first." He turned towards Mr. Auerbach and Lyle and explained, "This has been a tremendous experience, and I think I speak for everyone when I say thank you for allowing us to participate. Everyday taught me so much...and things that I never would have learned in school. I guess I realized a number of things about myself that I hadn't considered before."

"Such as...?" Mr. Auerbach encouraged.

"I guess I always assumed I'd be good at everything. My father always told me that I could succeed at anything I put my mind to. Now I'm beginning to question that. These simworlds have force me to accept that there are certain things that I can do better than other things. This wasn't a sad realization for me, though, because I also realized that everyone has some talent, but not everyone has the same talents."

Taylor paused in reflection for a moment. "The hard part is realizing where your true strengths lie and not settling before you've truly discovered them. The only thing that concerns me is that if you're not careful, you could use this as a convenient excuse to take the easy way out in life. You know: just give up and say 'I didn't do well the first time so I'm just not good at it and shouldn't bother trying again.' I guess the real challenge is in finding your strengths but not shying away from challenging yourself."

"Very well put," nodded Mr. Auerbach appreciatively. He paused a moment to let people reflect on the thought. He continued, "And what about a career choice? Did you decide whether you'd prefer to be a police officer or a CEO? I'm curious because your choices were so...how shall I put it?... different from one another."

"Definitely not a cop." Taylor responded without hesitation. "I can see that I'm not cut out for that. Besides, I didn't like many aspects my job: patrolling bored me and the paperwork annoyed me. Maybe that's why I didn't do so well. As for being a CEO, I had mixed feelings about the whole thing. I didn't really like getting too heavily involved in the strategic thinking and politics. My favorite part of the job was studying the financial records of both companies before the merger. It was like reading a mystery, or decoding a secret language. I noticed that because I enjoyed it, I approached that part of my job with much more enthusiasm. I'm sure that's part of why I did so well at it. I think, therefore, that when I go to college next year, I will study accounting, with the hopes of someday becoming a Chief Financial Officer, rather than a Chief Executive Officer. I'm now content to leave the top billing to someone else."

Marco almost choked on his drink at that announcement. Half-teasingly, he commented, "Wow. I'm amazed that you of all people have chosen what sounds like such a boring job! Don't get me wrong, it's a great choice, but it's so sedentary. I'm surprised you didn't decide to become a private detective solving all sorts of crimes. After all, you did such a great job catching Frankie for me. Thanks, again, for that."

"No problem." Taylor deflected casually. "Actually, I only did that because I don't like it when people get the better of me. I can see where you'd be surprised by the choice, buddy, but I guess anything can be exciting, if you're truly interested in it."

Marco considered Taylor's comments. "That makes sense." He nodded. "You know," Marco added, "I think I learned some of those same lessons. One of the things I'd like to thank you all for is helping me to realize my own potential. I've never been much of a student and so never thought I could accomplish anything. Now I realize I do have talents and that's given me a lot of hope."

"Well, if you come out of here having gained self-confidence, then I think the experiment has been successful for you." Mr. Auerbach commended.

"Definitely," Marco agreed. "But that's not the biggest lesson I've learned. That was just a great side-effect. Taylor's right when he says that life seems to go better when people follow their inner callings. But I think there's more to it than that. It's not enough just to have fun doing what comes naturally. I had that at the beginning of my second career. It was fun, but also a little boring. I think that's why I started doing the drugs.

"I found that to be happy, I had to come up with and

follow my own plans, rather than relying on others to make decisions for me. Kicking my drug habit and cutting the record with Karla means the most to me of anything I did this year. You know why? Because I set the goals myself and then I worked really hard to achieve them. It was tough while I was doing it, but the progress I saw kept motivating me. The accomplishment of those goals was my favorite part of this whole experiment."

Karla slammed down her juice glass on the table and huffed, "Is that so?"

"That, and getting to know Karla!" Marco added extremely quickly.

"Good save!" chirped April from across the room.

"What about you, April? Did you find what you were looking for?" asked Lyle, sensing that this would be a very good time to change the subject.

April pondered her response for a moment. Slowly, she answered, "Yes. I think I did, to a degree."

"What do you mean?" Lyle asked to the one who intrigued him the most.

"Well, I was glad to see that, as I suspected, I could be successful at anything I put my mind to doing."

"So all you got out of this was confirmation that you do everything well? Nothing else?" Mr. Auerbach asked incredulously.

"No. I didn't say that. I saw that fulfillment in life doesn't come just from being successful in one's career. It's bigger than that. You need to have balance. Time for work and time for leisure; time for oneself and time to give to others. My first career didn't give me that. I was so busy working hard that I wasn't really happy. I kept feeling like something was missing...and I was always tired.

"I almost got it right toward the end. Between working and volunteering, I found the time balance that let me live in the style I wanted and do what I enjoyed. Writing provided a wonderful outlet for my thoughts and gave me another focus. Even though I was busy, I found I wasn't anywhere near as tired. Of course, it would've worked out even better if I also had balanced the amount of focus I gave to each. I spent too much time thinking about what wasn't paying the bills, and that ultimately caused my misstep at the office.

"Still, I really owe Taylor a debt of gratitude for showing me that you can have multiple goals and accomplish them through various means. They don't all have to be done while at the job. His idea to volunteer helped me find balance and fulfillment."

April felt a light go on inside her. She added, "The more I think about it, the more I understand what you were trying to tell us about "driving our future", Mr. Auerbach. When I took control of my actions and perceptions, and when I planned a little more, I was able to make life work out more towards my liking. I finally felt like I was in the driver's seat, rather than just being a passenger in my own life."

Mr. Auerbach just smiled and nodded sagely.

"So does this mean you want to pursue any of the careers you've tried this year?" Lyle inquired.

"Actually, I'm not quite sure what I want to do. Although I was successful at medicine, law, and even writing, none of them really sung to me. I hate to say this, because, in some ways, I'm no further ahead then when I started. One thing I do know is that no matter what I choose, I will continue to volunteer. It really was so rewarding."

Cheyenne turned to her old friend, "That leaves you, Karla. Are you glad you did this? Did you find the life of an artiste to be everything you expected?"

"Oh yes, I'm definitely glad I did it. It certainly taught me more than I was prepared to learn in school this year. Did I enjoy the artistic life? Not as much as I thought I would. It really was much more difficult than I imagined. And I don't mean just the financial aspects. Creating a work of art, whether a painting or song, requires a lot of patience and determination. I thought you would just get an idea and write it down and that would be it. You know: inspiration does the work. I found that inspiration gives you the first 30%, but then determination and rework gives you the rest. I was also surprised at how much there was for me to learn, even about songwriting. I thought I had these great tunes, and then Marco would tinker with them a bit, and they'd sound better than I'd ever imagined. It was both humbling and annoying."

Karla paused for a moment as she considered her thoughts. Finally, she added, "Which I guess brings me to my second big lesson: It's ok to trust people. In fact, if you are willing to give someone a chance, you can achieve more with two than with one." She smiled softly to Marco as she said this.

Cheyenne was pleased at her friend's discovery.

Her face quickly turned from happiness to puzzlement and she felt compelled to ask, "You know, I can't tell from what you are saying: do you want to continue to be an artist or not?"

"Yes and no. I know now that I just don't have the talent or desire to be a successful painter. It was so difficult to even get an inspired idea. Songwriting was better, but it's too hard to make it in that industry. One other thing I did discover along the way is that I really enjoy cooking."

"I'll say!" Marco confirmed enthusiastically. "You should have tasted some of the meals she was making by the end of her time. They were delicious!"

"Thanks," she smiled. "So what I've decided to do…and Cheyenne, don't fall off your seat… is go back to school and get my high school degree. Then I want to go to a culinary institute so I can eventually become a chef."

Cheyenne was thrilled by her friend's about-face. She leaned over and gave her a hug. "Oh, Karla! That's a wonderful idea. You can still express yourself creatively through your recipes, and you can make a good living as a chef. I'm so happy for you!"

Karla returned the hug equally enthusiastically. "Thanks, Cheyenne, for being such a great friend and especially for recommending this to me. You saved my life."

The whole room basked in the warmth of the moment. All four participants agreed to themselves, that they, like Karla, had had their lives changed by this experiment. Breaking the silence of the moment, April turned the tables. "Lyle," she began, "we've told you all about what we got out of this experiment. But how about you? Did you get what you wanted from it? Did you learn anything unexpected?"

"Yeah," added Taylor, asking the question that was on everybody's mind. "What are you going to do now with this machine now that the experiment is over?"

Lyle stroked his chin and nodded his head. "Fair enough questions, I suppose. Based on what you've told me so far, I think we've achieved our mission of testing the equipment. I already have a list of adjustments I'd like to make on the machine, and I think I will probably end up with an even bigger list. I'm glad to see this has given you some good insights into what careers you might want to choose. It sounds like you all saved quite a few years of real time to discover that the careers you wanted were not the best ones for you. To me that makes this a success. However, the unexpected outcome was seeing just how much this helped you learn about yourselves. I never dreamed this machine could help people understand themselves so much better. It makes me feel proud that I was able to help you."

Cheyenne now stepped in, hoping to help out her co-founder. "As to what we're going to do with the machine now that the experiment is complete, we're thinking about starting a company that offers this as a program to high school students, kind of like being an exchange student overseas. Do you think this would be viable?"

"Most definitely," April asserted. " I think it

should be a requirement for most junior year students."

"I agree. I'd recommend this to anyone," Marco concurred.

"When you need help running it, let me know," Taylor volunteered. "Maybe I could be your CFO! Wouldn't that be a great testimonial?"

Mr. Auerbach smiled proudly at this group of teens and their accomplishments. Wanting to end on a happy note, he glanced obviously at his watch, stood up, and announced, "Well, it's getting late so we better start heading towards the airport. Before we go, though, I need to remind you that there's still one more requirement of you for the experiment: Within the next two months, I need each of you to write up a summary -- in any format you want -- of what you did during your ten months, what you learned, and also what you think we need to improve on the machine. We will use them to improve the program. We will also send your papers to each of your schools so you can get credit for the missed year."

Hearing this, Marco slumped in his chair and rubbed his face with both hands. "Oh man! We gotta write a report??" he whined. "I guess we really are back in the real world!"

ABOUT THE AUTHOR:

Like the characters in her story, Karen Adler Feeley's quest to find her ideal job started at the end of high school and has taken her across the country. She has worked as a secretary, a Wall Street stock analyst, a police officer, an English teacher in China, a travelling management consultant, and a writer. Her travel and work experiences form the backbone of this story. This book was written mostly aboard airplanes while travelling the USA between her job and homes in Seattle, WA; San Francisco, CA; Folsom, CA; Los Angeles, CA; Bakersfield, CA; Beaverton, OR; and Arlington, VA. She has written and edited articles which have appeared in magazines, journals, and newsletters. This is her first novel. Born and raised in Toms River, NJ, Karen currently lives in Arlington, VA, with her husband.

To contact the author, e-mail:
p2020experiment@comcast.net